I0554384

YOURS AFFECTIONATELY,

JANE AUSTEN

YOURS AFFECTIONATELY,

JANE AUSTEN

SALLY SMITH O'ROURKE

Victorian Essence Press
Los Angeles, California

Victorian Essence Press

First Printing of Trade Paperback: September 2012

Printed in United States of America

Cover by Rebecca Young and Diane Fraser

ISBN 1-891437-03-8 Trade Paperback

ISBN 1-891437-04-6 Electronic Book

FOR JANE AUSTEN
JENNIFER EHLE AND COLIN FIRTH

BUT MOSTLY FOR MICHAEL

Acknowledgements

I want to acknowledge with grateful appreciation
Victoria Lucas and Harvey Stanbrough
whose guidance and abetment have helped make
Yours Affectionately, Jane Austen
a better book and me a better writer.

And a hearty thanks to friends and colleagues for their
unstinting encouragement and enthusiasm during the
long process of getting my
little story to press.

Last but most definitely not least was the sage
advise of Abigail Reynolds and Regina Jeffers.

With much gratitude I thank
Ann Channon and Isabel Snowden
of **Jane Austen's House Museum**
for their generous help in creating this
little work of fiction.

And most particularly my appreciation to
The Jane Austen Memorial Trust
For the use of the 1809 watercolour of
Chawton Cottage that graces the cover

*If any one faculty of our nature
may be called more wonderful than the rest,
I do think it is memory.*

Jane Austen

A Short Foreword

With January 2013 seeing the two-hundredth anniversary of the publication of Jane Austen's *Pride and Prejudice*, it seems the perfect time to explore just who Elizabeth Bennet's Mr. Darcy really was. In tribute to the iconic author and in answer to that question I offer *Yours Affectionately, Jane Austen*. This trifling bit of fiction is the continuation of *The Man Who Loved Jane Austen*. *Yours Affectionately, Jane Austen* delves into the complex nature of the man who became the embodiment of, arguably, the most romantic character in English literature.

Let it be known and understood that this story is entirely fictional. Some small liberties have been taken with the known history of the famed novelist; for example Jane and her sister, Cassandra shared a bedroom in Chawton Cottage but as she did in *The Man Who Loved Jane Austen*, Jane has her own room in *Yours Affectionately, Jane Austen*. That said, while the purists will, no doubt, find flaws in Jane's history here, I have made every attempt to capture the spirit of the beloved author who after two hundred years, still captures our hearts.

Truly, a woman of two centuries.

Prologue

Torch flames danced in the still summer night as liveried footmen ran ahead to light the way for the beautifully restored horse-drawn carriages. Gravel crunched under the wheels as the remaining guests of this year's Rose Ball made their way to the gates of Pemberley Farms. It was meant to look like a scene from the past, and Eliza Knight had no doubt that it did. In fact, she was sure this was how it looked and sounded in 1795 when the first Rose Ball was held.

The story behind the Rose Ball was very romantic. Fitz Darcy's ancestor had established this amazing estate in the lush Shenandoah Valley of Virginia well over two hundred years ago. To win the hand of a Baltimore debutante, he built this magnificent house and invited the cream of American society to a fancy dress ball. According to the story, it worked; Rose Elliot became the bride of the first Fitzwilliam Darcy of Pemberley Farms. To honor her and the history of the family, the Rose Ball has been held every year since, just as it was being held tonight.

Eliza pushed herself away from the railing on the balcony of her bedroom in Pemberley House as the grandfather clock on the second floor landing struck the half hour. Darkness fell over the estate as the young men doused their torches, leaving only moonlight. The footfalls of the remaining servants faded into the distance and all was quiet. The mournful cry of a hoot owl signaled the close of the amazing fairytale evening.

The ornate and slightly cloying Rose bedroom had been so named, she'd been told, because every available surface was covered in either floral botanicals or rose coloured fabric and paint. Eliza was pretty sure it was actually named for the woman in the portrait on the wall opposite the French doors of the balcony: Rose Elliot Darcy, the Baltimore debutante wooed and won by Fitz' great, great plus grandfather and namesake. Family legend held that when Rose saw Willie—that's what Rose called her Fitzwilliam—riding up to the house on horseback she would slip into a bathtub. There she would wait for Mr. Darcy to join her in the rose-scented water. Eliza smiled. It was a fun story.

The New York artist kicked off her shoes and sat down, falling back onto the fainting couch—not a chaise lounge, mind you, but a fainting couch and glanced back at the painting.

"Well, Rose, did you marry him because he built this house for you, or were you comfortable when you were together?"

She leaned her head back, admiring the hand-carved ceiling panels. *Comfortable.* Eliza didn't know if that's how Rose felt about Willie Darcy, but for some strange and inexplicable reason it was how she felt when she was with Fitz Darcy, the current master of Pemberley Farms.

She'd only known him for forty-eight hours and the entire time had been a whirlwind of activity and a roller coaster of emotions; still she was more at ease with him than with anyone else. Was it possible it had been only two days? She glanced at the clock on the bedside table. Three in the morning; that made it about forty-two hours, so not even two days. She looked up at the portrait again. Yes, it *was* just last night, under the watchful eyes of his ancestor, that Fitz had told her his tale of leaping through a portal that took him from twenty-first-century Hampshire, England to nineteenth-century Chawton and Jane Austen's bed.

Certain he was crazy when he started telling her his absurd story of time travel, she considered leaving and going home. But there was genuineness in all he said and an openness she could not ignore. She would never know whether it was the champagne and the ambiance of the centuries-old southern estate or Fitz himself, but by the time he finished his epic tale, she truly believed that he had fallen through a rip in the fabric of time. Despite her inbred New York cynicism, she was convinced this uber-wealthy Virginia horseman had been the model for Austen's Mr. Darcy in *Pride and Prejudice*, and Mr. Darcy was arguably the most romantic figure in English literature.

Wearing her favorite extra-large tee-shirt Eliza sat down on the small upholstered stool at Rose Darcy's dressing table. Releasing her hair from its up-do, she shook it loose and ran her fingers through it. In the mirror she turned her head to the left and right, then rested her chin on her hand. She wasn't a classic beauty, but her dark hair and eyes did make her look a bit exotic. Two vines of hand-carved roses twined around the oval frame of the mirror, joined at the lower right edge by a bow. A small smile curved her full lips as she reached behind the silvered glass. *Nothing.* She laughed out loud at herself. Finding two hundred-year-old letters behind an old mirror happened only once in a lifetime. She shrugged, but it had happened—to her, and only two weeks ago.

Alone in her New York City apartment overlooking the East River, Eliza sat crossed-legged on the floor examining her newly acquired treasure, a late-eighteenth-century vanity table. She'd purchased it at a dusty antique shop against the advice of her financial advisor and part-time boyfriend Jerry.

The back of the mirror appeared to be slightly warped, however, further examination showed that it was not warped at all but separated from the frame by two letters. The silk of the green ribbon slipped through her fingers as she untied the delicate bow, releasing the two small documents. Were they love letters?

Intrigued, she read aloud, "Miss Jane Austen, Chawton Cottage." She paused. "That can't be right."

She picked up the other letter. "Jane Austen again... to... Fitzwilliam Darcy?" She turned it over; the seal was still intact. "She didn't mail it, Wickham. Maybe it's a Dear John letter and she changed her mind... but then why keep it?" She looked over at her big, gray tabby cat, who was totally uninterested. "Or maybe it's a mushy love letter. Well, let's look at the other one; maybe it will tell us. It's already open and it was obviously written by a man."

She read aloud. "May 12th, 1810." "Dearest Jane, the Captain has found me out. I am being forced to go into hiding immediately. But if I am able, I shall still be waiting at the same spot tonight. Then you will know everything you wish to know. F. Darcy."

It certainly wasn't a love letter. Who was the captain and what did Jane want to know? Was it really possible that Jane Austen was corresponding with a fictional character she'd created? The simple, obvious but completely outrageous answer was that he wasn't fictional at all.

The beautiful penmanship on the sealed letter was enticing, but the thought of opening it was fleeting. If the years of watching *Antiques Roadshow* had taught her anything it was that things were far more valuable monetarily as well as historically if left as original as possible. Reluctantly she re-bundled the letters.

The golden glow from a street light outside her window was the only illumination in Eliza's living room until she turned on her computer. Determined to discover an explanation for the existence of the letters, she sat at her desk and signed on to the Internet. The first thing she found was the New York City Public Library website advertising a current exhibit: *The World of Jane Austen – A Woman of Two Centuries*. She definitely would go there tomorrow and find out what the world of Jane Austen was like. But she probably wouldn't find an answer to the question she most wanted answered, so she continued to scroll through what turned out to be thousands of websites all claiming to have some association with the novelist.

One seemed a bit more promising than most:

AUSTENTICITY.COM
THE *EVERYTHING* AUSTEN SITE
Can't get enough Jane Austen?
Dying to know what she ate and wore, what books she read,
songs she sang? Post your question on our message boards.
One of our Austen experts is sure to have
the answer you seek.

She examined several topics on the message boards, finally selecting "Jane's Life & Times" and started to type.

POST MESSAGE:
Was Darcy from *Pride and Prejudice* a *real* person?
Please reply by e-mail to: *SMARTIST@galleri.com*

Smiling, she sent the message.

"There!" she told Wickham. "With any luck we'll get to the bottom of this and find out the truth."

The truth was that the Fitzwilliam Darcy of the letters was a twenty-first-century time traveler and not Jane Austen's nineteenth-century lover; at least he claimed not to be her lover. Lover or not, Eliza was sure that the unopened letter from Jane Austen to Fitzwilliam Darcy really had been meant for Fitz and not written to his ancestor as she initially had assumed. Because of that certainty the decision to give him the letter had been easy. Austen had written to him, so the letter was his.

The reflection of a single candle flame from the bedside table flickered in the soft summer breeze, one candle. The ballroom of Pemberley House had been ablaze with hundreds of candles tonight and with costumed guests whirling around them, Fitz had held Eliza in his arms as he waltzed her around the dance floor. She was almost sorry she'd told him that she'd made a decision about the letter at that moment because he'd stopped dancing. He'd whisked her out of the ball room and to the front porch.

Commandeering an open coach, the Virginia horseman took her for a short moonlit ride down to the lake. In the silver glow of the moon she pressed the unopened letter into his hand.

He had read the short missive aloud, and it had ended with Jane's wish and admonition for him: "Somewhere in that faraway world of yours, I know, there awaits your one true love. Find her, dearest! Find her whatever else you may do, and when you find her, you must tell her she is your dearest and loveliest desire. Be happy, my love. Jane."

Staring at the ground Fitz had refolded the letter and slipped it into the pocket of his hunter green frock coat, and then took the step that separated them. With grateful tears glistening in his eyes, he cupped her face in his hands and whispered, "Dearest, loveliest Eliza." Then he kissed her—a long, passionate but gentle kiss that had made her knees weak. Even now her heart beat hard in her chest and she had to take a deep breath to calm it.

She had wanted him to kiss her again, but at the bedroom door he had bowed gallantly and kissed her hand.

She didn't know what to say. "Thank you... it's been... amazing."

He smiled. "Yes." Then, with a feather-soft touch he traced the contour of her jaw and gently lifted her chin, brushing her lips with a kiss. "I'll see you in the morning."

She hadn't been kidding when she'd told him it had all been amazing, but she was still having trouble processing it. Hopefully sleep would make everything much clearer. Not bothering to remove her make-up or brush her teeth, she climbed into bed and fell asleep imagining she was in his embrace.

Chapter 1

Chawton, England
Summer, 1813

The slender, dark-haired woman walked alone on the same woodland path they had once walked together. Was it really three years ago? Then the slightly warm spring weather had brought forth the first blooming of the wildflowers. Today her muslin dress clung to her body in the moist summer air and flowers no longer coloured the meadow.

As she stood atop a wooden stile, a small smile curved her bow-like mouth as Jane imagined him reaching for her, his hands strong at her waist. Her eyes closed, she jumped down from the weathered step, pretending that he had set her down gently next to him. Her heart beat rapidly and she breathed deeply to calm it.

She had landed in a small mud puddle, and the hem of her gown was now quite dirty. Her sister, Cassandra, and her mother would strongly disapprove of such carelessness, but the thought of their disappointment was lost in the memory of that long-ago afternoon.

Jane reveled in the reminiscence. The walk was one she had made many times since he'd left. Her hand went to her bare throat where he had fastened the gold chain his late-mother had given him in his youth. She tried to imagine him as a boy but was unable to drive the image of the man from her mind: tall, lean and tanned as he lay in her bed recovering from his injuries—injuries that were not nearly as bad as he had led them all to believe. She smiled at the memory of his deception.

The trees hanging over the low-lying wall were nominally larger than they had been when she was here with him. They had sat together on the wall, holding hands and kissing in the sunshine, the breeze stirring the leaves overhead. He had held her in her arms; she had wanted to stay there forever and he had said he never wanted to let her go. But the world had intruded and he was gone.

It was the strength of that memory, his arms around her, his breath on her neck, the beating of his heart against her, that caused sensations of joy and sadness. His disposition and temper were nearly opposite her own, but the loving tenderness and gentle passion underlying everything he did still made her feel the excitement she had experienced when he touched her. She relished every moment of the time they'd had together and would not trade it for anything.

A warm breeze rustled the leaves of the two trees that created the arch through which Mr. Darcy had come and, she assumed, gone. The hope that someday he might return—

The thought and her heart stopped as a horse and rider came over the wall through the space between the two trees. In her hurry to retreat Jane tripped over a partially buried rock and fell to the ground.

Reining the black horse to a stop, the young man jumped down and was almost instantly at her side. "I'm sorry, Miss. Are you okay?"

Okay. That was a word she had only ever heard *him* use. She turned her head and their eyes met. Her brother's stableman turned his eyes away in deference to their different stations.

"When did you last see him, Simmons?" Her heart beat faster with a surge of irrational hope that the groom had seen him recently.

"Who, Miss?" He reached to assist her to her feet.

"Why, Mr. Darcy," she said, accepting his outstretched hand and rising.

Escorting her to the stone wall he said, "Not since the Captain come after him, Miss Jane. Why Miss?"

"I have never heard anyone else use 'okay'."

"It is a good word, I think."

"Indeed."

Simmons looked around. "Will he ever come back, Miss?"

"Mr. Darcy?"

Her brother's servant nodded.

"I fear it may not be in his power to return."

"If that is true then I wish I'd went with him." He stood next to the horse, rubbing the animal's neck.

"You wish you'd gone with him?"

"When he prepared to leave I asked to go with him to take care of Lord Nelson. But he said it would be too dangerous for me to go."

"It most likely was too dangerous."

A glimmer of realization flashed across his face. "He's not really a spy, Miss."

Surprised at the statement, she asked, "How do you know?"

"He gived me his word that he was no spy." He shifted his gaze to the ground and almost whispered, "He's a true gentleman, Miss, and I believe him."

"So do I, Simmons... so do I." She paused. "You would have gone with him to America?"

"Oh, yes, Miss"

Jane was astonished at the admission. Simmons held a position of some importance in her brother's stable, caring for his favorite horses, teaching the younger children to ride and hunt and having the special privilege of driving her mother, her sister and herself on local travels. It was a great honor in a household of so many servants to have the responsibility of caring for those most dear to his master's heart. But despite the fact that he was a young man of no education or particular background and no connections to speak of, Simmons had been willing to leave it all to follow a man he had known only a few days. She was unable to hide the shock. "Why would you have done such a thing?"

The young man straightened himself. "He treated me like he was no better than me, and he shook my hand, Miss, as if we was the same."

Jane smiled at him. Mr. Darcy had made quite an impression on her brother's groom. It reminded her of the American's declaration and his treatment of her as an equal as well. "I believe he considered you his equal, Simmons."

The young man's face beamed with the compliment. "I have often thought of going to Portsmouth and hiring onto a ship to go to America."

"Even after all this time?"

Simmons said quietly, "Sometimes it don't seem like such a long time."

Jane nodded.

"I want to be a horse doctor, Miss Jane, and I think Mr. Darcy might help me get the learning I need to do it."

"Since Britain is at war with America, I fear going there now could pose a great danger to you."

"You think because I am English Mr. Darcy wouldn't help me?"

"I have no doubt he would help you in any way he could were you to reach him, but if you went there now it might be seen as an act of treason, or you would simply be pressed into the service of the Prince Regent."

"I was afraid you meant he would turn me out. If the Prince is all I have to fear then someday I will take my chances."

Failing to dissuade him with logic or fear, Jane tried cryptic truth. "I am afraid, Simmons, that a ship out of Portsmouth would not lead you to Mr. Darcy's America."

"I do not understand, Miss. There is only one America, is there not? And he lives there, doesn't he?"

She had never considered telling anyone Darcy's story, but it was Edward's stableman who had found Darcy a hiding place so that her naval captain brother had been unable to capture him. Simmons had also gotten the American paper and ink so he could write her about his departure. A surge of emotion and fear for Simmons caused a tightness in her chest. He had also become a party to the deception she and Darcy had perpetrated so that they could have one last meeting. The young man's guileless face made it clear that he could be trusted. Had he not kept their secret all these years? In fact he had risked his life for Darcy and her, so perhaps she did owe her young champion the truth.

"Miss?"

She was aroused from the self-discussion by the sound of Simmons' voice. She looked up at him.

"Why do you say I couldn't get to America from Portsmouth?"

She smiled. "You could get to America on a ship from Portsmouth, but you would not find Mr. Darcy there... at least not our Mr. Darcy."

"But you said he was in America."

"And so he is. However, it is not the America of today."

The fear that he might be insulting Master Edward's sister made Simmons pause but didn't stop him from saying, "You confuse me, Miss Jane."

"Yes." She realized why Darcy had found it so difficult to explain the circumstances of his arrival to her. She had been incensed at his reticence, but now she understood. How could she explain to this young man, a boy really who had never even been to London, that Mr. Darcy had traveled from a time two hundred years in the future? She began an explanation she hoped would end his dreams of finding the tall Virginian. "After Mr. Darcy dined at my brother's house he requested a meeting with me." She smiled remembering the circumstances of the request, a hastily written note folded tightly and slipped into her hand under the pretense of finding her gloves, which Darcy himself had taken. Jane caught the hint of a smile on Simmons' face but he said nothing. "You knew?"

Simmons nodded. "I saw him give you the note, Miss." He looked at the horse. "That was why I had Lord Nelson ready for him when he come to the stables that night."

Startled by the admission, she said, "You were so sure I would meet with him?"

Stridently, he said, "Oh, no, Miss! But I was certain he would go... in hopes that you would."

Jane nodded, continuing to be surprised by the young man's insight.

"I told him that he needed to be careful of the Captain for he was a far different man than Master Edward and would not take kindly to someone playing loose with his sister." He blushed slightly. "Sorry, Miss."

Smiling to ease the groom's embarrassment, she said, "You were right; Francis is very protective of us and definitely did not like Mr. Darcy, so it was a good warning." After a short pause she added, "I am afraid my brother was not alone in his dislike of Mr. Darcy." Remembering that night....

The knocking started softly enough but with Jane's refusal to answer, Cassandra finally struck the door quite hard. "Jane, talk to me." She made no response. Plaintively her sister pleaded, "Jane, please. I am sorry if I injured your sensibilities. I only wanted to remind you—"

"That I am a middle-aged spinster with no right to—Oh, go to bed, Cass!"

"I will not be able to sleep if you are angry with me."

Grudgingly Jane opened the door but pointedly did not invite her sister into the room. Instead she kissed Cassandra's cheek. "I am not angry. Go to bed." Without waiting for a response Jane closed the door again. Leaning against it she waited until she heard her sister's reluctant footsteps as she walked down the hall to her own room.

Cassandra was only trying to protect her, but still it hurt. Cass had accused her of stupidity, declaring that Jane had long since passed the age for such childish romanticism if she truly intended to meet with Darcy. Jane could not deny that she had

had thoughts of romance; however, she also knew that Darcy simply wanted the location of his fall. He had made it very clear that he wanted nothing more than to be out of the country at the earliest possible moment. Romance was certainly of no interest to him. She did concede that the late hour and woodland location was a bit suspicious and highly inappropriate, but still it never occurred to her not to go.

As midnight approached, Jane stepped out into the hall, taking note that no light shone from under Cassandra's bedroom door. She felt secure that as she left the house under cover of darkness her sister would be none the wiser. Glancing up the stairs one last time to be sure Cass was not following her, Jane threw her blue gauze cloak around her shoulders and pulled the hood up to protect her head from the light mist that had started to fall just as they'd arrived home from her brother Edward's dinner party.

Chapter 2

In the deep shadows at the edge of the wood, Jane waited as the moon started its descent, casting an iridescent glow on the meadow. The tall American steered his great horse off the road and into the soft grass. He rode straight and tall as though he'd been born astride the animal. He was looking around, obviously in search of her but also making sure he had not been followed. When he was within a few feet she stepped into the moonlight.

He dismounted and cautiously walked toward her. "I was afraid you wouldn't come." He stopped no more than two feet away from her, still holding Lord Nelson's reins. He looked handsome and vital even in Edward's ill-fitting suit. She pushed aside the thought and the romantic notions she'd been entertaining since receiving his note and questioned his choice of time and place.

He apologized and added, "I believe dawn, the sunrise, is the crucial time for me to go back."

"Go back? Where?"

Darcy hesitated, unsure how much he should reveal about his situation.

Taking his pause as evidence that what would follow would be a carefully crafted story—a lie—Jane was surprised when he said, "Back to... back to the place where I fell."

She was irritated by his evasion and certain that he knew precisely what she wanted to know. "It is close. I will gladly show you exactly where it is... *after* you tell me where you came from, why you are here and why you're behaving so oddly."

"Miss Austen, I really can't explain. You wouldn't understand." He paused briefly. "I'm not at all sure I do."

Ignoring his apologetic admission, Jane spat, "What? Because I am a woman you think me too stupid to understand?" She turned and walked away. "Feel free to stumble around in the dark and find the place yourself!"

Almost panicked, he dropped Nelson's reins and went after her. "Miss Austen... Jane, please wait."

Expecting yet another insult but ready with a few of her own, she stopped and turned toward him. But he hurled no aspersion.

"Miss Austen, I believe you are one of the most intelligent women—in fact, one of the most intelligent *people* I've ever met."

Cautiously she returned and stood toe to toe, looking up at him. Her eyes glistened in the moonlight with a combination of suspicion and curiosity, and before she could say anything he began to tell her about her books.

"I know that *Sense and Sensibility* will be published early next year and it will do very well."

Suspiciously she asked, "Why would my brother tell you that?"

"He didn't, nor did he tell me about the one you're working on now, *First Impressions*, the story of five sisters hoping to marry well. It will be published in three years, after you re-title it."

His knowledge of *First Impressions*, on which she was still working, caused her curiosity to flare into anger at the reasonable assumption that he had rifled through her personal papers when he was alone in her room feigning his head injury.

Before she had the chance to throw any well-deserved invectives at him he told her about another book. "*Mansfield Park*. It will be considered your masterpiece by many people although, Pri—" He cleared his throat. "*First Impressions* will be the most popular, then and now."

Mansfield Park was but an idea in her head, she had not yet put pen to paper. How did he know? Jane accused him of madness as she took a few steps backward away from him.

Afraid she might bolt before he got the information he needed, he grabbed her arm. She tried to pull away but he held firm, "Jane, please…"

What had she been thinking meeting this mercurial and possibly dangerous man in the middle of the night?

Overwhelmed with guilt at having caused the fear he saw on her face, Darcy released her. "I'm sorry."

Suppressing the fear she said, "I have no idea how you know so much of my past but you cannot know what my future holds. No one can tell the future!"

Quietly, he said, "Yes… and that is my secret… it's all in the past for me." Sadly he looked away, then directly into her eyes. She saw the truth reflected there as he said, "*This is* the past for me. I came from the future."

Literally scratching his head, the dumbfounded Simmons asked, "The future, Miss Jane?"

She nodded. "Two centuries into the future."

"How is that possible, Miss?"

Jane told him what Darcy had told her. "He jumped the wall with Lord Nelson, and both were blinded by the rising sun. The great stallion stumbled, throwing Darcy to the ground where he hit his head on a rock. When he awoke he was here."

Simmons just stared at her, waiting for more.

"The day after that midnight meeting we came here and he attempted to enter the portal, but it was not open. That made him even more sure that the sunrise was instrumental in the opening of the gateway through which he and Lord Nelson had come." She paused. "Although it appears now, the sunset was just as effective." Her voice grew quiet. "At least I hope it was."

Simmons stepped to the wall and looked through the arch of hanging branches, "But I just come through here Miss and it was only Master Edward's fields."

"As I said, he was sure the sunrise or possibly the sunset was responsible for the opening of the portal."

The young horseman looked behind him. "It's almost sunset now, Miss Jane."

Jane nodded. "So it is."

She took three steps and stood next to him, after a few moments a fine mist started to rise from the grass on the other side of the wall. The mist turned to a thick fog, and as the fog cleared slightly Jane and Simmons peered through an opening. A large green machine was moving across the far meadow. There were no horses or oxen driving it and it made a grinding noise as black smoke billowed out of it. They looked at each other in awe and amazement. When they looked again, a smaller wheeled vehicle with no horses was kicking up dust on a dirt road next to the field. They remained where they were, transfixed until the image started to fade as a blaze of sunlight filled the space. The brilliance seemed to reflect as if off a mirror, and when they regained their vision Edward's field was just as it had been before.

Almost in a whisper Simmons asked, "Was that the portal, Miss?"

Sitting once again on the warm rock wall, Jane said, "I suppose so. I believe those things were some of the machines Mr. Darcy told me of... machines that replace horses."

"Replace horses, Miss?"

"Yes. Mr. Darcy told me about all manner of machines in his time. Automobiles are carriages without horses." She glanced over her shoulder at the meadow. "The big green one must have been a plough of some kind."

"But Mr. Darcy breeds horses."

"Indeed, but for sport and recreation."

Still standing at the wall looking through the arch of tree branches, Simmons said, "So the opening is still there."

"It appears so, Simmons... it appears so."

"Why do you think he hasn't come back, Miss?"

"There are many possibilities. It would still be dangerous for him. Perhaps he does not know he can. It is possible he does not want to revisit this time. Even worse, it's possible that he did not return to his own time safely."

After several minutes of quiet thought, Simmons ventured, "What do you think would happen, Miss, if I went through it?"

Jane looked over her shoulder at the meadow beyond. It was still and quiet. There was no sign of a rip in the fabric of time. It looked like the Hampshire countryside of Regency England. She turned to Simmons.

"Mr. Darcy said that his coming here was accidental. He had no idea how it happened or why. If the portal was open when my brother was chasing him and he went through it, we have no way of knowing whether he returned to his own time or some other time. And we cannot know what might happen to you. He told me there is no way to control it, at least as far as he knew." She paused a moment. "If you were to go through, what would you do if you could not return?"

"If I found Mr. Darcy I would not want to come back."

"And if you did not find Mr. Darcy?"

"I would secure work in a stable somewhere."

With the sun down, evening began to fall on the English countryside. Simmons took a deep breath. "I must be getting back."

"And I must return to the cottage before dark."

"Shall I see you home, Miss?"

"No, thank you, it is not necessary."

Simmons tipped his hat and swung up into the saddle, guiding the horse away from the wall. Suddenly he wheeled around and spurred the animal to a full gallop, charged the wall and sailed over it with ease.

Jane smiled at the image. Memories of that night with Mr. Darcy flooded her mind. Memories that she had not included in her telling to Simmons. After she had finally accepted his explanation for his sudden appearance in Chawton, he told her of the many changes that were to come. The ones that fascinated her most were societal, particularly the relationships between men and women. Alone in the early evening dusk, Jane's memory returned to that night three years ago.

As the moon started its descent he told her that he must return to the Great House before he was missed and then offered to see her home.

She declined, then coyly asked him to kiss her good night.
Hesitantly he gave her a light kiss on the lips.
"Is that how you would kiss a woman in your time?"
He smiled. "Maybe after a first date."
"And after a second or third date?"
He gathered her to him and kissed her more thoroughly.

Jane heaved a deep sigh. It had been the first kiss but she
was ever grateful that it was not the last. The growing dusk
reminded her that it was getting late and she started home.

The cushioning of the summer pasture again brought back
memories of the afternoon she was here with Darcy. She'd run
off, as a sort of test to determine whether he really preferred
women who were spirited and independent as he had declared.
He'd caught up with her, picked her up and whirled her around,
then fell with her in his arms, tumbling onto the soft grass.
Although she was fully aware that anyone seeing them this way
would be outraged, she did not care; lying there with him was
intoxicating. When he kissed her, her heart fluttered, then beat
so hard she was breathless. She closed her eyes and sighed at the
memory of his gentle passion. It was a good thing he was a true
gentleman, as Simmons said, for at that moment, in the soft
spring grass, she had not felt very ladylike. However, gentleman that he was, he did not take advantage; instead he stood
and offered her his hand to help her to her feet.

The reluctance she felt as she stood up with his help caused
a tightening in her chest, and as the years passed she often wondered what it would have been like if he had made love to her
that afternoon. She chuckled. Somehow the idea that it would
have happened in her brother's field made it all the more exciting.

She walked home in her own world thinking about what
might have been.

Chapter 3

Eliza didn't know who painted the portrait of Fitz's ancestor, Rose Darcy, but it was an exquisite example of Federalist era portraiture. She glanced at the dress hanging on the door of the armoire, another exquisite example of the era. She had worn it to the ball last night. It was the same gown Rose was wearing in the portrait. The tiny embroidered rose buds all over the delicate pink silk were just as lively today as they had been then. She laughed out loud. *"Lively" was a Jane Austen kind of word*, she thought. But then the whole weekend had been like falling into a Jane Austen novel. It's the kind of story you tell your grandchildren, and she would... if she ever had any.

The painted gaze of the Darcy matriarch followed her as she crossed the rose bedroom to the bathroom. She had no idea how she'd managed to rationalize to herself not brushing her teeth before she went to bed, but she did and her mouth was all fuzzy and tasted as yucky as it felt. Using more toothpaste than necessary, she scrubbed her mouth with vigor. That done, she slathered on cleansing cream (because her grandmother told her never to use soap on her face) to remove the sticky, crusted on make-up she'd also managed to rationalize away last night.

Rinsing the shampoo out of her hair she stood in the shower tiled with hand painted roses which were obviously not original to the two hundred year old house, and let the pulsating water pound her back and neck. She'd slept well unlike the night before and actually felt rested and relaxed for the first time in weeks.

The counter in the bathroom held several small etched glass bottles of liquid soap, lotion and body spray; all lavender fragranced. She was surprised but rather glad that it wasn't rose and used the body spray all over including her hair. She slipped on the jeans she'd worn the day before along with the only clean shirt she had with her. She ran the brush through her hair and put on just a touch of blush and pink lip gloss. She gave her hair one last spritz of lavender, and then set the bottle down on the weathered marble counter.

In the bedroom she looked at the portrait of the Darcy Grand Dame that hung over a naturally patinated copper bathtub. What she wouldn't give to see the look on Fitz' face to find her in the tub with rose petals floating atop warm water. Would he join her as Willie did Rose? In the bright light of morning it suddenly became a real question not just a fantasy. What *was* their relationship?

They'd held hands, danced and he had kissed her once but that was all there was to the relationship. It had been so long since she'd allowed herself an emotional connection to anyone outside the family that she wasn't at all sure what the signs were. Was she reading him right, did he like her as much as she liked him? Was he simply being a southern gentleman? Or was he just being nice because she gave him the letter? The memory of his kiss last night made the hair on the back of her neck stand up. It definitely wasn't a kiss of simple appreciation; but was it any more than a kiss?

Did his love of Jane Austen override any feelings he might have for her? Did Jane's plea for him to find his true love in his own world mean she didn't love him, or did she simply assume she would never see him again? Would they have married if he'd stayed in Regency England? Jane never did marry; was it because Fitz was gone and no one else could compare? He had never married either; was it because if he couldn't have Jane he didn't want anyone?

She glanced in the mirror and chuckled. She was doing exactly what her mother said: over thinking things. Still, it was very difficult to believe that the man who loved Jane Austen could or would ever love her.

She hit the open palm of her left hand with her right fist. *Enough! He obviously likes you. Why obsess over unanswerable questions? Take Mom's advice. Let nature take its course and simply move on to the next step, whatever it is.* She sighed. She needed coffee.

Dirt flew up in the wake of the vintage Jag as it sped down the drive and into the ground fog held by the woods near the gate. After the early morning departure of two of his overnight guests, Fitz poured himself a cup of coffee at the table that Mrs. Temple had set up on the veranda for his other guests.

Leaning against one of the Doric columns of the porch he was glad Heritage Week was over. It always took a lot out of him. He smiled at the thought that his mother would have thoroughly enjoyed it all, and he was sorry she never got to see it. His spirits were lifted by the fact that it would be almost a year before he had to deal with it again.

His coffee in hand, Fitz walked to the barns. He'd had a good night's sleep, helped no doubt by the fact that he had gotten virtually no sleep the night before. He was fairly refreshed and looked forward to seeing Lord Nelson. As he passed the tack room he grabbed his favorite saddle, one too worn for anything but exercising. It was the most comfortable one he had. He also grabbed a pad, a bridle and a small apple.

Fitz opened the door of the stallion's stall and set his tack just inside. He released the top of the Dutch door and it swung open on its large brass hinges leaving the bottom half in place. He set his coffee mug on a small shelf inside the stall. The horse remained in the corner but turned to him as the latch caught on the door.

"Good morning, boy. How are you today?"

Lord Nelson nuzzled Fitz' shoulder.

With his hand open Fitz offered Nelson the apple. The horse greedily munched his treat as Fitz gently put the saddle pad and saddle on the horse's back, adjusting the girth so it was secure but not tight. Pulling the bridle over the animal's head and gently slipping the bit into his mouth, Fitz threw the reins over his shoulder. Together the duo walked out of the barn into the early morning sun.

With a fluidity of motion not common in a large man Fitz swung gracefully into the saddle. Then horse and rider walked past the paddocks and out into the open fields. When Fitz spurred the great horse on, they galloped across the summer grass, the strong muscles of Lord Nelson taking them over white rail fences with ease. It was almost as if they were flying, the moist air rushing around him as they went. He loved being out at dawn with his horses. It allowed him to shake off the residual haziness of sleep and think more clearly, and he had a lot to think about this morning.

Chapter 4

No one was in the kitchen, but the coffee was brewed and smelled wonderful. Putting her sketch pad on the island, Eliza took a mug from the cupboard above the coffee pot and poured herself some of the hot, dark liquid.

"Miss Knight?"

Mrs. Temple, Fitz' housekeeper, looked none too pleased to find someone had invaded her domain.

"I just needed some coffee, Mrs. Temple."

"There's coffee, juice and muffins on the veranda."

"Sorry, I didn't know."

"Next time you want something, ask me and I'll take care of it."

Eliza finished getting her coffee ready with milk from the refrigerator and sugar from the bowl on the counter. "Sorry. It never occurred to me to ask for something like coffee. My mother says we come from good peasant stock and shouldn't expect others to do things for us."

Mrs. Temple's look softened. "That's commendable I suppose, but Mr. Darcy would want me to serve you properly."

Conspiratorially, Eliza said, "Then let's not tell him. I feel weird being waited on." She picked up her pad. "Thank you, Mrs. Temple."

The woman smiled. "Thank you, Miss Knight."

"Eliza, please. Miss Knight is so school marmish."

"Yes, Miss—Eliza." The two women smiled at each other and Eliza left the kitchen.

The brilliant light of morning made last night and the two days before seem even more dreamlike. A tractor in the far field, a single-engine airplane overhead and the three vehicles, including her little rental car, parked in the circular drive reminded Eliza that the real world didn't include horse-drawn carriage rides, candlelit rooms and romantic leading men.

Leaning against one of the porch columns she sipped coffee from a heavy crockery mug. The mug wasn't as pretty as the delicate china cups they'd been using all weekend, but the stoneware vessel felt real in her hands.

She turned at the sound of light footsteps behind her, and her stomach and throat tightened in anticipation. Fitz' teacher friend, Jenny Brown, came through the door, the picture of southern gentility in a simple yellow sun dress that made her ebony skin glow in the morning sun.

Eliza released the breath she'd been holding. "I was afraid you were Faith."

Jenny's dazzling and very friendly smile eased Eliza's tensions considerably. Walking to the coffee cart, Jenny casually said, "No, Faith and Harv are gone."

"Where did they go?"

Jenny turned toward the pretty New Yorker, a mug of coffee in her hand. "Home I suppose. Fitz evicted them, or so Mrs. Temple told me."

"Evicted them? Why would he do that?"

"I don't know the particulars, but Mrs. Temple said they left at dawn." She leaned forward and added in a hushed voice, "Apparently Fitz didn't talk to Faith at all. In fact, as far as Mrs. T could tell he didn't even look at her." Jenny grinned. "So relax. I don't think you have to worry about Faith for a while... probably a long while."

"What makes you think he evicted them? Maybe they just needed to be somewhere."

"Believe me, Honey, Faith would never have left voluntarily. At the very least Fitz asked them to leave or they'd still be here."

"But why would he ask his best friend to leave?"

"Well, he couldn't very well get rid of Faith and not get rid of Harv—they came together—as for why he did it; I'm pretty sure he found her threatening to kill you unacceptable."

Eliza still didn't understand. "But that happened the night before last, and she *did* apologize to me... sort of."

Jenny sat in one of the wicker captains' chairs.

Eliza took a seat in a bentwood rocker.

"For the last seven years, Faith has been instrumental in the plans and arrangements for the Rose Ball." She paused. "For Heritage Week in general, she's one of the few people Fitz allowed to give tours of the house, and until last night she'd always been his date for the ball so she'd come to fancy herself his hostess. She always made sure that everything was perfect in the hopes of showing him that she would be the perfect mistress of Pemberley. It never worked, of course, but she kept trying.

Because he is the way he is, Fitz allowed her to stay in spite of all her shenanigans on Friday. I'm sure he figured it was only fair since she'd spent so much time and energy organizing everything. But once it was over all bets were off. So she's gone."

"Certainly it wasn't just because of me?"

"I don't imagine it helped that she destroyed crystal that had been in his family for over two centuries. But you're the main reason."

Eliza shook her head.

"You still don't believe he really likes you, do you?"

"Oh, Jenny, we've only known each other three days, two if you don't count today, how much can he like me?"

Jenny raised an eyebrow. "How much do you like him?"

Eliza blushed.

"That's what I thought. Time has very little to do with it; three days, three months, three years, it doesn't matter. Haven't you ever heard of love at first sight?"

"Yeah," she said with a chuckle in her voice. "In movies and books, but this is real life."

"Don't they say that the best writers write what they know?" Getting herself more coffee, Jenny added, almost under her breath, "and life often imitates art."

"How long have you known Fitz?" Eliza queried.

"All my life. I don't remember a time when we weren't friends. We played together as kids; his father taught me how to ride a bike when he taught Fitz. My father taught Fitz how to fish. He's one of my favorite people."

"Is he really as nice as he seems?"

"You think he's hiding something?"

"Well, sometimes he just seems too good to be true. And you know what they say... if it seems too good to be true it probably is."

"He's not perfect if that's what you mean, but he does have a very strong sense of fairness and justice. In the old days they called it honor. He has a strong sense of honor. His word is his bond. On the other hand once you've crossed the line and lost his respect or affection, there's pretty much no going back."

"So he's hard-headed, implacable?"

Jenny shrugged. "When he's pushed too far, yes he is."

"What was he like as a kid?"

"Pretty much the same except he was always happy. Had a ready smile for everyone. She chuckled. "We called him sunshine."

"Really? Until last night I'm not sure I saw him smile. He seemed somber, almost sad."

"Yes and he was. It started when he was in the ninth grade and his grandmother died, the one who did costume restorations. He bounced back from that pretty well even though he was very close to her. But then it all seemed to come apart, and with loss after loss he turned in on himself more and more. He became distant even to those of us who were already close. By the time his mother died he had pretty much stopped smiling altogether and couldn't find the good in any situation or person. His life became his horses and making Pemberley Farms a thriving business. Not much else mattered to him."

"What other losses?"

"He doesn't like to talk about it, so it isn't really my place to get into the details; just know that his life was pretty well devastated and he's basically been alone ever since. And he's alone on purpose; it's safer than risking further loss. You only noticed it last night, but for me, over the course of the last two days he was gradually becoming the kid I grew up with again." Jenny got up and poured a second cup of coffee, then looked at

Eliza and smiled. "And I'm pretty sure *you* are the reason." She turned to walk back into the house.

"Where are you going?"

Jenny raised one of the mugs of coffee. "Going to take Artie his morning java. He's something of a bear until he's had his coffee. See you later, Sweetie."

Eliza didn't know whether she was responsible for Fitz Darcy being happy this morning, but he was very definitely the reason she was. Looking out at the expanse of beautifully mani-cured lawn, she grabbed her sketch pad and skipped down the steps, singing, "Oh, what a beautiful morning...." Suppressing the urge to continue the song, she giggled.

Chapter 5

Although the sun was fully up in the Virginia summer sky, it was not yet hot. Fitz found jumping exhilarating; the cool morning air caressing his face, and Lord Nelson, so strong and graceful, took all the jumps with no effort.

Heritage Week was over so things could get back to normal. He shrugged. *Whatever normal is.* He realized there was a very good chance that his normal was about to change radically. Eliza's letter—the one she had found written to him from Jane—had ended his search for the truth of his Regency encounter. But Eliza did much more than give him the letter.

He had been merely surviving, not living, in the years since his mother's death. He'd thrown himself into the business of Pemberley Farms to the exclusion of almost everything else. Eliza's arrival had heralded an acute awareness of that fact. It was as though a light was suddenly shining so he could see the world around him. She made him want to live again. And she had given him the letter... Jane's letter.

Fitz reined Lord Nelson to a walk as they entered the cool shade of the woods on the edge of his property.

Jane. He had spent more than three years seeking proof of his meeting with her and of her feelings for him. Almost as if he'd been transported again back to Chawton in 1810, the image of Jane's sweet face flooded his mind. He thought back to that morning and his inauspicious entrance into Jane Austen's life.

The combination of his head injury and the laudanum prescribed by Mr. Hudson, the Austen family physician, caused Darcy to slip in and out of consciousness. He tried to sit up, the effort making him dizzy.

Jane gently laid a hand on his chest. "Please, Mr. Darcy, Mr. Hudson wants you to remain still."

Through a cotton mouth, his head spinning, Darcy asked, "Mr. Hudson?"

"The doctor," Jane said. "You must rest now Mr. Darcy." The American looked at her face. Her curiosity was palpable even in his drugged state. Unable to think clearly, never mind responding to questions he wasn't sure he could answer, he closed his eyes completely and turned his head away.

Jane returned to her vanity table where she continued to write; a single candle and the flames in the fireplace her only light. Interrupted in her writing by a low murmur from Darcy, she took the candle and quietly approached the bed. He was tossing back and forth, his face flushed and contorted; he was speaking in quiet tones, a hodgepodge of words that meant nothing to her. He spoke what she could only suppose were the nonsensical ramblings of a sick brain; she attributed words like *television* and *jet* to his head injury and delirium. She placed her hand softly on his cheek and was distressed by the heat radiating from him. Using fresh linen soaked in water from the pitcher on her wash stand, Jane swabbed his face and neck, then laid it across his forehead. It seemed to calm him and she went back to her writing.

Each time he grew restless Jane stopped writing and went to the bed to refresh the linen with cool water. After three episodes in close succession she remained on the edge of the bed so she was at hand, and each time he started to toss and turn she would caress his face and neck with the cool, damp linen in hopes that it would, in time, reduce his fever.

She stayed there until Darcy's features turned placid and he was breathing more evenly. He finally seemed to be sleeping comfortably. She laid her small, soft hand on his cheek. The fever was broken. She dropped the cloth into the basin. Stiff from sitting in one position for so long without support, she stood up and stretched. She was not particularly tired but needed to get some rest.

Quietly she crossed the wooden floor and slipped the small pages of writing she was working on into the drawer of the vanity, then took a nightgown from the closet next to the fireplace. Glancing back at the bed she stepped behind the screen.

He opened his eyes just enough to see her slender, full-breasted figure silhouetted on the muslin screen, back-lit by the remnants of the fire as the light fabric of her nightgown floated down to envelope her.

Jane stopped at the bed before making her way to Cassandra's room for a few hours of sleep. As she stood over him he watched surreptitiously through the veil of his eyelashes. She leaned down and whispered, "Good night, Mr. Darcy," almost brushing his lips with her own. In spite of his continuing laudanum haze, he could see that her eyes were filled with a tenderness that caused him to grab her hand as she straightened up; he didn't want her to go.

Without opening his eyes or letting go of her hand he said, "Please don't leave me."

Unsure whether this was further evidence of the delirium or whether he was actually requesting her presence, she pulled her hand away. He did not move to take it again but said, "Please, stay."

Cognizant of Mr. Hudson's admonition of keeping the injured American calm and concerned her leaving might agitate him, Jane sat once again on the edge of the bed. Darcy smiled in the flickering flame of the dying fire. He said nothing more but gently took her hand. He did not relinquish it again until she rose to move to a chair by the side of the bed where she finally slept.

The movement woke him. His mind finally clear of drugs, he scanned the room in the dim, pre-dawn light. There were no electrical outlets or switches, no lamps, television or telephone, and the only clock appeared to be pendulum driven. Everyone he'd seen wore costumes similar to the ones people wore to the Rose Ball. Those things and the medical treatment he had received led him to the inexplicable conclusion that somehow he'd fallen into another time—a time when Jane Austen was alive.

And there she sat, serene in what had to be an uncomfortable position for sleep; his nurse, his savior and much prettier than she was depicted in the only portrait of her to survive to the twenty-first century. She was not the brazen hussy of Darcy family lore but a sweet and loving woman who took care of him without concern for her own safety or expecting anything in return. His mother would have said she was a true Christian.

As he watched her in the pale light of the dying embers his head started to throb as though a nail was being driven through it. He closed his eyes and blessed sleep overtook him.

Jane was an incredibly strong, intelligent, willful and virtuous woman who followed the propriety of the day... mostly. During the last three years he'd often wondered what might have happened between them if he'd been forced to stay in early nineteenth-century England. Of course with the way her brothers felt about him, he probably wouldn't have seen her again.

If the circumstances had been different would he have married her? He could have been happy with her, he supposed, but over the years he'd come to realize that the love he felt for her was based on who she was, the awe in which he held her, caring for him when she certainly didn't have to, loving him. Then again, *did* she love him? She had never said it and the letter Eliza had found and given him showed obvious affection but she urged him to find his true love. Apparently she didn't think she was it. Had they ever loved each other or had it just been a fling across the ages?

He laughed. What difference did any of it make? Jane Austen had been dead for almost two hundred years. Still, the undisputed icon of witty English romance had kissed him whether she loved him or not. He still had to pinch himself to believe it had ever happened.

He had no such questions about Eliza. Everything felt right when he was with her. This was no fling. He had no idea where they were headed, but for the first time in years he was looking forward to the rest of his life. As long as Eliza was with him he didn't care where they were headed.

Fitz and Lord Nelson crossed the bridge at a leisurely gait; the ground fog was burning off in the warm morning sun. Had it really been only two days since he and the great stallion were galloping across the bridge before the fog had lifted and run Eliza off the road and into a muddy drainage ditch? He hadn't even realized she was there until it had happened. When he did, he brought Nelson to a stop and, without questioning who she was or why she was walking along a road on his property, he had lifted her onto Lord Nelson's back and then swung up behind her. She was slightly light headed from the sudden fall, and once on the horse she had leaned against his chest and he'd had to control a strong desire to kiss the top of her head. He still didn't understand how a complete stranger could make him feel that way, but he didn't really care. From the first moment, being with her felt right and wonderful and that was all that mattered.

She had touched something in him that no one else ever had, including Jane, even before he knew her. At the Austen exhibit at the New York Public Library he had found himself staring at her. He laughed remembering that he had thought of her as a raven-haired beauty. Then two days ago she had come out of the fog and into his life.

He had told her his story about jumping through a rift in time and meeting Jane Austen. It had been very difficult at first, but once he started it tumbled out and had been a relief that he wasn't carrying it around anymore. It was as though a weight had been lifted and this slight, feisty New Yorker had done the lifting. She had listened to him with an intensity that had made her a part of the story. She had been kind and compassionate—he had seen real grief when she asked him about leaving Jane—and she had given him the letter that answered his questions about whether he'd actually met Jane Austen and how Jane felt about him.

Jane would always hold a special place in his heart, but Eliza held his heart. Maybe it was too early to take it all for love, but it certainly felt the way he'd always thought love is supposed to feel.

Horse and rider stepped out from the cool canopy of the woods and into the warm summer sun. Spurring his favorite horse to a full gallop Fitz guided him over every fence and stream on their way back to the barn.

Chapter 6

Chawton, England
Summer 1813

Staring at her image in the dressing table mirror, Jane turned her head to the right and then to the left, assessing the different profiles. She was not homely, she supposed, but her sister Cassie was the pretty one in the family with her bright, clear complexion and eyes the colour of a summer sky.

She touched the cool glass; Darcy had taken notice and complimented her many times when she had stopped wearing her dust cap. Almost everyone she knew considered her dark, curly hair her best feature, and she had wanted him to see it glistening in the morning sun. But he had said her best feature was her eyes. Although the golden flecks made them seem almost honey coloured, it was the fire of intelligence he saw there that made her one of the most beautiful women of his acquaintance, and she suspected there were many women. For a man to admire her mind, her curiosity and her talent and consider her beautiful because of them had been a heady experience, indeed.

She looked over her shoulder and glanced around the room. Assured that she was alone she reached behind the mirror and extracted the small packet of letters. She read the one he had sent her just before his departure.

12 May 1810
Dearest Jane,

The Captain has found me out. I am being forced to go into hiding immediately. But if I am able, I shall still be waiting at the same spot tonight. Then you will know everything you wish to know.

F. Darcy

She had known even before she read it that she might never see him again for when Simmons delivered it she had seen Frank, her naval officer brother, ride by on the way to the Great House with a contingent of his men. There could be only one reason for it: he had come after Mr. Darcy. She hoped that the American had made his getaway in time and was safe. She had started a letter of her own and now quickly finished it in the hope that Simmons could get it to him before he was forced to flee. She had written urging him to open his heart and find someone to love, but he never received the letter for it remained on the dressing table in front of her, still sealed in wax with the fanciful letter A made by the brass seal her brother Henry had so generously given her.

She outlined the red wax with her index finger. Simmons, unable to deliver it, had kept it to himself and returned it to her, assuming she would not want her brothers finding out that she had been communicating with the supposed American spy. It had been a great relief to find, at the time, that her brother's servant not only had understanding but was capable of discretion as well.

Jane popped the seal off and opened the folded document. A small calling card fluttered to the surface of the dressing table. She watched in fascination as the holographic horse changed to the Pemberley Farms crest in the depths of the glass-like paper. She read the letter she had not seen for three years:

12 May 1810
My Dearest Darcy,

Though you agreed that I should wait with you tonight, your expression told me you feared I might be breaking my heart for a love that can never be. Oh how wrong you are to think like that. Do you not know that I of all women would gladly trade a single moment of love for a lifetime of wondering what such a moment might have been? And though you have concerned yourself with my heart, let me now concern myself with yours. For somewhere in that faraway world of yours, I know, there awaits your one true love.

Find her, dearest! Find her whatever else you may do, and when she is found, you must tell her she is your dearest and loveliest desire. Be happy, my love.

Yours forever,
Jane

Had he found his true love, his heart's desire?

Once again she watched the horse change to Darcy's family crest and back again. Although their love, if it was love, had not been that of husband and wife, she was wont to relinquish one of the few keepsakes she had of him. This card, the gold chain and his letter were the only items she had to represent their time together. She had considered simply writing the information on a separate piece of paper and keeping the card, but decided against it. The actual card would give far more credence to Simmons' search for Darcy than a few scribbled lines should someone question whether or not the young stableman knew the American horseman.

Slowly she refolded the letter minus the card and carefully tied the ribbon around the two small documents, then slipped them back into their hiding place behind the mirror of her vanity.

Still in a mood to reminisce, she removed the gold chain he had given her from the hiding place in her handkerchief drawer and held it up to her neck. It was a beautiful piece. She had worn it only the one afternoon when they were together after he had draped it around her neck. Since then she had kept it hidden away. Sadly she tucked it beneath the small linen squares again and closed the drawer. It was such a generous gift and she had never given him anything in return. She had nothing that matched its value in money or sentiment. She thought a moment—there was one thing she could give him that he could receive from no one else.

From the very bottom of her sewing basket, slipped beneath a tear in the lining, Jane pulled a piece of the fabric that she, her sister and mother had chosen as the background for the quilt they were making. She spread it out on the bed and ran her hand over the embroidery she had done the winter after Mr. Darcy was gone. She'd had no reason to do it and until this moment had no idea what she would do with it, now though it would become part of the gift she would give him. Hopefully Simmons would be able to deliver it to him in person.

Simmons was waiting when Jane arrived at the wall shortly before dawn. She made one last attempt to dissuade him, but his mind was set.

"Very well." She handed him the calling card. "As you are determined, this has Mr. Darcy's contact information on it. The directions to his estate are right here." She pointed to the street address on the card. "And he told me of an instrument of communication called a telephone and said that his telephone number is also on the card. Hopefully something here will enable you to reach him."

Simmons took the card; however, with it was a gold crown which he immediately attempted to return. "Oh no, Miss. I can't take this."

"You cannot go out into an unknown world without some resource."

"Are you quite certain, Miss Jane?"

"Yes, but I ask you to do something for me."

"Anything, Miss."

She handed him a small package wrapped in brown paper and tied with twine. It had Mr. Darcy's name and the directions on it. "Will you please give this to him, when you see him?"

Simmons looked up at her. "Of course, Miss Jane."

"Thank you."

The two stood at the low lying stone fence, the time just before the sun's ascent casting radiance on the surrounding countryside. The meadow beyond lay still and quiet, not even a breeze moving the grass and leaves. A knapsack slung on his shoulder, Simmons held tightly to the package his master's sister had given him. He took a deep breath and waited for the sunrise.

The sky above the horizon glowed pink, then orange as the great orb started to rise. Jane said, "Take care and wish him well for me."

A fine mist swirled up and over the wall, and Simmons turned and smiled at her. "Thank you, Miss Jane. Farewell." Then he stepped up onto the stacked field stones and off into what, he was not sure.

Jane shielded her eyes to protect them from the intensity as the sun blazed into white brilliance. It took a few seconds for her to regain her vision, and when she did there was nothing in the field except grass. "Simmons?"

There was no response. Simmons was gone.

Summer, Now

The brilliant flare of white light blinded Simmons as he stumbled onto the damp grass of the meadow. There were voices in the distance and what sounded like musket fire.

Suddenly someone asked in a deep voice, "Here, where did you come from?"

Simmons squinted into the light ground fog and made out the image of an older gentleman in a regimental uniform. The gentleman had extended his hand.

Simmons looked back over the wall; Miss Jane was gone. Accepting the man's hand, he rose. "Chawton Great House, Sir."

"Well, take care young man, we're using live ammunition."

"Yes, Sir."

The officer returned to his men. Holding a sword over his head he intoned, "Ready... level weapons... fire!" The sound was deafening. Through the smoke-filled air the line of red-coated infantrymen shouldered their muskets after firing them into hay bales.

Past the line of regimental riflemen two rows of white tents dotted the field. What seemed to be hundreds of soldiers were marching in formation or gathered in small groups around campfires. There also was a canon, and several men in kilts were leading horses to a fenced area. The officer who had helped him to his feet cleared his throat, indicating that he expected the youngster to move away.

Gathering his bearings, Simmons started off across the field wondering why the men were here on his master's property. He walked slowly, giving the milling throng of redcoats a wide berth as he made his way to a narrow dirt road at the edge of the pasture. As he slowly hiked along the dusty path he was beset by confusion. *Where am I? Hampshire, of course, but when?* There were no horseless machines in this field as there had been earlier in the week. What did it mean that it was now teeming with a military encampment?

Behind him he could hear the sound of a horse-drawn wagon, so he stepped to the side to give it room to pass, but instead the vehicle stopped. The man driving the rig was not much older than himself. He flashed a friendly smile. "Need a lift?"

Simmons looked up. "What?"

"Do you need a lift? I'm driving up to the manor if that's where you're headed."

The manor. A ride to the Great House would bring his apparently failed adventure to an end, which seemed a good thing, but the man was unfamiliar. He was not a servant of Master Edward, and Simmons knew most of the stablemen and grooms in Chawton and surrounds. Still, he'd rather ride than walk. He warily climbed into the wagon.

The young driver introduced himself. "I'm Dave Keenan." Simmons nodded.

Dave asked, "And you are?" When the young Englishman made no answer Dave pressed, "What's your name?"

"Oh... Robert Simmons... I'm Robert Simmons."

"Where are you from, Bob?"

"Bob?"

"Isn't that what people call you? I mean that's the usual nickname for Robert."

"I'm called Simmons." He quietly added, "My mother calls me Robert."

Dave laughed. "My mother calls me David... David Alan when she's mad at me." He paused. "So where are you from, Simmons?"

It had been an automatic response when he told the regimental officer that he was from Chawton Great House, but heeding Miss Jane's warning to be careful what he talked about so as not to arouse suspicion, this time he chose instead his place of birth. "Derbyshire."

"Never been there."

The distant sound of bagpipes was punctuated by musket fire and cannon blasts. Simmons was baffled by all of it and wanted to understand where, or rather, when he was. "Why has that Army regiment moved in here?"

"It's not an active regiment of the army. It's the Coldstream Regiment of Foot Guard 1815. And they haven't moved in; they're just here for the day."

Simmons knew little of the military, but he was fairly certain the army didn't make day trips into the country. "I don't understand."

The young driver watched his passenger with curiosity. *If he doesn't know about the faire why is he wearing a costume?* Dave shrugged. He didn't suppose it mattered much. "It's the annual history faire." He looked out over the festivities as they entered the wood. "The estate is opened every year for the faire. The Coldstream Regiment of Foot Guard 1815 comes and does demonstrations of musket and canon use. They also drill and ride, stuff like that. Over on the other side of the grounds they're setting up a faire with food, games and stuff for sale. It's supposed to be mostly for the kids, but everyone from around here comes."

Simmons still didn't understand. He'd driven the Misses Austen and Miss Fanny to the faire many times but there had never been a regiment of soldiers there. Dave's explanation did make it appear that he had gone further into the future than he had thought if 1815 was history, so he allowed himself to relax a bit. He had noticed that Dave had an unusual accent. "You're not English are you?"

"Nope. From the good ole U.S. of A. I hail from the great commonwealth of Virginia."

The traveler looked down at the package still clutched in his hand and visibly perked up at the mention of Dave's birthplace. "The only other American I ever met is in Virginia. Mr. Darcy breeds horses."

"Whoa. You know Fitz Darcy?" Simmons nodded. "Boy it really is a small world."

"How do you mean?"

"Well, I used to work for Fitz. Came over here with him a few years ago to take care of a horse he bought at auction."

Simmons said suddenly, "Lord Nelson."

Dave looked over at the young man sitting next to him. "Yeah. How did you know?"

"I took care of the horse for a few days when Mr. Darcy was here."

A look of realization spread across Dave's face. "That week he was gone... he was with you, huh?"

Miss Jane had told him that it would be best to keep his origins to himself. She said if people knew about the portal it could cause all sorts of trouble. The young Englishman simply nodded.

They broke out of the woods and Simmons was astonished at what he saw. It was not Chawton Great House Dave had meant when he said the manor, this was a house he'd never seen before. It was a large house, though not as big as Master Edward's, and parked around it were vehicles of varying kinds. In addition to small ones like the horseless carriage he and Miss Jane had seen, there was a lorry and lots of people milling around the lushly landscaped grounds. Dave drove the wagon to the barns where he jumped down, telling Simmons to come with him.

Cautiously Simmons climbed down from the wooden seat, trying to take in the surroundings without seeming too astonished even though that was exactly how he felt. He wished that Mr. Darcy was here; he would have felt much more at ease with the tall Virginian.

As the two young men neared the house Dave called out "Linda!" and an attractive woman dressed as Miss Jane dressed but without bonnet or gloves, turned toward them and waved.

When they reached the woman Dave made introductions, "Simmons, this is Linda Clifton, lady of the house. Linda, meet Bob Simmons, a friend of Fitz'." In a stage whisper he added, "He prefers Simmons to Bob."

Linda stretched out her hand as if to shake his and he was taken aback. Mr. Darcy shaking his hand had been strange enough but he had never had a woman extend her hand to him before. Afraid to make a mistake that would cast a light on his situation, he accepted her hand, making a shallow bow at the same time.

"Welcome, Simmons; any friend of Fitz' is a friend of ours." She turned, shouting to a man not far away, "Roger, come here."

The man came over and Simmons was introduced once again as Mr. Darcy's friend. Roger was just as friendly as Linda, shaking his hand and welcoming him. He couldn't believe these people actually thought he might be a friend of the American horseman, but he accepted the compliment with grace.

Roger asked, "How do you know Fitz?"

Dave interjected, "He took care of Lord Nelson that week Fitz went missing."

"You're a horseman then?"

"Yes, Sir."

"And where are you staying?"

Surprised by the question Simmons admitted to not having made any plans.

"You should stay here for the night at least." Roger turned to Dave. "Take him up to the house and settle him in one of the guest rooms."

The house! I can't do that! he thought. But how could he tell these kind and generous people that he didn't belong in the house. Finally he said, "Thanks for the kind offer, but if it's all the same, the stable is good enough, Sir." Linda and Roger looked at each other and shrugged "If you prefer," Roger said. Then he turned to Dave. "You can show him the old tack room then."

Simmons thanked them again. "It's only until I can arrange to get to America."

"Ah, a traveling man. You're welcome to stay as long as you like." Roger patted him on the shoulder, then returned with Linda to their guests and the festivities of the faire.

Dave took a key off of a hook at the entrance to the barn and led Simmons to the far corner where he unlocked a door; behind it was a room like he'd never seen. He was sure it must be as grand as any in the house. There was a bed with blankets and a table with a vase topped by a strange fabric cone. In one corner were two upholstered chairs and another table. Hanging on the wall was a picture frame without a picture that Dave called a TV. In a small recess with no door was something the American said was a kitchenette and in the opposite corner of the room was the bathroom, he said. Unwilling to ask what all these things were, he hoped to be able to figure them out once he was alone.

"Well, I got stuff to do. Take your time settling in, rest, and get comfortable. I'll be exercising the horses later if you want to join me."

"I'd like that. Thank you."

Dave smiled and left the room.

Simmons tried to take it all in. He opened a cupboard in the kitchenette and there was cold air inside with bottles made of something that looked like glass but was soft, and they had labels that said they held water. The cupboard above it had a glass plate in the bottom of it, he didn't know why; Dave had called it a microwave. He walked to the door that Dave said was the bathroom and peeked around the jamb. In the dim light he saw immediately why it was called a bathroom, at the far end of the space was the outline of what appeared to be a bathtub made of something white.

His knapsack still slung on his shoulder and clutching Miss Jane's package, Simmons turned around and around. He was surrounded by wonders he'd never imagined possible. Finally he dropped into one of the upholstered chairs. As he took several deep breaths, the reality of the situation began to sink in. The gateway had opened into the right time. The Cliftons must be the friends Mr. Darcy was visiting when he crossed through the portal. He took the American's calling card from his coat pocket, but he didn't know how the jumble of numbers and letters would help him contact the Virginian.

He leaned back in the chair trying to make sense of it all.

Chapter 7

Chawton, England
Summer, 1813

Jane leaned back in her mother's donkey cart, just holding the reins, allowing the donkey to walk at his own slow pace rather than chance having him get overheated as the humid air started to warm. With Simmons off on his grand adventure, and she certainly hoped it was a grand adventure, she could do no more than say a prayer for his safe passage. She was not adventurous by nature, but the idea of seeing a future of technology and equality had made her consider, albeit fleetingly, going with him. However, convention, propriety and fear of the unknown had stopped her. Her life's adventure would have to be the five days she'd spent with Fitzwilliam Darcy of Virginia right here in the Hampshire countryside; a brief moment that she would treasure always.

Mansfield Park lay on the seat beside her. It was the novel Mr. Darcy had told her about while it was still only an idea. As ludicrous as it seemed at the time, his knowledge of the details of the story she had yet to start coupled with his clothing, which had zippers and elastic, as well as a watch that talked certainly gave credence to his claim of coming from the future. His description of the future with societal upheavals giving women independence of mind and person were proven by his treatment of her.

He had considered her his equal. It had not been the condescension of a proud, wealthy landowner to someone he considered inferior, but true equality of person. He had treated her with the same kind of respect with which he treated the men, and for that she would always love him. That was when she had decided to use him in *Pride and Prejudice*.

It was Darcy who made her realize that a man could love a woman who was strong and independent, someone intelligent with thoughts and ideas that went beyond clothes and balls. In fact, it had given her the confidence to make Elizabeth Bennet of *Pride and Prejudice* a bit more individualistic and insightful than she had originally been, even if some of her insights turned out to be incorrect. She was still lively and playful, though, and Elizabeth's Mr. Darcy was desirous of just such a woman: someone who read extensively to improve her mind.

She smiled and laid a hand on the wrapped manuscript beside her. Jane had written Fanny Price, the heroine of *Mansfield Park* as an intelligent, strong and independent-minded girl. While still demure and modest she was not the insipid and vapid creature she might have been, thanks to Mr. Darcy. But even beyond Fanny's character and personality, Darcy's influence was reflected in *Mansfield Park* with the talk of slavery. Jane had not originally planned to include slavery in the book but the American's vehement denial and intense outrage at the institution itself when she had accused him of being a slave holder had left an indelible impression, so Fanny's uncle now had a sugar plantation and slaves. Jane's sister, Cassandra, had wanted Fanny Price to proclaim slavery an abomination when she finds out her uncle holds people in bondage in Antigua, but her circumstances as the poor relation made Fanny's diffidence reasonable. Besides, *Mansfield Park* was meant to be a story of virtue triumphing over immorality in society—a story of manners, not a political narrative.

The sun was rising higher in the summer sky as Jane reached the Winchester Road. She steered the donkey left where the road split from Winchester to Alton. The sounds of nature were all around her: the wildlife that called The Butts home, the leaves rustling gently in the dark-green horse-chestnut trees that lined the avenue, and the clopping of the donkey. An occasional bird flew overhead and she wondered what the air machines Mr. Darcy had told her about sounded like. She imagined a harsh, unpleasant noise.

On High Street she stopped in front of her brother Henry's bank, handing the reins of her donkey to the boy standing outside. Jane asked Mr. Grey, the bank manager, to include her package in the pouch going to London. She had written Henry a note asking him to take *Mansfield Park* to the publisher if he thought it strong enough. Mr. Grey assured her that it would be in the city later that very day. She thanked him. Her business-minded brother would take it from there.

Leaving her small cart in the capable hands of the boy at the bank, Jane walked up the street. With the pink gloves and shawl she'd promised to purchase for Cass already bundled securely in a package, she stopped to look in at the milliner's shop. From the doorway she saw, on display, a bonnet she liked exceedingly well, but as it was far more appropriate for her niece, Fanny, than herself, Jane did not try it on.

Walking back toward the bank she questioned her reaction to the bonnet as being unsuitable for a woman her age. In the twenty-first century did society still dictate that a middle-aged unmarried woman should restrict her attire and actions? A tiny smile highlighted her face; Mr. Darcy had considered her a young woman, and she had often felt young with him. *Ah, to live in a time where thirty-seven is young!* she thought, for she felt no different physically or mentally than she had when she was eighteen. She heaved a deep sigh. *Why must I alter my appearance and behavior simply because of something as arbitrary as the number of years I've lived?* Somehow it seemed unfair.

She gave the boy looking after the donkey cart a small gratuity for his service, then climbed in and continued her drive up High Street.

The light from more than a dozen wax candles mixed with the waning sun cast a golden radiance over the dining room at Chawton Great House. Small shadows danced on the brocade chairs and hand-carved oak table as the diners rose to gather in the upstairs salon.

Sated by an excellent meal of roasted meats, salads and fresh fruits picked from the estates orchards, Jane stood at one of the tall, narrow windows that provided a delightful view of the grounds surrounding the mansion. The stables were in the forefront of the view and she wondered how Simmons was faring. The thought was interrupted by Fanny, Edward's eldest child and her favorite niece.

"Are you coming, Jane?" Fanny asked.

Jane glanced at her. "Lovely, is it not?"

"Not as lovely as home." Fanny paused. "I miss Godmersham."

"This is your home as well."

Sadly, Fanny shook her head. "It is not the same. It feels different here. Mother surrounds me at home. I do not remember a time when she was here with us, so there is nothing of her here. I miss her, and home is where her heart is." Fanny turned away to join the others.

Jane stayed a moment longer at the window as the sun started its slow descent in the western sky.

At the whist table a bit later in the evening Jane sat with three of her neighbors playing a game for which she had little or no facility and even less enjoyment. But playing was expected and as she fanned out her fourth hand of cards, she leaned back in the chair. Glancing around the elegantly appointed room, Jane found herself more than a little pleased that Edward's estate at Godmersham, which was going through some updating and redecorating, was not yet ready for the family's return. According to her brother's Kent physician, Mr. Scudamore, the threat of painter's colic was still far too great. Edward's steward had told him it might be two months or more before it would be ready for the family to move back in. Although she was glad for the delay because it would keep her brother's family at Chawton, she did hope for the sake of all the children it would not be quite so long, for Fanny was not the only one who longed to be home.

Her attention was drawn back to the game when it was her turn, absently tossing a card into the middle of the table; her partner claimed the trick and started a new one.

Annabelle Rodgers was her partner and neighbor; the Rodgers family lived no more than two miles from Chawton in Holybourne, and often Jane, Cassandra and Annabelle would exchange visits. Tonight Annabelle and her parents were Edward's guests. The young woman was proudly regaling the card table with tales of her brother's exploits in the Far East. A naval officer, Thomas Rodgers, had recently arrived home bearing wondrous gifts from some exotic part of the world.

For his sister, Tom had brought back four lengths of embroidered silk. His favorite was teal blue with a border of stately cranes. Jane looked at her friend; teal blue would accentuate Annabelle's lovely eyes quite nicely. She was sure that was what Tom had in mind when he chose it. There was also one the colour of emeralds, but it was the white one that made Annabelle blush a delicate pink and cast her eyes to her lap, for Tom had brought with him white silk shot with silver for his newly engaged sister's wedding dress.

Annabelle looked across the table. "Oh, Jane, Tommy brought me pink silk with rose buds and leaves scattered across the whole of it, but it does not suit me at all, for it is much too pale. It would look very well on you, if you would like to have it."

Amazed by the generous offer, Jane accepted the gift with much gratitude. The women then discussed when next to meet and decided that Jane would visit Annabelle the following day.

Annoyed by the women's inattention to the game, one of the other players demanded, "Are we to play at whist or talk of pale fashions?"

Jane and Annabelle apologized and play resumed.

Edward returned to the salon and his remaining guests after attending to the early departure of Lord Moore-Jeffries. A family friend since his father's days at Oxford, the old gentleman had been something of a mentor to Edward and Henry, making his lordship a favorite visitor when the Austen-Knights were in Hampshire.

At the refreshment table the genial host poured himself a glass of port. Sipping the dark, heavy liquid, he watched as candlelight reflected from the edges of the cut crystal. Laughter from the other side of the room drew his attention to the card table. His sister was not one of those laughing, and Jane's obvious disinterest in the activity was frustrating the rest of the card party.

He smiled, remembering an incident when they were children and his father was teaching them the game. In the midst of it Jane had thrown down her cards and run away, shouting that she hated the game, that it was stupid. Edward, his father and brother were at first a bit shocked by her outburst; however, they were unable to stop themselves from laughing at her reaction. His father, admitting to the same feelings for card games, later found Jane alone in his study, reading. Explaining to her the necessity of forbearance in the activities and ceremonies of polite society, especially when something unpleasant was expected or required, had elicited an apology and a promise to behave better. Although the discussion had been lively according to his father, Jane had accepted the deserved reprimand, and she had never again jumped up from a card table to run and hide, no matter how much she wanted to do it. But she had made it clear to the entire family that cards were a tedious waste of time.

With the object of relieving her ennui Edward motioned to Fanny to come to him, and together they approached the card table. "If no one has an objection, I would very much like to substitute my sister with my daughter in this game so Jane may entertain us at the piano."

Even though she did not like to play in public, she knew her brother meant to rescue her from the tedium of the card game. Jane squeezed Edward's arm as he escorted her to the wonderful musical instrument that was the focal point of the room. She sat, took a deep breath and began to play. Although her ability could hardly be called expert she was well beyond proficient; her technique had a lightness and gaiety that brought the music to life. This was most particularly a productive activity and she smiled as she allowed the music to envelop her. After the appreciative applause ended, Jane gave up her seat at the piano to another of Edward's guests and slipped quietly away from the party, finding sanctuary in her favorite room at The Great House. Making small talk with the assembly in her brother's salon had taken more effort this evening than Jane had been willing to expend since her mind was occupied by thoughts of Simmons and Mr. Darcy.

After saying goodnight to his other guests Edward found his younger sister in the Oak Room. He was not at all surprised to find her there as it was where she entertained his children with tales of adventure and excitement, creating characters that were vibrantly alive to them. They loved their Aunt Jane and she loved them; he was grateful for that.

But tonight Jane was alone, looking out the window and unaware of her brother's presence. He had found her many times in this contemplative state during the last few years and suspected she was thinking about Darcy. He had never been of the same opinion as his brother Frank that the American horseman was a spy. On the other hand he was hard-pressed to explain why the man had used someone else's name. His banker brother Henry had made it clear that the Fitzwilliam Darcy of Pemberley Farms in Virginia had never been in England, at least not after 1776 when the colonial uprising led to their declared independence from Britain. Although he had been considered an American patriot, to the British government he was a traitor and so had not set foot in the British Isles.

Still, the man who called himself Darcy was a gentleman and he knew as much if not more about horses as Edward himself. He smiled at the memory of Lord Nelson. Darcy's stallion had been the finest specimen of horse flesh he had ever seen. But a spy? What in heaven's name would the man have been spying on in Hampshire? There certainly had been no reason to believe that the Hampshire countryside had suddenly become a hotbed of political intrigue. No, although he could explain nothing of the man he was sure Darcy was no spy. It mattered not; Frank had forced the Virginian to flee; Darcy was gone.

Edward interrupted his sister's reverie, whatever it was about. "James is bringing the curricle around to take you home. He should be here presently."

Jane turned. "Oh, Edward, it is such a short walk."

"I prefer that you not be walking alone at night. James will see you home safely."

The hem of her gown brushed the tongue and groove oak floor lightly as she seemed to float toward him. In the doorway she reached up and kissed her brother's cheek. "Thank you."

Brother and sister stood on the porch and watched as carriages took the last of Edward's guests down the tree-lined drive. James arrived as the final equipage made its way out of sight. Climbing in with her brother's help she gazed into the starlit sky and wondered what was happening right now in Mr. Darcy's Virginia.

Chapter 8

The narrow path branched off the main graveled drive and wound around the stables. After finishing a sketch of them from the top of the inclined path Eliza closed the pad and slipped her pencil into the pocket of her jeans. The gravel crunched under her sneakers as she made her way toward the massive edifice.

The patina of the old bricks gave the largest of the buildings a rustic look. The freshly painted green wood sliding door crisscrossed with white trim was at least twelve feet high. Inside the place was immense and immaculate. The polished stone floor was so clean she could have eaten off of it. Each stall was enclosed by a hardwood Dutch door, and on all but one the bottom half of the doors were closed, the top half open. With fire sprinklers and smoke alarms, lights, heaters, and a misting system, the place was better equipped than her condo. The technology and pristine condition of everything made it hard to believe the building was more than two hundred years old.

Her sneakers made no noise as she walked, and she chuckled at the thought of stilettos clicking against the blue gray slate floor. Each stall had a small brass plaque on the bottom part of the Dutch door identifying the horse within. Lord Nelson's stall was open and empty. Eliza looked up and down the length of the building. There appeared to be animals in every stall but she'd only ever seen Fitz on Nelson. *Does he ride the other horses?* Warm breath on her neck and a rustling noise caused her to look over her shoulder. She was face to face with a gray and white horse. She froze.

"Just relax, she won't hurt you."

She squinted at the animal and tried not to appear completely terrified. "I'm afraid I'm not much of a horse person."

The man laughed. "I can see that." He reached behind Eliza and took hold of the animal's halter.

Eliza stepped away and turned around. "Thanks."

"You're welcome, though I didn't really do anything. As you can see she's still in her stall. One step and you would have been out of her reach. I'm Jake Williams, barn manager. You must be Eliza Knight."

Hesitantly she nodded.

He grinned. "Employee grapevine."

Eliza wasn't sure whether she was pleased or disturbed to find that she was the topic of conversation for the employee grapevine, but before she could decide Jake reached for her hand. He placed it on the end of the horse's nose, which surprisingly was soft and velvety. Unconsciously, she stiffened.

"Relax" Jake said. "She won't bite."

Eliza took a deep breath, willing relaxation.

"Stroke her the way you would a dog or cat. She's just a big pet."

Tentatively, Eliza petted the horse, rubbing the area between her ears. "What's her name?"

"Windsong. We call her Windy."

Eliza continued petting the horse. "She isn't the same kind of horse as Lord Nelson. She's a lot smaller."

"Windy is a Hobbie horse."

"She seems pretty real to me."

Jake laughed. "They used to be called Irish Hobbies—I'm not sure why—but now they're called Kerry Bog Ponies. I just like Hobbie horse better"

"She's very friendly," Eliza said when Windy nuzzled her shoulder.

"Yep. She's gentle, too. She'd be a good choice if you ever decide you want to ride."

"Thanks, I'll remember that."

Jake gave Windy a final pat and said to Eliza. "I've got to get back to work. It was nice meeting you."

"You too," Eliza said, forgetting her concern about the employee grapevine.

As Jake started toward the barn entrance, Eliza looked in Nelson's stall, then hurried to catch up with Jake. He glanced at her as she fell into step with him but didn't say anything.

"I noticed Lord Nelson is gone. Does that mean Fitz is riding?"

"Yeah, when Fitz is here he's pretty much the only one who rides Nelson."

"Do you have any idea how long he'll be gone?"

"I wasn't here when he left but generally he doesn't ride more than a couple of hours, so he should be back soon."

They continued in silence. Eliza finally asked, "How come you're working on Sunday?"

Jake grinned. "The horses' appetites don't take a day off."

"So many people work here... isn't there someone who does that?"

"Sure. We have several people employed in the stables but they worked above and beyond their regular jobs during Heritage Week so I gave everyone the day off."

"That was nice of you."

Jake grinned again but didn't say anything.

"So you're the one who did all the carriages?"

"My part is the horses, harnesses and drivers. The carriages are Lucas' pride and joy. Years ago he found most of them in an old outbuilding that we were getting ready to bulldoze. He spent several years doing much of the restoration work himself."

"They're beautiful. I wasn't here for Heritage Week, but last night was pretty spectacular and the carriages were a large part of that."

Jake agreed. "Even after all these years I still find it an amazing sight."

"Hard to believe it's been going on uninterrupted for centuries."

He laughed. "Well I haven't been part of it for all of them."

Embarrassed, Eliza stammered, "I-I didn't mean—"

"I know. And you're right; it is hard to believe it's been going on for so long." He paused. "It hasn't been uninterrupted though."

"What do you mean?"

"The ball wasn't held during the Civil War or either of the World Wars."

"Right, Jenny mentioned that... but they did Heritage Week during the wars?"

"Heritage Week didn't start until after the Second World War."

"So it's been going on for almost seventy years?"

Jake shook his head. "Interest waned in the mid-sixties; too much else going on I guess. About twenty years ago Fitz started The Heritage Association and Foundation by convincing the other horse breeders and plantation owners to start the historic tours again. He suggested they do it in conjunction with the Rose Ball, which was already a highly anticipated event."

"He must have been just a kid when he did that."

"He was twenty-one, about the same time he started the Point to Point."

"What's point to point?"

"Here, come with me." Jake walked into the office next to the barn door. From his desk he handed her a flier. "Point to Point is a steeplechase kind of horse race."

"Like the Grand National?"

He smiled at the *National Velvet* reference, the only one most people outside of horse country had of steeplechase. "Yes, except that a steeplechase is an actual course with fences and water features constructed for the event. Point to point is usually run in the countryside using whatever there is to jump over, like fences, brooks and downed trees. It's what they do now instead of the fox hunt."

"And you do that here?"

"Yep. It's another of Fitz' charity events."

"Another?"

"The Ball... Heritage Week."

"A scholarship program, right?"

"No. Right after Fitz graduated from college the local school district abandoned their arts programs so the kids didn't have drawing classes or music or drama—anything. Fitz started the point to point to raise money for the schools."

"Was the Ball always for the scholarship fund?"

"Originally the ball was just a society function; Fitz made it a charity event after his mother died. The scholarship is a memorial to her, The Kate Darcy Scholarship. Heritage Week was started because some of the plantations are not self-sufficient, and it raised money to help maintain them. For most of them it still is the reason. Fitz was more concerned that the rich history of the area was being lost, which was why he started the Association in the first place. Pemberley Farm's portion of the proceeds from the tours goes to the scholarship fund because we are self-sufficient."

Fitz' world was amazing: balls, charities, pretend fox hunts. Eliza couldn't imagine living like that. The pictures on Jake's office wall made it evident that the family had been living that way for generations, including real fox hunts. Several of the photographs were of people in riding costumes holding a dead fox by the tail or what appeared to be a dead fox on the ground in front of them.

A display case next to the photo gallery was filled with ribbons and trophies. One in particular stood out.

"What's this?"

"The trophy?"

"Yes."

"Ah... that's the Virginia Gold Cup. Very prestigious. They've been running the race since 1922 and there's always been a Darcy in the field, but Fitz is the only Darcy to win it."

Eliza gestured toward the glass-enclosed case. "Why is it more prestigious than the rest?"

"You have to win the race three times before they let you keep the trophy."

"Oh. The others are all for races, too?"

"Races and shows... horse people love to compete."

"And Fitz won all of them?"

"No. All the Darcys have been equestrians. Those awards span a very long history for the family."

Looking at all the ribbons, trophies and photographs it was clear that the Darcys weren't just equestrians. Horses were the family's life blood.

"You said the farm is self-sufficient. What does that mean exactly?"

"It means we make enough money to maintain the place. Here at Pemberley we breed horses, sell them, train them and have several stallions that stand at stud."

"Stand at stud?"

"People will pay a hefty fee to have a champion like Lord Nelson impregnate their mares. It's one of the reasons horse people compete. The more a horse wins, the more valuable the semen; hence the more expensive the stud fee."

Jake said it very matter-of-factly but his explanation embarrassed Eliza a bit. "That kind of thing really keeps a place like this running?"

"Indeed it does and has for generations." He paused. "We've had some tough times, though, particularly after Bill died."

"Bill?"

"Fitz' father. When Fitz took control we didn't have any champions, and that meant no stud fees. Most of the mares were aged, too, so we were unable to breed them, but he managed to turn it all around."

She would have asked how but was pretty sure she wouldn't understand it anyway.

"He even converted one of the agricultural fields to windmills and solar panels, which provides enough electricity to

supply Pemberley Farms and several of the surrounding proper-
ties. He charges only what we need to maintain the equipment."

"Fitz did all that?"

"Yes, he did, and more."

"I had no idea."

Jake smiled, his eyes sparkling with undiluted pride. "He's
quite a young man."

Eliza shielded her eyes as she left the dim lighting of the
barn and stepped out into the bright sunlight. The story of the
Darcy family and Pemberley Farms was incredible. Her rational mind had questioned whether it was possible for Fitz to be
as kind and sensitive as he seemed, on top of being rich and
handsome. Now she'd learned that when he was not much more
than a teenager he had succeeded in bringing his centuries-old
home into the twenty-first century, at the same time restoring
and maintaining its history and charm. He seemed to get better
and better. Could he possibly be real?

Relationships were not her forte, but she did have to question whether all the projects and charities weren't just a way
to avoid getting close to people, as Jenny said he'd been doing
since high school. In spite of Jenny's optimistic assurance that
Fitz had suddenly become his old cheerful self because of Eliza,
logic told her that people don't change overnight if they change
at all. Breathing-in the moist morning air she dug the pencil
out of her pocket, determined to stop her mind from driving a
relationship that didn't even exist yet into the ground.

Chapter 9

Sitting on the top rail of the fence, Eliza waited for Fitz. Pushing aside all the questions whirling around in her head about him, she opened her sketch pad. The landscape was amazing from the trees, bushes and grass that surrounded the barn to the majestic mountains in the distance; there were so many beautiful sights on the estate that it would take her years to run out of scenes to paint here. She smiled at the thought that she might be welcome here for years.

Holding the sketch pad at arms-length, she was pleased with the just-completed scene: Jane Austen's Chawton Cottage surrounded by Fitz Darcy's Pemberley Farms. She closed the pad. She'd finish it later when Fitz could describe the immediate area around the cottage so it would look as it had when Jane was living there.

As she slipped the pencil into her pocket she heard a sound that was becoming surprisingly familiar. The thought that a city girl from Manhattan could find horses' hooves on packed dirt and gravel a familiar sound made her giggle.

The look that greeted her wasn't what she'd expected. He smiled, but there was a question in his eyes. Still, in her exuberance Eliza jumped down from her perch on the split-rail fence when horse and rider were but a few feet away.

Lord Nelson stopped suddenly, startled by the unexpected motion. He reared, snorting, then started backing away from the frightened visitor.

Jake rushed out of the barn to Eliza. "Are you all right?"

"I guess." Innocently she asked, "Did I do that?"

Before Jake could answer Fitz replied sharply, "Yes, you did."

The barn manager glanced up at Fitz, then back to Eliza. "Nelson is very high strung. He can be extremely skittish when he's startled by something or someone unfamiliar. He just doesn't know you." He looked back at Fitz and pointedly said, "So, no, you didn't do anything. It wasn't your fault."

As everyone took a deep breath, the horse continued to snort and whinny, obviously still agitated. Eliza, having plastered herself against the fence, was afraid to move.

The tall Virginian dismounted, obviously as agitated as his horse. If Eliza had hoped for some comfort and reassurance from her host she was sorely disappointed for anger had filled his clear green eyes. It was the second time in their short acquaintance that he had appeared imposing and intimidating, and both times it seemed to come on suddenly; one moment he was fine and the next seething with anger.

"What the hell are you doing down here anyway?"

Surprised by the hostility of the question, Eliza said, "I beg your pardon?"

"I want to know what you're doing at the barn. You don't ride." Through a snide chuckle, he added, "And you're obviously afraid of horses, so what do you want?"

Her abject terror turned to anger. "I don't *want* anything. I wasn't aware that there were restricted areas. Perhaps you should have given me a list of places you don't want me to go. You know, you can be a really arrogant ass." She turned and walked quickly up the path.

Realizing too late that he might have been unnecessarily harsh, he called, "Eliza?"

She did not respond and quickened her pace. She was almost running by the time she reached the lawn.

Fitz looked at Jake "Was that as bad as I think it was?"

Jake raised an eyebrow as he took Nelson's reins. "Worse... a *lot* worse. I can't believe you blamed her for that, like you thought she did it on purpose. She had no way of knowing Lord Nelson would react like that. You know he bolts when he sees a rabbit in the field."

"Yes, but—"

"There is no but. She doesn't know horses and you know that. You overreacted, plain and simple, and you owe her an apology."

Fitz stared at the ground.

"She isn't going to hear your apology from here."

Fitz looked up the empty path and back to Jake. "Do you think I'll ever learn?"

"You haven't up to now, so I doubt it." He led Nelson into the barn.

Small puffs of dust and bits of gravel followed Fitz as he trudged up the dirt path, his head down. He ran his hand through his hair and rubbed the back of his neck. *What was I thinking?* Of course the obvious answer was that he hadn't been thinking at all.

He'd spent a good part of the morning fantasizing about Eliza, thinking about how much he liked her and enjoyed being with her, how right it felt. He even thought he might be falling in love with her. Then this one unexpected thing happened and he'd lost it. *What's wrong with me?*

The veranda was empty. *She probably returned to the Rose bedroom*, he thought. *Of course, she might be there packing to leave; if she is, I hope I can convince her to stay.* He wasn't sure how he was going to apologize adequately for any of it, but avoiding it wouldn't help. He took a deep breath and headed up the stairs for what would surely be a volatile confrontation, if she would speak to him at all.

He hesitated in the doorway; her overnight bag was still on the floor next to the armoire, a good sign. The French doors to the balcony were open and Eliza was leaning on the railing, her dark hair shimmering in the morning sun. *My raven-haired beauty*, he thought. He smiled, then breathed deeply and stepped into the room.

As he walked across the hardwood floor she continued staring straight ahead.

Her sketch pad lying on the bed caught his attention. It was open to the drawing she had been working on at the barn. "This is Chawton Cottage."

She glanced at him over her shoulder. Without comment she directed her gaze out toward the lawn again. *Does he think I don't know what I drew?* She was trying desperately to control her anger.

"It's very nice. But this isn't what the Hampshire countryside looks like. This looks more like—" He stopped, suddenly realizing what she had actually drawn. He looked beyond her at the mountains that matched her picture, then looked at the floor. "Oh."

Her only response was a none too pleasant look and a shake of her head. Then she looked away again.

He walked out onto the balcony and stood next her. "I'm sorry, Eliza.

She made no response. "I didn't mean for that to happen." Still she said nothing. She glanced at him. "You aren't going to make this easy for me are you?"

"Is there a reason I should?"

"No, I guess not. It's just that Lord Nelson is very excitable, temperamental."

"And very expensive... yes, I know."

"That didn't have anything to do with it."

"You weren't afraid he'd get hurt?"

"No. Well yes, he could have gotten hurt... but I was afraid *you* might have gotten hurt."

"My getting hurt didn't cross your mind."

"Yes it did. I even asked if you were okay."

"No you didn't, Jake did."

She was right, of course, so he said nothing.

She turned slightly so she was looking directly at him. "I'm sorry I upset your horse. I didn't do it on purpose, but tell me, why was today so different from the other day when I first arrived and surprised Lord Nelson? You didn't get angry then."

"We startled you, you didn't startle us... besides, you were injured."

"So your being startled and my *not* being hurt made you angry?"

"No, of course not."

"What then? Explain it to me."

"Look, the bottom line is that I didn't expect to see you at the barn. If Nelson hadn't been so disturbed I probably would have overlooked it."

"Overlooked my being at the barn? Well, as I said before, you really should have given me a list of where I could and couldn't go." She paused. "Maybe I should just go home."

"No, please. I mean no... I... I don't want you to go, and of course you can go anywhere on the estate you want. It's just that since you don't like horses it never occurred to me that you'd go to the stables. It just surprised me to see you there. I wouldn't expect to find Faith in my study since she doesn't read and I would question her intentions if I found her there."

"So you were questioning my intentions?"

Unable to deny the truth of the statement, he was overwhelmed with remorse, "No. Yes. I'm so sorry. I really didn't mean it the way it sounded."

"To satisfy your curiosity regarding my intentions, I figured at thirty-four years old I shouldn't be afraid of horses just because they're bigger than I am. What better place to try to get over it than a horse farm? After meeting Jake and Windy I decided to wait for you so we could walk up to the house together." When he didn't respond she added, "But I still don't understand what happened or why."

Fitz shook his head. "It's not a justifiable excuse, I know, but I tend to be suspicious of what people want from me, particularly people I don't know but even people I do."

This was the kind of thing Jenny had said he did to protect himself from getting too close to people. She decided she wouldn't let him losing his cool over something relatively unimportant ruin an almost perfect weekend. She took a step toward him and slipped her arms around him. "I don't know what those other people want from you that makes you so suspicious, but be assured that I only want your body."

Having expected a far more drawn-out exchange, Fitz was pleasantly surprised by her playful comment. He smiled broadly and held her in an embrace, followed by a deep and passionate kiss.

"So you were afraid I'd steal a horse, huh?"

His reply was another enthusiastic kiss.

"Good morning," he whispered as their lips parted.

"About time," she teased.

Chapter 10

Jenny and Artie were enjoying a second cup of coffee while they awaited the return, from wherever he was, of their host. Mrs. Temple had laid out a sumptuous breakfast buffet and Artie was ready and more than willing to eat it, but Jenny insisted they wait for Fitz and Eliza.

When the couple stepped out of the house and onto the porch hand in hand, Jenny whispered to Artie, "See? What did I tell you?"

Fitz laughed. "Talking about us, were you?"

Jenny flashed a radiant smile. "Us? There's an us?"

Eliza and Fitz smiled at each other and Eliza turned very prettily pink.

Fitz said, "Yes, I think it's safe to say there is an us." He squeezed her hand, and she squeezed back.

Artie smiled. "Well, now that we've settled that, may we have breakfast?"

Jenny reached over and patted her husband's hand. "You're such a romantic, y'big palooka."

"That's why you love me isn't it?" He paused. "Let's eat."

As with all the meals at Pemberley Farms, breakfast was superb. Perfectly poached eggs on toasted homemade egg bread, country fried potatoes mixed with lightly seasoned sausage and a fresh fruit salad of melon, berries and peaches. Fresh from the oven blueberry muffins smothered in butter made the coffee taste that much better.

The paraphernalia for the previous week's activities was ready to put back into storage, and even though it all remained on the lawn in plain sight, any thought of Heritage Week or the Rose Ball was being put off until next year. With the farm returning to normal, Fitz and his guests were enjoying the calm after the storm of preparation and celebration.

Jenny was the first to break the comfortable quiet. "We'll be out of your hair soon. Being the Chief of Orthopaedics doesn't, unfortunately, allow Artie to be late for surgery, and since he has an early case tomorrow we need to get home." She flashed a playful grin. "You'll have the house all to yourselves... well, except for the servants."

"Employees, Jenny. They are employees," Fitz said.

Jenny got up, walked over to her host and kissed the top of his head. "You're funny. Call them what you will, but politically correct or not they are in your service. To wit, they are servants. I doubt that it bothers them as much as it bothers you."

"Nevertheless, if you find it necessary to refer to them at all and you don't want to use their given names, I'd prefer you referred to them as my employees."

Jenny stepped back and curtsied. "Yes, Massa."

Fitz straightened in his chair, his back tense, his jaw tightened. His eyes filled with the same anger Eliza had seen at the barn when she upset Lord Nelson, only this time the anger was suppressed—barely, but suppressed. Jenny saw it too. "I'm sorry, Babe. I was just teasing you. After all, I'm the one who's descended from Pemberley Farms slaves, so if I can't joke about it who can?"

"I just don't think it's something to joke about."

"I know you don't. You feel guilty for what your ancestors did and I love you for it, but it wasn't your fault so lighten up. I don't care, you shouldn't either." Jenny threw her arms around Fitz' neck and kissed him. She took a step back. "Okay, enough of this. I have to go throw our stuff in the suitcase so we can be off." With a slightly wicked grin, she added, "And leave the two of you to your own devices."

Eliza said, "Actually, I'd better go pack up my stuff, too."

They all turned to her. Fitz, obviously surprised, asked, "Why? I mean, where are you going?"

She smiled at him. "I need to get back to the city."

"Right now?"

Jenny looked over at Artie and tilted her head in the direction of the front door. Her husband took the hint and got up. "Guess I'll give the ol' ball and chain some help."

As his friends entered the house Fitz took Eliza's hands in his. "I want you to stay."

She flashed a dazzling smile. "I would love nothing more than to stay, but I have responsibilities."

"Like what?"

"Well, I have a business for starters."

"You can run your business from here."

"Well, I could I suppose… if I had my computer here and my studio. My work is in New York."

"Can't it wait a few days?"

"The work probably could, but I'm pretty sure Thelma can't... or won't."

"Thelma?"

"Klein, the document expert from the New York Public Library. You remember, the one you recommended?" She smiled again.

"I hardly think it was a recommendation. I simply said she considered herself an Austen expert and had done an acceptable job putting the exhibit together."

She chuckled. "Right. Anyway, there's Sotheby's too. Tomorrow they plan to announce the pending sale of a previously unknown and *unopened* Jane Austen letter and her personal vanity. Obviously that can't happen now."

He dropped her hands and turned away, walking toward the porch railing. "I should go with you. After all, if it wasn't for me you would still have the letters to sell."

"On the other hand, the one letter would have been opened and immediately declared a fraud since your business card was in it."

"I guess the truth is out of the question."

"Who would believe you traveled through time and met Jane Austen, who then wrote you a letter with which she returned your business card? It's still hard for me to believe."

He turned to face her. "But you do, don't you?"

She went to him, took his hand and kissed the back of it. "Of course I do."

He slipped his arm around her shoulders and sighed.

She said, "Unfortunately that doesn't make it any easier for me to tell them."

Fitz grinned. "You could tell them I made you an offer you couldn't refuse."

"That would make me no more than a mercenary."

"I didn't mean it that way, but it *is* what people like that would understand."

He was right; no one seemed particularly interested in the history or truth about any of it. Thelma had a book deal, and the contract with Sotheby's gave them a sizable commission. She nodded. "You're right. From the beginning everyone kept telling me how valuable all of it was, monetarily. Thelma told me Sotheby's was expecting to get a million and a half dollars for the unopened letter alone, and the vanity could easily go for a hundred thousand. I've never even imagined what it would be like to have that kind of money, so I got swept away by it I guess. I had even decided not to give you the letter."

"Really?"

She nodded. "Yes, but when I was getting ready for the Ball I was sitting at your great-great whatever grandmother's dressing table looking at her portrait and couldn't help wondering what kind of woman she was... what she thought about when she was standing on the balcony waiting for her husband to come riding up on his steed." She smiled. "Then I thought about my little vanity table having really been Jane Austen's, and I realized that what captivated me was that I was looking into the same mirror she had looked into, that it had been her hands that had opened the drawers. Even the idea that she had written while sitting at the vanity wasn't what fascinated me. It was what she thought about when she looked in the mirror, what she kept in the drawers. It was the person who had used it that I wanted to know. And then I remembered that when I found the letters they made me want to know... you. That's when I decided to give them to you.

My father always said you must take responsibility for your own actions, and now that's what I have to do. I gave the letters to you so I have to deal with the fallout. So it's best if I go and try to smooth all the ruffled feathers. And believe me, you don't want to get involved in that."

"But I *am* involved."

"Only because of me and I don't intend to drag you any further into it. But I do need to get home to take care of it."

He squeezed her shoulder. "I suppose you're right. But does it have to be right now? There's a flight tomorrow morning."

She certainly didn't want to go right this minute. On the other hand she was afraid the longer she stayed the harder it would be to leave. Her pause was encouraging so he turned her in his arms and kissed her. His gentle passion melted her resolve. As their lips parted, she said, "If you keep this up I might never leave."

He whispered, "Promises, promises."

Reluctantly she pushed away from him.

He suggested, "How about that morning flight?"

"I was thinking more like tonight."

"Were you?" He flashed a slightly lecherous grin.

Coyly she said, "But I might be able to be persuaded to wait a few hours more."

Once again and without warning he pulled her into his arms, and his kiss made her spine tingle.

As their lips parted a small whimper escaped her throat. "Your powers of persuasion are remarkable, Mr. Darcy."

He smiled. "I'm glad."

Jenny's voice startled them. "Couldn't wait 'til we left, huh?"

Fitz released Eliza and turned toward his friends. "Actually, I forgot you were still here." He grinned at them.

"Nice to know where we fit into the scheme of things."

Artie said, "Right where we belong." With a wink to Fitz, he turned to Jenny. "Come on, Woman. Let's leave the love-birds alone."

Eliza and her host walked his guests to their car and Fitz opened Jenny's door. She hugged him. "I'm really happy for you, Fitz."

"Thanks."

When he went around the car to shake hands with Artie, Jenny hugged Eliza, whispering, "I told you so."

Chapter 11

Simmons was still sitting in the chair, for how long he had no idea. He was trying to make sense of everything he'd seen and heard. He ran his hand over the arm of the chair; even little things seemed so strange. He'd never sat in a soft chair; the ones in his mother's house were all wooden, like the ones in the kitchen at the Great House. This one had a fabric cover like ones in the manor houses at home, with soft stuffing underneath. It amazed him to find it here in the barn. He didn't have any kind of chair in his room at Master Edward's, and unlike most of the stablemen of his acquaintance, the Austen-Knights had given him a room of his own with a bed. He looked over at the bed with its fluffy comforter and pillows. His bed wasn't anything like this one. He couldn't imagine actually living in a place like this, but Dave had acted as though everyone lived this way.

From out in the barn he heard a sound he recognized immediately and wondered whether he should do something. He waited a few minutes but did not hear anyone come into the barn and the noise continued. Simmons opened the door and carefully looked out into the stable. There wasn't anyone around so he stepped out of the room and closed the door.

Halfway down the barn a horse was very agitated. She was scooting around her stall, pawing at the straw and occasionally kicking the walls. He dropped his bag and package just inside the Dutch door and closed it, to make sure Jemma (the plaque next to the door said) couldn't bolt and run away. As he approached she backed away from him, but he soon gained her trust and was able to stand beside her. When he started to leave, suddenly she started all over again.

Trying to find a cause for her fear he finally spied a field mouse. Although most horses would just ignore it if they noticed it at all, Jemma seemed genuinely frightened by it. Before he could venture out in search of the barn cat, although he hadn't actually seen one, the large animal became very agitated again so he bent down, grabbed the small creature by its tail and rushed outside. The mouse squirmed violently at the end of his arm, and he threw it as far as he could away from the building.

When Jemma was calm and before he left her alone, he raked through the straw on the floor, going out of his way to show her that the mouse was gone. He leaned the rake against the wall. He didn't know whether coming through the portal had used up his energy or whether the excitement that had kept him awake most of the night had sapped it but he suddenly realized he was exhausted. He petted the horse one last time, telling her that the mouse was gone and she would be okay, then left. He had just one stop to make before returning to the room.

The dense shrubbery around the barn afforded Simmons the much needed privacy his activity required, but as he was coming back into the open and readjusting his trousers he was met by Dave. Startled, the young Englishman said nothing.

Dave grinned. "Better not let Linda catch you doing that."

"Linda?"

"Mrs. Clifton." He paused. "Look, I know we're guys and sometimes it's just easier to deal with nature's call out here rather than trekking inside. But from now on use the commode in the bathroom because Linda gets really ticked off about stuff like that."

"Commode?"

"Loo, john, toilet, chamber pot, commode—whatever you want to call it, just don't do it out here."

His mind reeling from the sudden flood of information and the embarrassment of apparently making such a mistake, Simmons could think of nothing to say except, "Okay."

"Good. I'm going to get the horses off the hot walker. I'll stop by later and get you for dinner."

Simmons nodded.

The Regency horseman remained still, taking deep breaths. He didn't move until Dave disappeared around the other side of the barn. Then he rushed to the room where Dave had said he could "bunk," whatever that meant. Closing the door he leaned against it, trying to regain his bearings. He was trembling. Having made such an egregious error, he'd been afraid to say anything lest it might be wrong as well.

He sat in the same chair as before and ran his fingers through his hair. *What am I going to do?* If he couldn't even manage during the first few hours of his visit here, how could he ever get to America and find Mr. Darcy? His throat started to close slightly and tears welled in his eyes. *What will happen to me if I stay here? Will the portal open tonight?* As a tear streaked his cheek, he stood up and sniffed to stop the possibility of more. *Whatever might happen, I'm a man and men don't cry... not out of fear, anyway.* But fear definitely had a grip on him.

From the doorway to the bathroom, where Dave said he'd find the commode, he could see only the outline of the fixtures since there was no window. He stepped in, running his hand along the wall to guide his way. Suddenly a loud noise started from overhead and the room was filled with a bright white light—not the radiant light of the portal but bright enough to see everything in the room clearly.

Willing himself not to panic at the unexpected occurrence and holding his breath, Simmons looked up. There was a glowing orb in the middle of the ceiling as well as several small ones near the mirror on the wall. Not far from the ceiling light was the source of the noise. It seemed to come from behind a grate where a windmill-like contraption was spinning around. Realizing that it could do him no harm he looked around the bathroom, taking note of the small white switch that he had accidently thrown. He purposely flipped it up and down, starting and stopping the noise and light several times.

The bathtub he'd seen earlier was at the end of the room and appeared to be white porcelain—very unlike the ones of copper and bronze that he was used to seeing—and silver pipes were coming out of the edge of it. At the other end of the room near the door was a porcelain basin on a stand. There was no pitcher, but it too had silver pipes on its edge. He ran his hand over the surface of the basin; it was cold, as were the pipes. He turned the handle that jutted out from one of three pipes and stepped back as water rushed from the center one. Gingerly he pushed the handle back and the water stopped. *Water inside....* He pulled and pushed the handle several more times, turning the water on and off, on and off. *Amazing!*

Another fixture sat between the basin and the tub. *That must be the commode that Dave talked about.* The only commodes he'd ever seen were chairs with holes in the seat and a chamber pot underneath, but this seemed to be all of it in one piece and there was water in it. Like the tub and basin there was a silver handle, which he pushed. He watched in amazement as water swirled around the pot then down the hole and out as the pot refilled with fresh water. Flushing the toilet a few more times, he realized that chamber pots didn't need to be emptied anymore; they did it themselves.

He assumed that the pipes at the edge of the bathtub had water running out of them, too. He turned one of the handles and watched as a torrent of water splashed into the tub. He found another handle, different than the rest, this one was on a round metal object which he turned and was more than a little surprised when rain-like water flowed from an overhead pipe. *Rain inside!* He reached out to turn off the water, but quickly pulled his hand back. He was almost burned by the heat emanating from the faucet. *Somehow the water is heated!* Carrying boiling water from the kitchen to the upper floors of the house was no longer necessary. Gingerly he turned off the water still running into the bathtub, then looked around. *Truly an amazing room.* He laughed at the number of times he'd thought the word *amazing* just since entering the bathroom, but it was the only word he could think of to describe everything. *Amazing... and all the more so because it's in the barn. What must the house be like?*

Simmons found the switch that turned off the light and fan and made the room dark and quiet once again. In the bedroom there were a couple of the same kind of switches, which he tried and found that they caused different lights in different parts of the room to ignite. He looked closely at the lamp on the table next to the chair and found that the light contained no fire, just a very bright globe that blinded him for a second when he looked directly at it.

He sat down on the bed after switching off all the lights. The bed was springy. He'd never slept on anything but straw; even his mother had stuffed their mattresses at home with straw when he was a child. This bed seemed to have springs and a very soft stuffing. It was like sitting on a cloud; at least it was what he imagined being on a cloud was like.

The twenty-first century was truly an astonishing place. *If there were so many unfamiliar things just in this room, will I be able to work with the newfangled contraptions that were everywhere?* Everyone would be able to see that he was unfamiliar with all these new inventions, making it almost impossible to not make more blunders that would surely reveal his secret. *If only I knew which numbers on Mr. Darcy's calling card would allow him to contact the American....* He realized suddenly that even if he knew which numbers were the right ones, he had no idea how to use them or what to do with them. *What am I to do?*

The emotions and efforts of the day finally caught up with him. After a snack of some of the bread and cheese he'd brought with him, he lay down on the soft bed.

Chapter 12

Three loud raps and then Dave's voice through the door brought Simmons out of a deep sleep.

"Come on, Simmons, we're having dinner with the Cliftons."

Making an effort to straighten his clothes, Simmons shuffled to the door; he was hungry but he was afraid of being around people. What if he made another bad error, and in front of his lordship? That would be terrible and probably would ruin any chance of getting to Mr. Darcy. However, he couldn't just ignore the people who had welcomed him as a friend of the American horseman and shown him such hospitality. It would be disrespectful. He took a deep breath and opened the door.

"Come on, I'm starving."

Simmons nodded and stepped out of the room that had become something of a refuge for him. As they were walking through the barn, a very loud bell chimed, startling the young man. "What's that?"

Dave said, "Phone."

Phone. Miss Jane had told him about a communication device called a telephone. He wondered whether phone and telephone was the same thing. Assuming that to be the case, he decided not to ask about it, fearful that too many questions would arouse suspicion.

The dirt path wound through some shrubbery and then around to the back of the manor house to a room unlike anything Simmons had ever seen. The walls of the space were made of a mesh-like material that seemed to allow air to flow through the room; overhead another windmill-like machine was spinning slowly above the trestle table where his Lordship and Lady Clifton were already seated.

Simmons stood near the door, taking it all in as people started to arrive and sit; people Dave had told him were neighbors of the Cliftons. Then the biggest surprise of all, several servants also sat at the table with the Master and his friends. Dave nudged him, indicating that they were expected to sit at the table as well, but Simmons had never eaten in the company of Master Edward or even Miss Jane so this was yet another new experience and one that made him exceedingly uncomfortable.

The housekeeper, the stablemen, and even the cook were sitting beside the gentry. He had thought Mr. Darcy unusual in his equal treatment of people, but here was a whole group who seemed to do the same thing. *Is everyone in this time like that? Will I be accepted everywhere?* The word *amazing* came to mind once again.

The women were all dressed like Miss Jane or Maggie and the men dressed like Master Edward or himself. It made him a bit more comfortable in spite of the situation and incredible food.

Dave called it a buffet. "It's self-serve," he quietly explained. "So the house staff can join the party and not have to serve."

Simmons had never seen such a feast, at least not for the servants; even Miss Jane's brother would only send out a leg of mutton or a shank from some game animal, and he was one of the more generous masters according to other servants.

The array of food was breathtaking: leg of lamb, gammon and roasted beef, cooked vegetables, salads, a rich brown soup and baskets of bread. On a smaller table were a variety of sweets, which he overheard someone say were made by Linda Clifton.

Simmons had never seen any of the ladies at Chawton Great House in the kitchen. He could imagine Miss Jane there but not the others. Only the cooks and maids were ever in the kitchen. He laughed thinking of Miss Fanny baking a cake.

The neighbors were first to leave and then the servants—or as Dave called them, the staff—started going in groups of two and three. That was when Simmons rose, but Dave stopped him. "Linda asked us to stay after everyone else is gone."

Simmons looked at the young man, and dread gripped him. "Why?"

"I don't know."

Simmons' stomach felt like it was tied in knots. Had the Cliftons somehow discovered how he had arrived, or were they simply going to ask him to leave? While he waited, his mind and heart filled with fear. The time seemed to drag on and on, but finally the only ones remaining on the sun porch were the Cliftons, Dave and himself.

"So Simmons, where do you come from?" Linda asked. Immediately she saw the confusion and question on his face. "I mean, where were you born? Where did you grow up?"

He remembered telling Dave he was from Derbyshire, so he repeated that information.

"Where did you come from this morning?"

"Chawton Great House, Ma'am."

"Did you work there?"

"I did, Ma'am, in the stables." It was a reflex to say it but now he wasn't even sure the Great House or stables were still there. He held his breath.

Linda looked at her husband. "I didn't realize they had horses." She turned back to Simmons. "So you like working with horses."

"I hope one day to be a horse doctor. I think Mr. Darcy will help me in that."

Dave chimed in. "Fitz is great about stuff like that. When I was working for him I told him that my sister wanted to go to college but my folks couldn't afford it and the job she had didn't pay enough or give her the time to go to school. Fitz made arrangements for her to get a scholarship. Now she's a teacher in some hotsy-totsy private school, the first one in our family to graduate from college."

"So your plan is to go to the U.S. and work for Fitz?" Roger asked.

"Mr. Darcy, yes, Sir."

"When do you intend to leave?"

"I'm not sure, Sir."

"Is Fitz paying your expenses for the trip?"

"Oh, no Sir. I want to make my own way."

Roger and Linda looked at each other. Roger said, "I see. So you want to work?"

"Yes, Sir."

"If you were working at Chawton Great House already, why did you stop?"

Simmons tried not to panic. What could he say to explain that without revealing his true origins? The only thing he could think of in this time of horseless vehicles was, "No more horses, Sir."

Linda added, "I wondered about that when you said it. I was pretty sure they'd gotten rid of the horses."

Roger said, "Well, if you'd like to work for us while you make arrangements for your trip to the States, you're more than welcome. We can always use a good hand with the horses." He turned to his wife. "Right, Sweetpea?"

"Definitely." She turned back to Simons. "You can stay in the room in the barn if that suits you."

Suit me? It more than suited him. Many of his fears started to subside and he thanked them profusely. After hearing some of the other servants talking, he realized that he would need money to make a trip to America and now the Cliftons were giving him the opportunity to make some. He couldn't believe his good fortune, but it would remain good only if no one found out how he arrived here. Keeping that secret seemed to be getting more difficult with each passing hour.

Dave got up and Simmons followed, bowing as he left the table.

Linda watched as the two young men left the room. "A very pleasant sort, isn't he? A bit shy though. He took care of Lord Nelson, which is why he knows Fitz—Dave mentioned it when he introduced us this morning—so it makes sense that he works with horses."

Roger chuckled at his wife. She hadn't taken a breath or left anything for him to say except to agree with her, which of course he did.

After bidding goodnight to Dave, who did not return to the barn after the meal, Simmons took his time and stopped to see Jemma. He was still excited by his good fortune in having found friends of Mr. Darcy who, like the American, treated him well.

With all the mistakes he'd made earlier in the day and his inability to contact Mr. Darcy, the Regency horseman had decided to return to his own time. But this new opportunity of working for the Cliftons had put that idea behind him, at least for the time being. He was confident that he would discover how the telephone worked and which numbers on the card would let him make the contact with the American.

Back in his room he sat in the soft chair, wondering what Miss Jane would think about all of the things he'd seen. He wanted to tell her all about his experiences here, and a sudden wave of sadness came over him; he might never see her again. He reached down beside the chair to touch the package she'd given him for the Virginian. He felt around with his hand, then got up and looked. It was gone. He looked everywhere; under the chair, under the bed, in all the cupboards and drawers. It wasn't there. What happened to it?

He sat on the edge of the bed trying desperately to remember what he'd done with it if he hadn't left it by the chair. Suddenly he bolted from the room and ran to Jemma's stall. He had taken it with him, he was sure of it.

He stopped only long enough to greet the horse, then pushed the hay around the floor. After he'd raked and sifted through all of the loose floor covering it became painfully evident that the package simply wasn't there. He leaned his head against the horse. "What have I done, Jemma? The only thing Miss Jane asked of me and I've lost it. What should I do?"

He hadn't been in the future for a whole day and already he'd made several big mistakes. *I don't belong here,* he mumbled. He made his way outside toward the low wall and sat in the tall grass. As darkness descended, the disappointed groom fell asleep while he waited for sunrise.

White puffy clouds dotted the dawn sky. Over the wall Simmons could see a small pasture and houses in what used to be the meadow on the edge of Chawton wood, which appeared to no longer be part of Master Edward's estates. A fine mist rose from the moist grass on the opposite side of the stacked field-stone fence. The mist thickened to a fog and suddenly the field looked as it had when he'd left the day before, acres of meadow with woods on the other side; the trees, flowers and the lay of the land were familiar to him. He hesitated, trying to decide what to do. It would be easy to simply step over the low lying wall and return home to the people and things he knew; but he would be returning to a life of servitude. *Nothing wrong with serving*, he thought. *It's honorable work.* But he wanted more, and home was not where that could happen. The sun's ascent was accompanied by the brilliant white light that seemed to be the portal closing.

As the remaining glare faded Simmons was already questioning his decision to stay. He didn't want to go back but things kept happening that made him think coming here had been a mistake. Still, knowing he could escape through the portal later if it became necessary gave him the confidence to go ahead with his plan. The Cliftons' generous hospitality and offer of work is what he needed to stay here for a while. In the meantime he would try to learn as much about this new world as he could, and just maybe he'd discover how to reach Mr. Darcy. So far the machines and other items he'd seen were surprising but fairly simple, and he was sure he could learn to use them. In time he could also learn what he needed to know to go to America and become a horse doctor.

As the sun rose higher in the morning sky, he turned back to the barn. Like yesterday the sound of horses caused him to step into the grass at the side of the path. Linda and Roger Clifton came up alongside him on horseback.

Roger said, "Good morning, Simmons."

The young Englishman doffed his hat and bowed, "Sir, Ma'am."

"Taking a constitutional I see," she said.

"Ma'am?"

"A walk."

"Yes, Ma'am."

"Enjoy the morning, then," Linda said as she and Roger continued on.

Simmons said, "Thank you, Ma'am."

The British couple rode ahead of him and turned into the woods. Under the canopy of intertwining branches above them, Linda and Roger walked their horses on their daily sunrise ride.

Roger chuckled. "Until last night, I can't remember the last time someone bowed to me."

Linda agreed. "I think it's kind of sweet. Did you notice he's still wearing his costume from yesterday? Well, it may not be a costume; I think he may belong to a sect of plain-living Mennonites. I was reading about them a few months ago. They live on farms and don't use technology; no computers, televisions or phones. They use some mechanical farm equipment but they still use horses for personal travel. They believe clothes should be modest, and it seems to me that they don't use zippers or Velcro or anything like that."

"That certainly would explain his discomfort in the modern world." Roger paused a moment. "If they don't have phones do you think he's actually been in contact with Fitz? Is there really a plan for him to go to the States or did he just decide to do this on his own?'"

"He has been vague about that, and I do think it's strange that Fitz didn't tell us about it if it was planned. On the other hand maybe it was done by post. Without access to phones or the Internet, the post is the only way. Maybe he's just gotten here a few days early."

"I don't know. His insistence that he make his own way is commendable but I suspect part of that is because he hasn't talked to Fitz about any of this. Perhaps we should call him."

"Let's wait a bit, in case it is planned. Fitz might just show up. He doesn't always tell us when he's coming."

"Well, if we haven't heard from him by the time we get back from Brighton we should definitely call him. I do want to know that this is all on the up and up."

Chapter 13

Chawton, England
Summer, 1813

Jane rolled over in bed and stared at the ceiling. Sometimes it felt as though morning came much too soon. She threw back the covers and slipped out of bed. Barefoot, she stepped lightly to the window. Cassandra's mignonette stood tall, waving slightly in the summer morning. The pale pink peonies at the base of the oak tree bowed their heads in the soft breeze. Jane stretched and yawned.

Wearing only her bodice petticoat she brushed her hair, it fell over her shoulders and down her back as the silver brush slipped through the dark tresses. She ran her fingers through it, then lifted it and allowed it to fall again. It felt free. *If only I could wear it loose,* she thought. *If only I were brave enough.* But propriety dictated that ladies wore their hair off of their necks, so with a sigh she called to her maid to help pin her hair up into its usual fashion.

At the vanity Sally put the finishing touches on Jane's hair and fastened the buttons at the back of her dress. Just as the young maid slipped the last button into its hole, Maggie shouted from downstairs for help with some unknown chore. Making a quick curtsy, the girl rushed out of the bedroom. Hearing her running down the stairs, Jane silently admonished her to be careful.

The drawing room was stiflingly stuffy, so Jane opened the window to let in the cool morning air. The piano sat at the end of the room opposite the window and as large as the room was, it took only a few steps to reach the small but lovely instrument she had purchased especially for the Cottage after moving to Chawton. Cassie often told people that music was her sister's true passion and a natural talent, but the truth was that Jane simply believed anything worth doing was worth doing well. To that end she practiced on the pianoforte daily, using one of the books into which she had carefully copied music she particularly enjoyed. Completing her regular hour of playing, she slipped the music book into the bookcase.

Maggie had started a fire in the dining room and left a rack of thickly sliced toasted bread on the small oak table. Along with the toast was a dish of fresh butter and a small fruit compote made up mostly of peaches, plums and apricots from the garden. She preferred such a meal for the start of the day rather than the heavy breakfast of meats favored by her brothers. The compote reminded her that they would soon have to start putting up preserves and making wines from the fruits and berries before they were too ripe.

Jane set the copper tea kettle over the hearth to boil and with a small iron key opened the cupboard beside the fireplace, bringing out canisters of tea and sugar.

As she leisurely sipped her tea, Jane's attention was drawn to the window when she heard the squawk of chickens. A man on horseback had caused the skittish birds to scatter in the roadway and flap into the yard. A post chaise rumbled by and she wondered at its final destination, Portsmouth perhaps. Two girls walked by, shielding themselves from the summer sun with a pink parasol. A black dog scampered across the dirt road.

Not for the first time in the last two days she pondered the possible result of Simmons experiment. Was he in America? Darcy said it only took five hours in the air machines. Was he safe? Pushing aside the unanswerable questions Jane completed her meal, put away the tea and sugar and carried her dishes into the kitchen where Sally relieved her of them.

In the drawing room again, Jane sat down at the small rosewood secretary near the window and withdrew a piece of paper from one of the shallow drawers below the glass enclosed shelves. She began to write.

Jane believed that the true art of letter-writing was to express on paper exactly what one would say to the same person by word of mouth, much like sitting with friends gossiping about the latest fashions, local activities and the people. She loved to write about people, real and imagined. So the letter to her brother Frank, aboard HMS Elephant, was filled with the goings on at the previous evening's dinner party. She did not spend too many words on the fabrics as men found such things dull, but she talked of Annabelle and her brother's exploits and Lord Moore-Jeffries' latest trip to the continent. She spent some time detailing the activities of her nieces and nephews,

Edward's children. She finished the letter by signing her name with a bit of a flourish just as the bell at the gate chimed the arrival of the post rider.

She cocked her head in anticipation of Maggie's footsteps scurrying across the wood floor of the entry. Dropping her pen onto the ink stand she heard the housekeeper's impatient exchange with the rider and then the front door close. Out the window she watched the young horseman astride his bay mare scatter the gravel in the road as they galloped off toward Winchester.

She turned at the soft knock on the drawing room door and smiled as Maggie came in with three letters. The housekeeper made a quick curtsy and put them on the small round table just inside the door. "There's one from Miss Austen, Miss Jane," she said, then hurried off to complete the task interrupted by the postal delivery.

Of the three letters Maggie had left, two were addressed to Jane; she turned one over and snapped the seal.

Her mother and her sister, Cassandra, had arrived at Great Bookham in good health after several weeks in London with her brother Henry. The weather on their arrival was excellent. Cousin Cassandra and Reverend Cooke were in tolerable health, but only tolerable. Their daughter Mary was in good spirits and glad for the company. Jane was pleased to find that her nephew, James Edward, who was already visiting at Bookham, very much liked the backgammon set she had sent along as a birthday gift. Not wanting to injure the feelings of his young sister, Jane also had sent a small china tea cup and saucer for Caroline to use on special occasions. Cass wrote that their arrival was occasion enough and the eight year old had felt like a grown up lady having tea with them using her own special cup.

After reading the second letter, a note from her publisher, Jane added a postscript to the long letter she had just completed writing to Frank:

> *You will be glad to hear that every copy of S&S is sold and that it has brought me £140, besides the Copyright, if that should ever be of any value. I have therefore written myself into £250, which only makes me long for more.*
>
> *I have something in hand, which I hope on the credit of P&P will sell well, tho' not so entertaining. And by the 'bye, shall you object to my mentioning the Elephant in it, & two or three of your other old ships? I have done it, but it shall not stay to make you angry. They are only just mentioned.*

Browning, the houseman and general help around Chawton Cottage, had hitched the donkey to the cart Edward had given her mother and was waiting at the gate. He helped Jane into the cart and then handed her the reins. "You be careful, Miss."

"I will. Thank you, Browning." Gently she tugged on the leather straps to start the donkey moving and then guided the small animal onto the road to Holybourne.

As the little donkey cart made its way down the beech-lined drive Jane smiled. Maywood was a small but charming park landscaped in the Capability Brown manner, naturalistic in style with sweeping lawns flowing into the trees and up to the house, free-form gardens very unlike the formal French gardens of her brother's estate at Godmersham. The park seemed almost to drift into the surrounding countryside.

Maywood house, designed by Robert Adams, was much larger than Chawton Cottage, though not as expansive as Chawton Great House. However, it was elegant in its simplicity.

The scored stucco exterior was painted what they called pink but was actually the colour of smoked salmon and was complemented by the grey bark and dark green leaves of the stand of birch trees directly behind the house. Jane had seldom seen a house as lovely.

Sitting as it did on a rise, Annabelle had seen her friend enter the park and was waiting for her on the trellised porch. The young woman looked handsomer than ever in a blue muslin gown. A groom from the Rodgers' stables was waiting as Jane brought the donkey to a stop.

The young man took the reins. "I'll brush and water him, Miss."

"Thank you, George."

He bowed slightly to Annabelle. "You just send Jimmy down to fetch me when Miss Jane is ready to go and I'll bring the cart 'round, Miss Annabelle."

Annabelle nodded and slipped her arm through Jane's, leading her into the house. "I have so much I want to tell you about the wedding plans."

Jane smiled at the exuberance of her young friend and squeezed her arm.

The interior of the home was as lovely as the exterior. The entry was made bright and cheery by yellow walls. The sun streaming in through the fan light over the front door warmed the vestibule. On the ceiling a brass and glass chandelier was filled with wax candles. A large oval mirror hung over a serpentine chest inlaid with leaves and flowers. Sitting atop the chest was a porcelain figurine of an oriental potentate whose hands, head and tongue moved with the slightest assistance. Removing her bonnet and gloves, Jane blew on it and giggled when it nodded. She set her bonnet and gloves on the chest next to the humorous porcelain piece.

"Tell Molly we will have tea in my room," Annabelle said to her maid as she led her friend up the stairs. "Come, I want to show you the silks."

Annabelle's bedroom was an explosion of flowers and floral motifs everywhere. The room suited her friend, but Jane preferred furnishings that were more utilitarian and simple.

Even before Jane had a chance to sit down Annabelle had spread out the pink silk and laid it on the bed. "Here it is, Jane. Is it not the perfect colour for you?"

Jane looked at the gossamer silk as it lay across the moss-coloured bedcover and imagined herself in it. "It is lovely, Annabelle, but are you sure you will not want it?"

"Oh, no. I cannot wear such a light colour as this. And see?" She held the material up under Jane's chin. "It is perfectly becoming on you. No, you must have it. Would it not make a perfect gown for Lord Moore-Jeffries' Michaelmas Ball? Yes, it is *just* the thing!"

Jane gave it some thought. Michaelmas was still several weeks away, so there was ample time and the pink silk would make a charming ball gown. The thought of being too old for such a youthful colour crossed her mind. What would people say if she should appear in public in such a colour? Why was she doing this to herself? A bonnet she liked but was too old to wear and now a fabric she was too old to wear? If a suitable style was used to make the gown it should be apposite to all respectable people. And why should she care anyway? She was not old and still had a pleasing figure that might be deemed youthful. She could hardly be condemned for the colour of such a gown.

Seemingly unaware of Jane's distraction, Annabelle hurried on. "Pink silk rose buds would be set off nicely by your pretty dark hair." She sighed. "I have always envied you and Cass, that you both have such beautiful hair."

Jane looked at Annabelle with some surprise. "I thank you for the compliment but you are the perfect beauty with your flaxen hair, fair skin and pale blue eyes."

Annabelle nodded. "My mother tells me all the time how pretty I am and how lucky I am to be so fair, but sometimes, Jane, I feel so *pale*... like a ghost. My hair has almost no colour at all, not like Cassandra's. Hers is like beech trees in the autumn... so lively."

Like so many of the young, Annabelle had moved on to other things before Jane could respond. "You are going to the Michaelmas Ball, are you not?"

Jane said, "Of course. My mother and sister will be home by then and Henry is coming into the country as well."

"Will Fanny be there?"

"We are yet unsure as to the date of their departure for Kent. However, if my brother and his family are still in Hampshire I am sure they will attend."

As Jane completed the sentence she watched a length of white silk float onto the bed. She picked up an edge of the diaphanous fabric, feeling the silver threads entwined in the stems and blossoms of the ribbon embroidery.

"Is it not beautiful? Tommy brought it to me for my wedding dress. I was going to wear blue, but now I will wear white. Oh, and look!" Annabelle draped a piece of Mechlin lace over her head. "He brought this so I can have a veil." The young woman twirled around the room, giddy with excitement and with the delicate lace—in a floral pattern, of course—still on her head. "And to think I was going to wear a bonnet!"

She finished whirling around and collapsed onto the settee covered by embroidered honeysuckle vines. As Jane sat down next to her, Annabelle took a deep breath. "Oh, Jane, I am so excited I can hardly wait!"

Jane smiled. "That is as it should be."

Annabelle touched Jane's hand. "But I am very apprehensive as well."

"Anxiety over such a milestone in one's life is a natural thing."

Quietly Annabelle said, "It is not the wedding about which I feel apprehensive or even the marriage." She looked over at the door then back to Jane. "My mother says the wedding night is a duty that must be borne. But duty or not it is frightening as one hears so many unsavory stories of brides imposed upon."

Jane remembered Mr. Darcy's telling her of the sexual mores in the centuries to come, a time when pleasure in the marriage bed for both partners was paramount. Women were no longer simply chattel, property to be used. Her anger that it was so was tempered by Annabelle's fear. "Does he love you?"

"Oh, yes. He says he loves me more than life itself."

"And do you love him?"

"I cannot imagine life without him."

"It is well for you, as I can think of no fate worse than marriage without affection. As there is affection on both sides I believe you shall be fine."

Jane smiled at the memory of Darcy's playful teasing and gentle touch, like a feather on her skin. The thought of his kisses made her heart beat fast. She took a deep breath and added quietly, "I have it on excellent authority that a patient and gentle partner can make such times quite pleasurable." She shivered at the memory of Darcy's tender caress. "Very pleasurable," she whispered.

"Truly Jane?"

The question brought Jane out of her reminiscence. "I believe so, yes."

Annabelle hugged her friend. "Thank you, Jane."

Chapter 14

The day had dawned bright and beautiful, but a distant roll of thunder tightened a small knot in Jane's stomach. Over the tops of the trees a band of dark clouds was gathering on the horizon. Having opened the window to fill the room with cool morning air, Jane now secured it against the coming storm. Glancing once more at the dark sky she was sure she would be at her brother's house before the storm reached Chawton so she gave it no more thought.

At the gate Browning handed her into the donkey cart, reminding her to be careful. He doffed his hat as she set off for Farringdon.

Mr. Woolls had proudly regaled the other guests at Edward's dinner about improvements he was making to his home. Jane's interest had been piqued when he mentioned an American garden. Her curiosity was further aroused when he said that many of the plants had come over by ship from Virginia where his cousin lived.

Mr. Darcy had never mentioned plants being different in America; of course, they had had little time to talk of such mundane details. She tried to imagine his estate, about which she knew virtually nothing, in fact, all she did know was that he bred horses and it was called Pemberley Farms, and as he had emphatically said, it was not an agricultural farm. That had been yet another way, she realized later, for him to stress the fact that he had no slaves, but then that was before she had known the truth about him. Her beloved Hampshire country-side was alive with horse chestnut trees, birch trees, grasses and wild flowers. An American garden—she was looking forward to seeing that.

As her thoughts were thus engaged the clouds she'd seen on the horizon earlier moved in far more quickly than she had anticipated. A flash of lightning followed by a clap of thunder startled her and once again her stomach tightened. The surrounding countryside seemed otherworldly, illuminated as it was by the lightning, which preceded every clap of thunder. As her agitation grew the rain started in earnest. She turned the donkey around; there would be no American garden today.

The donkey trotted quickly, unaffected by the thunder that was causing Jane's anxiety. His speed, however, was not enough to get Jane out of the pelter in time to avoid getting wet through.

Fanny was beside herself with concern when Jane arrived at the Great House. She rushed her aunt to her bedroom where a maid had just laid and started a fire. Fanny insisted, "We must get you out of these wet clothes and dried off."

An astonished Jane said, "But Fanny, dear, a fire? It is warm; I will dry in due time."

Adamantly Fanny insisted, "Dr. Phillips says that a chill from remaining in wet clothes can cause a cold in the lungs or worse." She paused. "No, we must get you dry. Martha finished dyeing your gown yesterday so we have something for you to wear, and you can borrow one of my bodice petticoats."

Fanny gave Jane a dressing gown and, along with the maid, helped her father's sister out of her wet things and positioned her by the fire. She sent the maid away with the wet clothes and ordered tea to be brought up immediately.

"I am not cold."

"But the heat will dry you. We should take your hair down so it will dry as well."

"Fanny, I am fine."

"You will be when you are warm and dry."

Jane finally relented and resigned herself to her niece's ministrations, admitting, if only to herself, that she rather enjoyed being fussed over. After taking her hair down she combed it through with her fingers, tilting her head toward the fire. The flames were hot enough that she was sure it would take only a very short time for her hair to dry.

While her eldest niece was pouring the chamomile tea they heard Fanny's younger sisters whispering. The two young girls were not allowed in their oldest sibling's room unless specifically invited, so they remained in the doorway.

Fanny sighed, "All right, you may come in."

Jane looked at them and smiled. "What were you two whispering about?"

Louisa timidly said, "Your hair."

"My hair?"

"The other day Marianne told me that she had found you once with your hair down and it was the most beautiful hair she had ever seen... and it is."

"Why, thank you, girls."

Louisa picked up Fanny's brush. "May I brush your hair, Aunt?"

"Of course, dear."

Her young niece ran the boar bristles through her hair over and over until it was completely dry. The natural curl made it fall in soft waves down her back almost to the floor, curled tendrils framing her heart-shaped face. Louisa asked, "Why do you not wear your hair down, Aunt Jane?" She pulled the brush through one last time.

Marianne said, "It is immodest. I told you, mother said so."

Jane said, "And your mother was right. The church says that a woman's hair is her crowning glory so to keep pride under good regulation a woman must tie up and cover her hair."

"But Marianne and I do not."

"You are not yet women."

"What about Fanny? She wears hers up but not covered."

"Fanny is a young woman. Generally it is married women who cover their hair, so only their husbands see it."

"But you and Aunt Cass are not married."

"True, but we are old so we are expected to dress and act in a more conservative manner like married women."

Louisa, in her innocence, said, "I do not understand that at all."

Jane hugged her young relative. "Frankly, Louisa, I do not fully understand it myself."

Fanny interrupted any further questions from her sisters by telling them that they all needed to allow their Aunt Jane some privacy so she could dress for tea. Jane smiled as Fanny took her younger siblings by the hands and the three of them left their father's sister alone.

The rain had stopped and the black clouds parted, revealing a rainbow arching over Edward's estate. It was brilliant against the rain-scrubbed sky. She sighed deeply. Her nieces had been a great comfort during the worst of the thunder storm. The darkness was vacating the sky, portending a sunny afternoon.

Jane turned at the sound of the door opening and Martha came in with the dress. It was one of Jane's favorite gowns, a white muslin that had unfortunately been stained by spilled tea. At her age white was no longer appropriate so she had, herself, used tea to dye it, just enough to cover the stain. But in time the ecru of the tea dye had become dingy and Fanny had suggested that Martha, the Austen-Knight family laundress, dye it for her. To her surprise the gown was now the colour of spring grass, a much brighter colour than she was used to wearing. Could she really wear such a colour in company? White, green—there it was again. She was allowing society and propriety to dictate what she wore based solely on the fact that she was no longer sixteen.

In the borrowed bodice petticoat Jane stared at the green dress as Martha laid it on the bed and left, sending Amy, Fanny's personal maid, to help Jane dress. Completing the chore, the young servant curtsied. "You look nice, Miss Jane."

Jane looked at the woman in the full-length mirror. The high cheekbones had some colour; the dark hair almost glistened in the newly revealed sun streaming through the window. She tilted her head for a different perspective and smiled at her own reflection. Since her fichu was as wet as her dress she would have to go uncovered, leaving the tops of her breasts exposed. In spite of feeling a bit naughty, she was well pleased with the way she looked. Then she reminded herself that *Pride goeth before destruction, and an haughty spirit before a fall*. She hoped her own vanity was not pride enough to cause destruction or even a fall.

In the second floor drawing room Jane entered to many comments from Fanny's friends and guests, espousing her pleasing appearance and high colour; the colour no doubt came from the blush of embarrassment at hearing such admiration from so many. Lord Moore-Jeffries insisted she sit with him after taking a turn about the room and making her compliments to each guest in attendance.

Sitting with his Lordship Jane felt at ease for the first time that afternoon, for while he too had made mention of how lovely she looked, it was as though her father was saying it and that brought her pleasure. Taking small bites of one of the many pastries being served by Fanny, Jane admitted to the Earl that she supposed she must leave off being young now, although as a sort of chaperon for her niece's party she had discovered there were many douceurs. For example she could sit in comfort with him rather than having to make small talk with people she did not know. "Then, of course," she whispered conspiratorially, "I could drink as much wine as I like." They laughed together.

As Fanny's tea party started to wind down, his Lordship sent his man out to the stable to make ready his carriage and to have Jane's donkey cart readied as well.

The Earl and Jane made their goodbyes to their hostess and went down to the porch where his Lordship's carriage was waiting. Fully expecting Jane's little cart to be waiting too, they were both surprised when they were met, instead, by James.

He bowed. "I'm sorry, Miss. The donkey is coughing. I wish Simmons was here; he would know what to do. Maybe he will return tonight and take care of him, but I don't think Simmons would want me to put a harness on the donkey. Sorry, Miss."

Before Jane could respond Lord Moore-Jeffries offered his carriage and she gratefully accepted. She thanked James and said she would return the next day to see to the donkey. James bowed and went back to the stable.

"Who is this Simmons the boy was talking about?"

"My brother's head stableman."

"He knows animals, does he?"

"Horses—he's excellent with horses and dreams of being a horse doctor, although he takes very good care of my mother's donkey and the dogs as well."

The Earl handed Jane into the carriage and then stepped in himself after telling the driver to stop at Chawton Cottage.

"This Simmons seems to have instilled good work ethics as well as good sense in those working with him, certainly where it concerns the health of the animals. Seems a good sort of man to have in your stable. Your brother is very lucky."

Jane smiled at her father's closest friend. "Indeed."

She said nothing of it but was fairly certain that Simmons would not be returning tonight to care for the donkey.

The cerulean summer sky was fresh and clear with only a few of the remaining gray clouds on the horizon. She wondered about the success of Simmons' trip. Was he in the twenty-first century? Saying a quick prayer that he had made the journey unscathed, she turned her attention to Mr. Darcy. What was he doing on this warm summer day?

Chapter 15

Eliza held Fitz' hand as they walked across the lawn toward the little lake at the edge of Pemberley woods, once again wondering why she felt so comfortable with him. After all, she didn't really know him. There were things she knew *about* him, but she didn't know him as a person. Still, she felt more at ease with him than she ever had with Jerry, or anyone else for that matter.

She was used to the sounds of street and river traffic, but here the trees rustling in the warm summer breeze and the water lapping softly on the shore of the lake brought to mind a pleasant childhood memory that made Eliza giggle.

Fitz glanced down at her. "What's funny?"

"Did you ever see the movie *Tammy and the Bachelor?*"

Hesitantly he replied, "Don't think so."

"Well, Debbie Reynolds sings a song in it called 'Tammy'."

He shrugged and shook his head.

"The first line is about hearing cottonwoods whispering above and another line says the breeze from the bayou murmurs low. And here I am on a southern plantation and—"

"Pemberley Farms has never been a plantation. It's always been a breeding farm. The farm has never grown crops for profit, but only for use here, mostly as feed for the livestock."

She understood that not having vast fields of tobacco and cotton meant that Pemberley Farms had never kept huge numbers of slaves working in the fields, but she was unsure why Fitz found it preferable to have had only a few slaves. Rationalization she supposed, something with which she was quite familiar. Still, it did seem kind of silly for him to get so upset at the mention of the farm's slavery past. One day she would have to ask him why, when he was so intent on keeping the history of Pemberley Farms alive, he seemed unable to accept that part of it's history. *One day… if there's more than this weekend.*

She grinned at the thought, then bowed her head in concession before continuing. "Southern estate then, like in the movie. Anyway, as we got closer to the lake it did sound kind of like the trees were whispering and the wind murmuring as it swept across the surface of the water. Silly, I know, but I thought it was kind of funny."

He smiled slightly but made no comment.

She added, "Of course, the whole weekend has felt like a musical to me."

"Brigadoon?"

She smiled at him. "I never would have guessed you were a fan of musical theatre."

"My mother loved movie musicals, so it was something we did together after my father died."

She flashed a sad little smile. "Me too."

He stopped and took her hand, bringing it to his lips and kissing it. "It has been strange, hasn't it? Surreal almost."

"Yeah."

"But it hasn't been just this weekend for me."

She looked at him strangely.

"I don't know whether love at first sight actually exists, but if it does, it happened to me in the Austen exhibit at the library. I haven't been able to get you off my mind since that day, and I had no idea who you were. I can't begin to tell you how many times over the last two weeks I wanted to kick myself for not having gotten your name and number."

She looked up into his sea-green eyes and saw the look that tightened her stomach. Finally finding her tongue, she said, "I thought it was all a dream. I couldn't imagine that you'd even like me after I emailed telling you to get lost, then sneaking onto your property and basically calling you a lunatic in your own house."

He laughed. "We did get off to a rocky start. I suppose my almost killing you with Lord Nelson and then coming close to terrorizing you when you wouldn't sell me the letters makes us even on that score."

She sighed. "I couldn't get you off my mind either... after the library." She looked at the ground and almost whispered, "I even did a portrait of you from memory of that day."

Gently he cupped her face in his hands and tilted it up to him, caressing her cheeks with his thumbs. "You really are my dearest, loveliest Eliza." He kissed her with the same smoldering passion as last night, but this time there was no moonlight, no horse drawn carriage, no champagne. She was wearing jeans, not a two hundred year old silk dress. It was broad daylight and it was real.

The woods were pleasantly cool. They walked hand in hand and she thought how nice it was that even though he was much taller than she, he was still able to match her stride so it was easy walking with him. Jerry always made her feel like he was pulling her around. She and Fitz hadn't said anything since they'd entered the shelter of the trees, but only because they didn't need to talk. The word *comfortable* came to her mind again, and she liked it. She breathed a contented sigh.

He smiled. "What are you thinking about?"

"You wouldn't believe it."

"Try me."

Far from ready to divulge her real thoughts and feelings, she said, "John Adams."

"What?"

"Did you know that Jane Austen was born about the same time that John Adams left Massachusetts for the Continental Congress? Mid-December, 1775. I was just thinking it was a strange juxtaposition, particularly with what happened to you."

"How do you even know that?"

"I had just finished reading McCullough's *John Adams* when I found the letters. In my research I read her biography. They pretty much start out the same way: December 1775."

"I take it you like history."

"Yeah. My grandmother says that you can't know where you're going if you don't know where you've been."

He stopped. "You might find this interesting then." He pushed aside a very leafy tree branch. Nestled in the depths of the woods was a stone house. Fitz called it a cottage but it seemed too big to be a cottage, though it was cute in spite of its size.

Eliza gasped. "It looks like something from one of my paintings!"

"It's Lucas' house," the tall Virginian explained as she started across the clearing.

She walked around the lovely structure. "Lucas the carriage driver?"

"Lucas is my steward."

"Caretaker?"

"Yes, but it goes well beyond just being a caretaker; he manages the estate."

"I thought Mrs. Temple did that."

"She manages the house and its employees: food, linen, that kind of thing."

"And Jake?"

"The horses and all that goes with them."

She smiled. "So you have someone who takes care of the house and you, and someone for the barn and horses. What's left, the dogs?"

"We have a master of the hunt to take care of the kennels and the hounds."

"Master of the hunt?"

"Yes. She's a woman, but tradition still calls the position master. Nicolette is a vet; she manages the kennels and dogs and cares for all the animals on the farm."

"What is it Lucas does again?"

"Everything else. Lucas manages the property itself. We still grow feed for the horses, and there's a fairly large greens crew to take care of the landscaping. Gardening is not my thing, so someone has to take care of the kitchen garden. Lucas also manages all the employees outside the house and barn, including Nicolette and her staff."

"So Lucas takes care of the windmills and stuff, too?"

Surprised by the question since he had never mentioned the electric plant, he was slightly annoyed that Jenny had said so much. He supposed it didn't really matter, so he simply nodded. "Technically, Mrs. Temple and Jake report to Lucas. He keeps things running smoothly whether I'm here or not."

"So he's like an overseer?"

"I don't like that term; he is my steward, plain and simple."

"What's wrong with overseer? It just means supervisor doesn't it? I mean, I've seen it in books."

"Generally books about the civil war, no doubt. In the old South an overseer was a white man who dealt with and controlled a plantation's slave population."

"Oh... sorry, I didn't realize." She returned to the subject of Lucas. "Jake told me Lucas is the one who restored the carriages."

Aha, Jake, Fitz thought. *He's the one who told Eliza about the electric plant.* He shook his head. Between Jake and Jenny, Eliza knew far more about him than he knew about her. "Yes, Lucas is very good with his hands."

Eliza shook her head. *How can he live like this? Steward, housekeeper, barn manager, master of the hunt—even his own personal veterinarian. How can he seem so normal? I guess everyone's normal is different.* This certainly wasn't hers.

As they continued their walk, Fitz said, "The first Fitzwilliam Darcy built the stone house for his huntsman or gamekeeper, whose job was to keep poachers off the land. The estate was far larger then than it is now. When a gamekeeper was no longer necessary, my third-great-grandfather updated it and made it a living space for his steward. Since that time it's been for the Pemberley Farms steward.

She looked at him. "So if Rose's Willie was the first Fitzwilliam, what does that make you?"

"I'm number eight."

Her first thought was that the Darcys didn't have much imagination when it came to naming the men in the family. Instead, she asked something that she had wondered about since she had first found out he was real. "Didn't you ever wonder why you had the same name as the character in *Pride and Prejudice*?"

"Of course. When I was young I didn't give it much thought, but when I was a junior in high school it was required reading in English literature. After enduring the torment of everybody bowing and curtsying and calling me Mr. Darcy, I finally asked my mother and grandmother why Austen had used the name."

"Of course, you actually *are* Mr. Darcy."

"Yes, as one of my teachers graciously pointed out, just before she curtsied. Some of the teachers teased me as badly as my so-called friends did, or worse. Anyway, my grandmother held to the family line, which had created a picture of Jane to rival Fanny Hill. But my mother said it was ridiculous to think they had ever even met each other. Willie was a foot soldier in the Continental Army, so he would have been unwelcome in England, and as far as anyone knows he never left the US after the war. And we know Jane never left England. So mother said that Gram's scenario, although far more exciting than Jane simply liking the names, was highly unlikely."

They continued their walk for a few minutes in silence; then quietly Fitz confessed, "Who would have thought I was the culprit who caused the generations-old family scandal?" He chuckled. "You know, even in my dazed state I could tell that she'd never heard the names before I said them. But I will *never* understand why she used them."

"Seriously?"

"Why, do you think *you* do?"

"I have a theory."

"Which is?"

"Besides the fact that she loves you—"

"Oh, she didn't love—"

Eliza held up one hand. "Besides the fact that she loves you, men of that era were considered superior to women. They were condescending. You know. You were the one who told me that women couldn't inherit and were forced into marriage for property and monetary gain. Men knew they held that power and they very often took advantage of it. You didn't and it was something she wasn't used to."

"Her brothers weren't that way."

"I noticed that in the biography. Neither was her father and I suspect that's why she was as successful as she was."

"That still doesn't explain why she used my name."

"Now we get to my theory. Although her brothers certainly were not the norm for the time, they still felt the need to take care of her and control her to some degree, but I imagine you treated her the way you treat me and all women as far as I can tell. She wasn't used to being treated as an equal. So when she decided to have the main male character in *Pride and Prejudice* re-evaluate his attitudes and actions, she made him more like you—and that's why she used your name."

For a while Fitz said nothing, then simply, "Interesting. That never occurred to me. I treated her the way I do everyone, men and women."

"Exactly."

Chapter 16

They stepped out of the shade of the towering trees and into the hot summer sun. The heat of the day was already getting fairly uncomfortable, so he suggested they return to the cool protection of the veranda. Eliza agreed. As they made their way back to the house, Fitz lifted her small, delicate hand to his lips and kissed it. The ring on the third finger of her left hand caught the sunlight.

"What's this?"

"My father's wedding ring." She added sadly, "Mom gave it to me after he died."

"Why do you wear it on your left hand? Won't people think you're married?"

"Legend holds that the vein in that finger runs directly to the heart. I wear it there to stay connected to him, at least in spirit."

"I don't remember seeing it before."

"'You weren't paying attention, then. I've had it on all morning."

"Really?"

"Really."

"Were you wearing it all weekend?"

"No. I had it on when I got here, but I took it off when I cleaned up after the mud bath. I just didn't put it back on until this morning. I didn't put any of my jewelry back on." She paused slightly. "Does it matter?"

"Well, it certainly would if you were married."

"You thought I might be?"

"Not really. Just for a moment when I first saw it. I was afraid someone might have already snagged you."

She looked up at him and smiled. "Nope." *Kind of nice that he feels that way.*

He slipped his arm around her shoulders and squeezed. Nothing more was said until they reached the covered portico.

"Coffee's still hot. Would you like some? Or I can have Mrs. Temple bring out some ice tea or lemonade. She makes a wicked limeade, too." He smiled.

"Coffee's fine."

Handing her the mug and then taking the chair across from her, he said, "Jake reminded me this morning that I'm not very good at relationships, of which you've seen ample proof."

"Why is that?"

"I'm sure a psychiatrist would tell you it's because I'm afraid to love, having lost both my parents and my three surviving grandparents before I was nineteen. On average I lost one person a year over a five year period. I do believe that ultimately it made me stronger and more resilient, but I definitely avoid even the possibility of getting close to people."

She reached across and laid her hand on top of his. "I'm sorry."

He covered her hand with his own. "It is what it is. Jake said I don't do people very well, but the fact is, I don't do relationships with people at all."

So is that what he's trying to tell me? That he likes me but he doesn't have relationships so this is pretty much all there will ever be? She didn't want to believe it. "So you haven't had any kind of long-term relationship?"

"Not really. Generally speaking my relationships, such as they are, have been transient; in fact, a better term might be liaisons. And quite frankly, most were only physical in nature, no emotional connection or commitment... especially no emotional connection."

She said, "It doesn't hurt as much when it's over that way."

"Yeah."

"So your liaisons are really just conveniences, then?"

"Yes, I'm suddenly ashamed to say."

"What about Faith?"

"Faith is a whole other story."

"Why?"

"I've known her all my life and her brother is one of my closest friends. That puts a completely different dynamic on the connection."

"Connection? She's not one of your conveniences?"

"Not the way you mean."

She grinned at him. "How do I mean?"

"Physically."

"You don't sleep with her?"

"No! It happened once when we were both drunk, but it's never happened again and it won't. I may be something of a cad, but I'm not stupid."

Eliza wanted to believe him. "She's very much in love with you."

He shook his head. "The only person Faith loves is Faith."

"She's in love with you; that's why she was so jealous of the attention you gave me."

"That wasn't jealousy."

"What do you call that episode in the ballroom? I mean, she was throwing the punch cups across the room and crying. I fully expected her to throw herself on the floor, kicking and screaming."

"Precisely—she was throwing a temper tantrum, something she does when she doesn't get her own way. It was the first time in years that she wasn't my date for the ball."

"Jenny mentioned that too. Why is that?"

"You were here."

"I mean why was she always your date?"

With a slightly apologetic grin, he said, "Convenience. I don't like having people here when I know I'm going to be too busy to pay any attention to them, so I've never invited anyone. And Faith always put so much effort into coordinating the ball that it only seemed fair that she was my date. But she knew where I stood and where she stood with me when it came to anything else. I'm afraid any hurt she felt was her own doing." He took a sip of his coffee. "So what's your story?"

"My story?"

"Come on. I've just bared my soul to you. It's your turn. Is there a man in your life?"

"Well, I'm not involved with anyone at the moment. I'm afraid we're in the same boat when it comes to relationships. I don't do them very well either."

"What's your excuse?"

She shook her head. "No excuse... I... I just don't believe in love. The whole happily ever after thing is just plain silly. People can't be happy forever; it's not natural. To think there's one person who can rock your world and that you would want to spend the rest of your life with is just not logical."

"Logical?"

"Yeah... logical, rational."

"I'm pretty sure love isn't supposed to be logical or rational." Eliza said, "You sound like my mother."

Fitz shrugged. "Maybe she's right. Love is subjective, a perception in the light of experience. It can't be defined by logic."

"Exactly. Subjectivity and perception by their very definitions mean things can change. If things change then the whole concept of anyone finding only one person for a lifetime doesn't make any sense. Besides, if there's supposed to be one person for everyone what are the chances of finding that one person in a world of millions? And what happens if you don't find that one person? You either have to settle or you end up alone."

"You're talking like true love can only happen once with one person. Simply because it *is* changeable, as are people, there are more than likely several people who would be right for every other person. I think you just have to be open to the possibility of someone actually being one of those people."

"This from the man who just told me that he hasn't allowed himself to love anyone for years?"

"Yes, and it's why I'm saying it. I don't want to be that man anymore." When she didn't respond, he asked, "Didn't your parents love each other?"

"Why would you ask that?"

"I'm assuming this cynical, negative belief or lack of belief has grown out of something. I thought maybe your parents hated each other and you got caught in the middle of it."

"No. In fact, according to them they were soul mates and from what I remember about them they probably were, but when he died she was devastated and she just kind of shut down emotionally. She said there was no point trying to fall in love again since all she'd do is compare everyone to dad and no one would be able to live up to him. So even though they were soul mates, it didn't last; there was no happily ever after. She found the one person she wanted to spend the rest of her life with and he died, so that little trip down lover's lane was pretty much useless."

"I assume you are a result of that trip, which more than likely means your mother doesn't consider it useless... and quite frankly neither do I."

She blushed slightly. "Are you sure you're not channeling my mother?"

He flashed an enigmatic smile.

"She says I'm all she needs but she has no one to share her life with; she's all alone." Eliza stopped to get control of her wavering emotions. "So she and dad may have been madly in love but what good did it do them?"

"Haven't you ever been in love?"

"I thought I was once... I even got engaged. But here I am, single, so obviously I was wrong."

"Why didn't you marry him?"

"He turned out to be a schmuck."

She was going to stop with that statement but she could see the unasked question in his eyes. She had noticed over the course of the last few days that he had a way of getting what he wanted without saying anything; she wasn't sure how he did it, but suddenly she found herself saying, "Marty was my so-called college sweetheart. We were engaged during my senior year; he'd graduated the year before." She glanced at him. He seemed very interested.

She shrugged. "It had always been my dream to be a painter, but I realized early on the chances of that were slim. I settled for the idea that at least I'd be able to make a living drawing as a graphic designer. A few months before graduation my academic counselor told me I was a gifted artist, that I should consider trying to make a go of it as a painter. Frankly, doing silly newspaper ads for some advertising agency never was what I wanted to do, so I told Marty what the counselor said and that I wanted to give myself five years to try to make a go of it as an artist.

To say he was less than supportive of the idea would be an understatement. He actually got angry; he considered the whole idea foolish and unreasonable. In order to live the life we had imagined we'd need two incomes. He suggested I 'play at being an artist' after we were established." She paused briefly, then added, "Of course, that was the life *he* imagined. He told me I needed to face reality and join the real world. I felt like I was in a modern version of *I Love Lucy*. He didn't want me to stay home, but he wanted me to be the good little wifey who was willing to work toward the suburban house with the yard, the dog and 2.5 children."

"You don't want children?"

"No, it wasn't that I didn't want a dog and a house and children; it was just that I was twenty-two years old and figured I had time to do the suburban stuff later, including having children. I mean, he thought I should do all the regular stuff first, and then later I could paint if I still felt I had to."

"He actually said that?"

"Yes. He obviously had no idea who I was, and I certainly didn't know him. I realized I'd gotten engaged because it seemed like the thing to do. I was graduating from college and starting the next phase of my life, and marriage seemed the logical next step."

Fitz grinned at her. "Logic doesn't seem to have served you too well in that instance, but I'm glad you didn't marry him."

"So am I."

Fitz seemed to drift off and she wondered whether he was thinking about Jane Austen. Every time she'd seen that faraway look on his face he was talking about the author. She cleared her throat and he glanced at her.

"What were you thinking about?"

"Nothing."

"Admit it, you were thinking about Jane, weren't you?"

"Not at all."

"Then what was it?"

"I'm afraid you'll think I just want to come off better than Marty."

She giggled. "Pretty much anything you say or do would make you come off better than Marty."

He looked at her trying to determine whether she really meant it. He decided he'd take a shot. "Did he never see your work?"

"What do you mean?"

"Did Marty ever see your paintings?"

"Of course he did. He thought they were nice little drawings."

Fitz shook his head. "I don't understand that. I mean, I know art is subjective and beauty is in the eye of the beholder, but I went to your website after I got your first email and I was amazed. Your counselor was right; you are gifted. Your pictures bring a lightness and pleasure to the world, which sometimes is a pretty dark place." He paused and glanced away, then back again. "Your paintings remind me of Jane's writing. Both of you find joy in the world around you and fill your works with the delights you see even if the rest of us don't. You don't dwell on the dark side of life."

Eliza didn't know what to say. She was astounded. His comparing her paintings to Jane Austen's books almost brought tears to her eyes and left her speechless.

He surprised her by adding something that she was thinking. "I'll bet you think your paintings fill a small niche and will soon be forgotten. Jane thought that too, that her work was trifling and would not be remembered. You're both wrong."

Quietly she said, "Thank you." She could think of nothing else to say.

Fitz nodded, then got up and replenished their coffees. As if the conversation had never gotten off course, he asked, "So no one after Marty?"

"No one to write home about." She paused. "My mother thinks I chose men I'd never get serious about so I wouldn't have to deal with the fall out when it doesn't work."

"Do you?"

"Not on purpose."

"Anything 'not to write home about' recently?"

"What do you mean?"

"Has there been anyone in the last year, the last month?"

"Sort of."

"What does that mean?"

With an apologetic grin she said, "It was really just a convenience, at least for me. Jerry is my financial advisor; he set up my on-line business and website, helped with investments and secured the financing for my condo. He's pretty good with money and contracts." She waited for some kind of response but got none. "Anyway, we'd go out occasionally and once in while we slept together. That was it."

"How long did it last?"

"Two years."

"When did it end?"

"Last week."

Skeptically he asked, "Suddenly last week it was over?"

She ignored the tinge of suspicion in the question. "Yes, it's most definitely over. When I found the letters he basically called me an idiot for getting so excited about them. He was constantly complaining that I was getting too invested in something that was utterly absurd and most likely a hoax of some kind. Of course once they'd been authenticated and appraised, he was suddenly all lovey-dovey and wanted me to put some of the money the auction was expected to realize into an obscure Internet start-up that he was involved in. I cut him off right then. No love lost there."

"So this is what led you to believe that true love doesn't exist?"

"It's not enough?" She added with a chuckle, "I don't need the kind of love you're talking about. If I do feel the need to get all emotional and mushy I read Jane Austen; she believed in love. But where am I going to find a man like...."

His roguish grin made her blush. "Yes, Jane had faith in love... and people; she was the ultimate romantic." He paused. "It would appear that neither of us has a grasp on the fine art of relationships. So where do we go from here?"

"You tell me."

"Fortunately or unfortunately, however you want to look at it and in spite of our best efforts there are some things we simply can't control and the unexpected happens."

"Like what?"

"Finding the happily ever after kind of love... in spite of ourselves."

Eliza frowned. "Jane?"

He reached across the space separating them, took her coffee cup, and set it on the table next to him. Leaning over again, he took her hand and pulled it to him. The look on his face made her knees weak and tied her stomach in knots. "You," he said quietly.

She suppressed a whimper and swallowed. Not willing to accept it at face value, she asked, "I'm not saying I believe it, but if it's true, what do we do?"

"I've been thinking about this a lot. We have the opportunity to change the way we do things, and I want to try. I think that's what we should do." He kissed her, and her heart triphammered in her chest.

When their lips parted, she asked, "Do you really think we can?"

"I think we can do anything we want to do."

She whispered, "I... I don't know whether I—"

He kissed her again. The conversation had ended with a kiss and an unspoken agreement.

Chapter 17

Chawton Cottage and Rosemont Hall
Summer, 1813

After practicing at the piano forte and writing to her sister Cassandra at Great Bookham, Jane was enjoying the luxury of a second cup of tea. She had described to Cass the beautiful pink silk Annabelle had so generously given her, then continued with the more mundane things she had done during the past days. She finished with a request that her sister remember the patches for the quilt, then promised to work on it herself.

She picked up a patch, threaded the needle and began the tiny stitches that would attach this new piece to the whole of the quilt. When the diamond-shaped section was complete she clipped the thread and returned the needle to its cushion in her sewing basket. The sun came streaming in through the window as she watched the traffic in the street, feeling a little melancholy.

Fingering the newly placed patch, she thought the vibrant collection of colours and patterns were very much like Eliza Austen, her much-loved sister-in-law, a favorite cousin who had married her brother Henry.

Jane smiled; Eliza had been such a spirited, happy woman. She had brought joy to Henry and all the family. Had it really been only four months ago that she had gone to London to be with Henry and his wife during her last illness? Tears filled her eyes. It seemed almost impossible that Eliza was gone.

Six weeks after the funeral while Jane was packing to return to Chawton, Henry had given his sister the material that his wife had never had the opportunity to have made into a gown. Jane, her mother and sister had decided to include it in the quilt as a permanent remembrance. She missed Eliza and ached for her brother's grief.

A loud knock at the front door startled her. By the time she had put the quilt away Maggie was at the door of the dining room with a note.

"James is waiting, Miss Jane."

"For what?"

"Don't know, Miss. He said he was told to wait."

"Thank you. Tell him I will be there shortly."

Jane quickly read the note from her niece.

Dear Aunt Jane,

Two of my young siblings have been brought down by a bad cold in the night. As my father has gone to Godmersham to collect the rents already delayed, I feel obligated to stay at home with the invalids.

Please convey our compliments and apologies to the Earl.
You need not be concerned, as James will see that you arrive at
Rosemont in safety and will stay to see you home.
                    Your niece,
                    Fanny

The plan had been for Jane, Edward, Fanny and the younger children to attend Lord Moore-Jeffries' picnic together. It was to have been a leisurely afternoon that Jane had been anticipating with great pleasure, particularly as the Austen-Knights were not often in Chawton and would be leaving in a few weeks to return to their Kent home, so she wanted to take every opportunity to spend time with them. Now, though, she was exceedingly disappointed that she would not be sharing the day with her family. In fact, after reading Fanny's note she fleetingly considered sending her own regrets, but she was wont to disappoint the Earl in such a way. She told her brother's servant she would be ready to leave directly.

Freshening herself in her room, she once again considered sending a note to his Lordship rather than attend the picnic alone. She sighed and an old memory surfaced. After the death of her father she had confided to the Earl that she often felt very alone even when others were present. Her father's oldest friend, whom everyone called Uncle Jeff, had told her that as long as he lived she would never be alone. So although she would not be with her brother and his family, she would not be alone.

Feeling better about the excursion, she returned to the young groom from her brother's stable who was waiting at the gate. After assisting her into the carriage, he climbed atop it and slapped the reins lightly against the hindquarters of the horses; Jane bounced inside the vehicle as it started off.

The gray stones of Rosemont Hall rose up in front of her as James helped her out of the equipage. The building stood out against the green hills and blue sky. Although it was from the Elizabethan era it had the foreboding look of a medieval castle even in the brilliant sunlight of the summer day. Lord Moore-Jeffries' summer home had always seemed like a castle to Jane, especially as a small child; however, her father had explained that it was not a castle at all as it had no battlements. It was simply the manor house in which the Earl and his family lived.

The park went as far as the eye could see and had woods, lakes and streams aplenty. Formal gardens were divided by hedgerows, and several greenhouses dotted the immediate area around the house, enabling the Earl's family to enjoy fruits, vegetables and flowers all year long should they chose to stay in the country. Otherwise the perishable edibles were parceled out to his tenants.

The edifice had been built by his Lordship's ancestor after he'd been granted the Earldom of Lasham for his service to Queen Elizabeth I in quelling one of the Irish rebellions of the era. Although succeeding generations had made great improvements within and without, it still seemed more castle than home even to the adult Jane.

The name of the estate, Rosemont Hall, was a tribute to the Queen who had bestowed the honor. As further proof of his devotion to Queen and country, Lord Moore-Jeffries' antecedent had incorporated the Tudor rose into the family coat-of-arms, which was cast in bronze and embedded in a stone over the front door.

His lordship had made many improvements to the estate himself. The one most notable to Jane was the Great Room. Originally used to intimidate sixteenth-century enemies with its vast space, vaulted ceilings and immense fireplace, it had been transformed into a Ball Room.

As a child Jane had been afraid of the room after her brother Edward told her that if she was too close to the fireplace she might be snatched up and carried away forever by a ferocious ogre who lived in it. She had run crying from the room and into the arms of the Earl, who had comforted her by reassuring her that there was no ogre in his fireplace and she need not worry for he would never let anything happen to her. His assurance had helped calm her at the time, but she still found herself skirting the fireplace whenever she was in the room.

And she was in the room at least once a year at his Lordship's Michaelmas Ball. Now the stone walls were covered with something—she was not at all sure what—but they were painted green with white plaster moldings and trims. The soothing colour made the immense room much more pleasant.

Although the Ball Room was one of the improvements his Lordship had made, Jane was thankful he had made only minor alterations to the library, her favorite room in the entire house. Muted red carpet ran from one wall to another. The carpeting, coupled with the rich, warm wood of the paneled walls, made the room feel cozy in spite of its size. A comfortable arrangement of a sofa and chairs near the fireplace made a perfect place for reading or conversation. Sunlight flooded the room through large casement windows and made writing at the lovely old secretary, which always was well stocked with paper and ink, a real joy. Then there were the books: hundreds, maybe thousands of books from the floor almost to the ceiling and the ceiling was high. She loved the room. She turned at the sound of footsteps behind her.

"Jane?" It was Annabelle Rodgers and her family. As they curtsied to each other, Annabelle introduced her brother. "You know Tom, do you not?"

"Yes, we have met."

Tom bowed. "Miss Austen." He turned away to join his parents and several other people who had been gathering in the foyer while Jane had wandered the first floor.

"Where is Fanny?" Annabelle asked, looking around.

"I am afraid two of the children became ill during the night, and with my brother away, Fanny stayed home to care for them."

Within moments Lord Moore-Jeffries appeared on the stair landing and hailed his guests. "The carriages are ready, let us away."

Annabelle linked arms with Jane, insisting she ride with the Rodgers family.

One of the greenhouses of which the Earl was particularly proud stood on the right of the party as they made their way to Fordam Ridge for his Lordship's picnic. He had created an African jungle inside for two parrots he had acquired on a trip there. As a young girl Jane had been fascinated by the jungle and the birds. She had thought many times that a trip to Africa would be exciting, but at the same time she hated to see the birds trapped in the glass building. What was the point of having wings if they could not fly free? She had embarrassed her parents when she had said as much to the Earl, but Lord Moore-Jeffries had been very philosophical about it and admitted that she was right. However, now that he had captured the birds he could not let them loose in England for they needed the tropical conditions he had created in the greenhouse to survive. As he had no plans of returning to Africa, the birds would have to live there. Jane had accepted his explanation, but had purposely avoided going to the greenhouse again.

The sun was warm on her back as she finished her luncheon of cold mutton and salad. The melancholy still had hold of her, and without her family she did not feel much like socializing in spite of the pleasant company.

She was grateful, therefore, when Lord Moore-Jeffries came over to her and offered his hand. "Walk with me, Jane."

She stood and curtsied. "With pleasure, your Lordship."

The old gentleman tucked her arm in his and they walked away from the others, who were playing parlour games or exploring. Wild raspberries were just coming ripe so a few people were off collecting the luscious fruit. Once they were far enough away that the Earl was sure no one else would hear, he squeezed Jane's arm against his side. "It has been a very pleasant summer, has it not?"

"It has, your Lordship."

"I have found the time to enjoy several new novels this season."

Jane smiled. "You have such a wonderful library."

"Yes." He glanced at her and smiled. "Two of the books, I found to be particularly enjoyable."

Jane was simply reveling in the Earl's company and the pleasant walk. "Hmmm."

He chuckled. "Imagine my surprise when I discovered that you are the lady who wrote the books."

Almost startled, she asked, "How did you know?"

"Henry sent them to me."

Jane blushed. "I am so sorry he imposed upon you."

His Lordship laughed. "Imposed? Jane, sometimes I do believe you are the silliest of creatures. My daughters, my sons and their wives all found the books so entertaining that they suggested I read them as well, so I had read them both long before Henry sent them to me."

Slightly embarrassed by the Earl's declaration that the books were entertaining, Jane said, "I am glad he sent them then."

"Henry believes the works are exceptional."

"Henry says such things in the warmth of his brotherly vanity and love. After all, what a trifle they are to the really important points of one's existence in this world."

"No, Jane, Henry is right. You have a strong mind and are quite gifted." His Lordship paused. "Your father would be very proud of you, my dear."

Jane felt the warmth of the compliment, particularly as it regarded her father. Her father's good opinion was precious to her. "Thank you."

"It is I who should thank you for your insight into every-day life. There is none of the dark foreboding of other current novels."

"I see no real purpose in writing about the dark side of life. I let other pens dwell on the guilt and misery."

"Well, that is your gift, Jane. You bring your world and the joy you find there to life for those who read your books. You will be remembered."

She thought about Mr. Darcy telling her that she was remembered even in his time, and she wondered whether it could be true. He *had* known more about her than a stranger ought. She shook her head; it was too ridiculous even to consider.

They walked for a while and then the Earl broke the comfortable silence. "May I take credit as the inspiration for one of the scandals perpetrated by Wickham?"

Taken aback by the question she paused, then quietly said, "I hoped you would not mind, your Lordship. I told no one and everyone thinks I made it up."

Her arm still entwined with his, he patted her hand. "I do not mind at all, Jane, and as we are alone, please call me Uncle Jeff, as you did when you were a child."

She bowed her head slightly. "Thank you, Sir."

He laughed as they continued their walk. "I believe your family was more surprised by the name you chose for your hero than the scandals you portrayed."

Jane blushed. Except for Cassandra's avowed disapproval for using Mr. Darcy's name and home, no one in the family had ever made mention of it. She had been grateful for not having to explain herself, but now she wondered that it was so.

Suspecting her question, the Earl said, "Edward and Henry convinced Frank not to confront you about it. Edward told him that Darcy had been a perfect gentleman during his stay at Chawton Great House. Of course, neither of them think he believed it, but rather than accuse you of unseemly behavior, Frank promised never to mention it to you."

Jane was glad the rest of the family had coerced Frank, by whatever means, to keep his opinions to himself after *Pride and Prejudice* was published, for he had made them well known to her after the American's departure in the spring of 1810. Brushing aside thoughts of her naval officer brother's displeasure, she silently reminisced about the afternoon Lord Moore-Jeffries had confided to her the painful memories of his young sister, memories that haunted him still. She had begun to re-write *First Impressions* even before Mr. Darcy had come into her life. The summer after he left, during a Rosemont picnic the Earl had told her the story of his sister, Georgina. The story became an integral part of the book, which she re-titled, as Darcy said she would, *Pride and Prejudice*. She was obliged that the Earl seemed not to mind that she had taken some liberty with the story he'd told her. Jane closed her eyes, remembering the story.

Chapter 18

In the summer of 1810 the Earl had removed a small stand of trees. He had led Jane toward a large stump situated in the shade of the remaining woods. When he had asked whether it was acceptable as a seat, Jane had told him that for a freshly hewn tree it was quite comfortable.

The Earl had smiled at her. It seemed a sad smile, and she wondered at the cause when he turned and took a few steps away. With his back to her he looked out over the landscape of his estate and said, "My sister loved this park."

"I did not know you have a sister."

"Had... I had a sister."

"Oh. I am sorry."

He turned back to her. "Thank you."

"Was she very young?"

"Fifteen."

Jane made every effort to stifle the gasp that escaped her. "Oh, your Lordship! Why did she die so young?"

He turned away and Jane, fearing that she had been too bold, apologized. "I am sorry; I should not have asked."

The Earl sighed and returned to her side, patting her hand as he sat. "You and Georgina share a spontaneity tempered by a gentleness of spirit." He paused a moment. "Where shall I start?"

Jane was insistent. "You need not tell me anything if it is difficult for you, your Lordship."

"Thank you, Jane, but I want to tell you. I believe Georgina would want you to know." He reached over and squeezed her hand. "I thought we agreed you would call me Uncle Jeff."

Somehow "okay" seemed the most appropriate response, but then she would have to explain what it meant and how she had come to know the word. Instead she smiled at him and simply said, "Yes, Sir."

He smiled, then began: "My sister, six years my junior, was an extraordinary young woman and an exceptional artist."

Jane wondered at the gentle smile that curved his lip.

"Her paintings were drawn from her imagination, from how she saw the world." He paused. "She found happiness in the world around her, as you do, Jane. She painted one painting that I particularly liked. It was of the ocean waves crashing on the craggy hills of the Derbyshire countryside. Those were two of her favorite places when she was away from home." The tears in his eyes glistened in the summer sun. "Georgina was sweet tempered and loved animals. It was easier for her to talk to the dogs and horses than to people. I suppose that was, at the very least, partly my fault for not wanting her out in society. I feared that with a fortune of fifty thousand pounds, men with unsavory intentions would be attracted to her and I wanted to protect her." His voice quieted. "I believe now that keeping her so sheltered made her easy prey for just such a cad."

Jane considered how commendable it was that he had been so protective of his sister and decided that it would be a good character point for the Mr. Darcy in her book, but she made no comment.

The Earl continued. "While I was away at school, our mother became even more protective, wanting Georgina to associate only with the right people."

Jane raised an eyebrow; she hated the term *right people. Who are these "right people," and who decided who was and who was not "right"? God made all people, they are all right to Him.*

Her attention was drawn back to the Earl's story as he told of his relationship with his two best friends at school and the easy company they offered. "For two years we were the closest of friends, almost inseparable: your father, Charles and me. That summer we planned to spend the school holiday here." The Earl spread his arms, indicating the landscape around them. "This was Georgina's home, her sanctuary... but I turned it into her tomb." He fell silent for a moment, then cleared his throat and continued. "The previous holidays had seen us all at the homes of Charles' parents, the Duke and Duchess of—well, never mind that. Who he was is an unimportant part of this account. Just know that Charles was the Duke's eldest son and very much looked forward to his inheritance."

"We often went to their London house, but we spent the longer summer holidays at the Duke's country home. It was a place where we could do what young men do, hunting, fishing, and playing at cards. We had a grand time."

Jane noticed that although it sounded like a happy memory, his Lordship was solemn, almost sad.

Still, when he turned toward her he was smiling. "We came here because your father wanted to be closer to home. He was paying court to your mother and was unwilling to spend the entire holiday so far a distance from her. The Duke's summer home is in the Lake District, so we all decided on the summer here at Rosemont."

The finely dressed young men fairly tumbled out of the carriage as it came to a stop in front of the gray stone edifice, still laughing at some unremembered story. Phillips, the Earl's butler, was forced to repeat his greeting over the rowdiness.

"Welcome home, your Lordship."

All three school chums looked at each other and laughed even more heartily. George bowed. "Your Lordship." The Earl in turn bowed to Charles. "Your Grace."

"Right you are." Guffaws from the three of them once again filled the afternoon air.

Phillips, attempting to bring some decorum to the situation, said, "All is ready, Sir. Shall I show the gentlemen their rooms?"

"That would be splendid, Phillips." He turned to his friends. "After you are settled come to the library." He pointed to the back of the house passed the stairs. "My mother will be serving tea."

As Phillips ushered George and Charles up the stairs, Lord Moore-Jeffries went in search of his mother and sister. From a window in the breakfast room he watched his mother cutting flowers, gently placing them in the basket hanging on her arm. His sister was sitting in the garden drawing. They both seemed so delicate and fragile, his heart filled with the love he felt for them and he was reminded of the solemn promise he'd made his dying father, to watch over them and keep them safe. He opened the doors leading to the garden. "Good afternoon, Ladies."

They both looked up, but before Lady Moore-Jeffries could even turn around Georgina had run to her brother.

"Oh, Jeff!" She stopped suddenly directly in front of him and curtsied. "Your Lordship." She straightened, her eyes downcast.

Surprised and slightly disturbed he reached out for her and held her in a bear hug. "Now what was that all about?"

Georgina stepped away from her brother and curtsied again as her mother approached.

"Welcome home, Son."

"It is always good to be here. Why the curtsey?"

Georgina said, "Mother says when other people are here I must treat you with respect."

"And a sister embracing her brother is somehow disrespectful?"

"When others are present we should treat you as we want them to treat you," their mother responded.

"But there are only the three of us here."

His mother said, "What about your school friends? Did they not come with you?"

"Yes, but it is just George, who is hardly a stranger, and Charles who soon will not be."

Shocked, Lady Moore-Jeffries said, "But he is the first son of a Duke."

"And he is conceited enough because of it. Until he is the Duke he deserves no more respect than George or I. Besides, he's a friend of mine. He is not a stranger."

Although he did not want to counter his mother's instructions entirely, he was unwilling to let them stand uncontested, so he said, "Shall we compromise then? If it is necessary for my family to treat me like a stranger, then I prefer you only do so when real strangers are present, not neighbors and school chums."

His mother was none too pleased with his directive, but she conceded; he was, after all, head of the house even if he was her son. Without saying anything more he put his arms around both of them and led them into the house.

George Austen was in the library when the three members of the Moore-Jeffries family entered. He immediately went to the Earl's mother and bowed.

"Lady Moore-Jeffries."

"Mr. Austen, how nice to see you again."

"Thank you for inviting me." He turned to Georgina and bowed, "Lady Georgina."

She curtsied, "Mr. Austen."

As the four exchanged pleasantries, two household maids came in and set the table for tea. Charles came in just as the two young women were leaving, each quickly curtsying with eyes downcast as they passed him. Before entering the library he looked back and watched the girls hurrying down the hall, his attention not leaving them until the Earl called his name.

Charles flashed a ready smile for Lady Moore-Jeffries and bowed gallantly, then turned to Georgina. After eyeing her for a few moments he finally made an exaggerated bow, then gently brought her hand to his lips and watched her flush a very pretty pink as he brushed her fingers with a kiss. "Jeff, the way you talk about her I thought your sister was a little girl. I had no idea she was such a beautiful young woman."

The Earl and Lady Moore-Jeffries smiled at each other for the compliment, seemingly unaware that Georgina was made terribly uncomfortable by the encounter.

Jane waited for the Earl to continue but he said nothing more, only stared out at nothing in particular, as though he were in a world of his own. He had made no mention of how or why his young sister had died, so she assumed he was not yet finished telling her what had happened. Finally she said quietly, "Uncle Jeff?"

He was almost startled by her voice. He took a deep breath to calm the rage that could still take hold of him. He turned to her and smiled. "I should have heeded your father, Jane. He warned me."

"About what, Sir?"

"Charles. Over the few weeks we were here, he was particularly attentive to Georgina. Every night after dinner he would play cards with her, talk with her, and read to her. Your father suggested that it might not be the best thing for Georgina to spend so much time with him."

"Why?"

"He said we needed to be careful, for Charles was a true man of the world. He'd traveled extensively, was on the social invitation list of every nobleman and woman in the country and took every opportunity to enjoy himself by accepting most of those invitations. My sister, as your father reminded me, was young and not at all worldly. She had never ventured out of England and seldom accepted social invitations."

Jane reminded him that he had said he sheltered her in order to protect her.

"Yes. Unfortunately I did not see Charles as the threat your father did. In fact, mother and I were grateful to Charles for helping to draw Georgina out since that autumn would see her presentation at Court and the attentions of a trusted friend would only help to create confidence in her." He paused a moment. "But your father was right, and if I had taken his suggestion to limit Charles' time with her, it is possible that none of it would have happened."

Jane's first reaction was to ask what had happened, but she didn't have to wait long.

"Only a few months later, after our return to school, I discovered that Charles had been visiting Georgina even when I was not present. My mother, assuming she could trust my close friend, allowed the meetings. In fact, considering the possibility that her daughter might marry the young nobleman, she even encouraged the association. Once again your father tried to warn me, suggesting the possibility that the secrecy of the meetings was because Charles' attentions were not simply those of a brother's friend."

The Earl shook his head. "I could not believe Charles to be that devious, and when I asked him about it he claimed that he simply had not had the opportunity to mention the meetings. I accepted his word that there was nothing untoward in his actions. Your father said nothing more about it, but I think, perhaps, it would have been better had he hit me over the head with something heavy, for I paid no attention to his warnings."

The Earl stopped to take a breath, and Jane leaned forward a bit, waiting for him to continue his narrative. After a moment he did. "Actually, the idea of a marriage between the two aristocratic families seemed a real possibility to me as well as my mother and sister. Of course I couldn't imagine that my friend's attachment to my sister was based on anything but honorable intentions. However, we soon realized the possibility of marriage existed only on our part, for Charles' surreptitious trips to Rosemont and our London house was for the sole purpose of seducing Georgina... a purpose fulfilled one stormy winter afternoon when Charles found her home alone. He convinced her of his love and devotion."

His Lordship looked at Jane and almost shouted, "What was a fifteen year old girl supposed to think when a friend of her brother, a man of noble birth, said he loved her?" He paused, then said in a quieter tone, "She believed him, and he took advantage of that. He took advantage of the fact that we all trusted him. Her love and my trust enabled him to have his way with her."

Jane waited, unsure what she could or should say.

After a bit, he took a deep breath and continued. "When I found out I immediately confronted Charles who, rather than agreeing to marry Georgina, laughed and said it had all been nothing more than a game, a sport. He had done it simply to see whether he could have her. Once he had, he no longer wanted any part of her and he had no plans of marrying anyone. Charles actually bragged about how easy it had been, and per-haps the worst thing he said was that had it been someone other than my sister I would have been laughing along with him. That made me almost as angry as his actions." The Earl grew quiet again for a moment. "But that was only because I feared he was right. Still, I did not allow that truth to dampen my outrage at his destruction of my sister's innocence. Our heated argument continued, eventually culminating in my challeng-ing him to a duel to avenge my sister's honour. When I arrived back in my own rooms I sent word to my mother that Charles refused to marry Georgina and that I would protect the family name on the field of honour."

Jane was taken aback; she had never met anyone who had actually fought a duel. She was bewildered by her own feelings. Although the barbarism of it was more than a little disturbing, somehow, in a strange way, it was very romantic. She smiled inwardly. *Perhaps I have read too many novels.*

Chapter 19

"That morning I waited for my second. Your father."

"My father?" Jane was astonished; she couldn't imagine her gentle father on a dueling field with pistols firing around him.

"Yes. He tried to barter a peaceful resolution, but to no avail. He arranged that the duel would take place at dawn two days hence."

The young Lord paced the floor of the parlour in his rooms at school. He had not slept and the hour remaining before George Austen would arrive was going to be unbearable. He stopped at the fireplace and leaned against the mantle, willing himself to stay as calm as possible. If he allowed his rage to take control he might miss his mark. The center of Charles' chest was the mark and he had no intention of missing. The deceitful bounder would die by his hand.

His valet brought in a breakfast tray, but he was in no mood for food; he just wanted to get on with it. Ignoring the tray and dismissing his servant, Lord Moore-Jeffries continued to pace. Within moments a carriage pulled up outside and he ran to the window. *Finally!* He had the door open before his friend had an opportunity to ring the bell. "I began to wonder whether you were going to come."

"I stopped to see Charles."

The man who would someday be Jane's father watched the anger rise in Jeff's face. "He would not relinquish his position. He will meet us at the appointed time." The anger drained away. George continued. "I had to try one last time. It is part of the responsibility of your second to bring about an end to it before shots are fired if it is possible."

Jeff turned away and gritted his teeth. He didn't want an end to it before he had a chance to kill the bastard. Without bothering to summon his valet he put on his coat and hat, walked past his friend without saying anything, and climbed into the carriage. George closed the door of the flat and followed his friend into the vehicle.

The Earl stared out the window. On the seat opposite him, holding the case with the pistols on his lap, George could think of nothing to say that might make his friend stop what he considered a foolish and probably tragic course of action. He certainly could understand the outrage Jeff felt by the injury done to his sister, and that the injury was perpetrated by a trusted friend was as hurtful as it was enraging. George had always seen something of the cad in Charles, but Jeff, generally seeing only the good in people, had never believed it.

There was no other carriage present when they arrived at the designated spot. The open field was far enough outside of Oxford to offer some privacy, particularly at such an early hour.

Dueling was illegal, but with two noblemen involved, even if they should be seen nothing would come of it. Still, they had to take care.

Having more and more trouble controlling his anger Jeff said, "I do not like the rules you agreed to. Three shots and it is to be over even if no one is hit? I know I can hit him, but I want him *dead*, George!"

"His death will change nothing. I hope only that this exercise will enable you to release some of your anger and carry on with your life."

"I do not *want* my anger released!"

"I know. However, it will not be a help to Georgina if you do not control your rage." Quietly he added, "She needs a brother far more than she needs a champion."

Unable to face the truth of that statement, Lord Moore-Jeffries went quiet. Once it was past the appointed time he said, "He is not coming. I knew he was a coward."

Pulling his watch from his pocket, George said, "It is only ten minutes. He has no reason to come in haste." He paused. "However, it might be best if he did not come at all."

"Best for him perhaps, but I would still demand satisfaction."

The words had barely left his lips when they heard the carriage. The Earl wasted no time getting out of his own vehicle.

As Charles alighted from his equipage he smiled at his two former friends. "You do not really want to go through with this, do you, Jeff?"

Saying nothing in response but very obviously insulted further by the question, Lord Moore-Jeffries took a step toward Charles, stopping only when George grabbed his arm. He could see no advantage in delaying the inevitable, so he suggested they begin.

While Charles and Jeff went to their respective carriages to remove their coats and prepare themselves, George Austen and Charles' second met and talked in another failed attempt to bring about a peaceful end. Finally, after agreeing that the pistols were indeed loaded properly and ready they called on the two opponents.

In the middle of the field each of the young noblemen took a pistol from the case in George's hand, they stood back to back as the seconds returned to the relative safety of the coaches.

Charles' second counted off the agreed upon twelve paces as mist swirled around them in the gray winter morning. Looking down the length of the black barrel, the Earl took aim at the stranger twenty-four paces away. He had been no friend. He waited no more than a fraction of a second. Slowly he pulled the trigger, willing his hand and eye to remain steady. The flint on the hammer scraped the frizzen, causing sparks to ignite the black powder. The resulting explosion forced the ball out of the end of the barrel. The sound reverberated off of the trees, and smoke hung in the air, captured by the morning fog. Charles' ball missed its mark, embedding itself into the tree just to the left of the Earl, but the Earl had not missed. George Austen ran to Charles' side as he lay in the wet grass, then reported to Lord Moore-Jeffries that it did not appear to be lethal but he could not continue. There would be no more shots. The duel was over.

Jeff looked across the field, then began to make his way toward his injured opponent. His pistol at his side, he stood over the man he had considered a friend. He had not reloaded the gun or he might have shot the man as he lay on the ground. It took all his willpower not to stomp on the blackguard's neck, finishing him off right then and there. The satisfaction of seeing him dead was lost. "I am sorry, Charles."

"For shooting me?"

"For not killing you."

The Earl shook with rage and frustration. George's hand resting gently on his arm stopped him from further action. At his friend's urging he turned and walked away. George assisted Charles back to his vehicle and, as he closed the carriage door, Charles suggested they get together later for brandy and cigars.

George, dumbfounded by the invitation, declined.

"Do not suppose for a moment, Charles, that my not wanting you dead is an indication that I approve of what you did or the tactics you employed to accomplish it. I no longer consider you a friend. Goodbye, Charles."

He turned and walked back to Lord Moore-Jeffries's carriage.

Inside the Earl asked, "What did he say to you?"

"He invited me to have a drink with him."

"He what?"

"He seemed to think that we were still friends. He no longer does." He paused, "Shall we be off? I have yet to eat this morning."

"I wanted him *dead*, George!"

"I know," his friend said quietly, then reminded him again that killing Charles would not repair the damage he had wrought and emphasized that retribution should be left in God's hands.

When they arrived back to Jeff's rooms, George asked whether he wanted to eat, but the Earl declined. George wasn't sure being alone was the best thing for his friend, so he stayed and went inside with him. As they walked through the door the valet handed the young Lord a letter.

"It came by express right after you left this morning, Sir."

Before removing his coat or hat he broke the seal from the paper and read it.

"Good God!"

"What is it?"

"Georgina ran away!"

"When?"

"Two days ago, after they received my letter. One of the tenants found her this morning but two nights without food or shelter has made her very ill." He dropped the letter on the table near the door. "I must get to Rosemont, immediately."

"Shall I come?" George inquired.

"Would you? I know you would be a great comfort to my mother."

Without further discussion the two young men went out and climbed into the carriage again.

"Why did she run away, Jeff?"

"She realized Charles did not love her and was certain, because of his refusal to marry her, that she had irretrievably damaged and disgraced the family ... and it is my fault."

"I am truly sorry, Jeff."

"What have I done, George?"

"What do you mean?"

"I promised my father I would keep her safe." He shook his head and looked at the floor of the carriage. "I should have listened to you when you warned me about him. You saw the truth. I am to blame; I am responsible for all of it."

"You are not to blame, Jeff. Charles is to blame."

"But I was supposed to watch over her, protect her. I failed. I failed her and I failed my father."

There was no consoling him and the rest of the trip was made in silence.

When he turned back to Jane the Earl's eyes were filled with tears. With a tremble in his voice, he said, "She was already gone when we arrived. She died believing she had been a disappointment to me and that somehow I blamed her."

Jane gasped and threw her arms around his neck. "Uncle Jeff, I am so sorry. I had no idea."

At first a bit shocked by this uncharacteristic display of affection, it took a moment before he raised his arms in a gentle embrace. As his hands touched her back, the realization of what she was doing struck her. She released him and took a large step back, dropping her gaze to the ground. "Forgive me. That was entirely too forward and very unseemly. I am sorry for it."

"You need never apologize for expressing your concern, Jane."

"Thank you for your forbearance, but there was little excuse for my actions. It was just that I... it seemed so—"

"Natural," the Earl said. "I know."

Her face still flushed from embarrassment, she nodded.

"Like Georgina, you have a loving and affectionate heart, Jane, so as we are alone and very old friends, let us say that natural is acceptable and always will be."

Jane curtsied. "Thank you, your Lordship."

He smiled. "Lordship? We already had that discussion, Jane."

Once again he wrapped her arm around his and they started walking back toward the other guests and the carriages.

"What happened to Charles?"

"I got my revenge after all. He died three weeks after I shot him. To try to avoid scandal, his family claimed that he had acquired consumption on a trip to the continent. But we knew that he had not gone to the continent, and George saw him before he died. He said it was unquestionably the wound I inflicted that caused his death." He paused slightly. "He died by my hand."

They walked in silence for a while. Finally his Lordship said, "Your father tried to get him to apologize on his deathbed but he refused right to the end. He also attempted to get me to see the blackguard and forgive him, but my stubbornness and pride would not allow it. In my youth I could easily have been called unyielding." He paused. "The truth is, Jane, I was glad he was dead."

Jane said nothing, only thought that it was a very unchristian sentiment.

"But your father was right; his death did not bring my sister back, nor did it heal the damage he did. And it certainly did not ease the pain inflicted by a man I had called my friend."

They walked on, Jane still unsure what, if anything, would be appropriate to say. Finally she said, "I am sorry you have had to suffer so much pain."

"The pain and grief will never go away. I am afraid I will forever be sorry that I made so many wrong choices then. Had I come home to be with my family rather than trying to exact vengeance for my wounded pride, my sister might still be alive. Even Charles might still be alive."

There was nothing she could say that would help. He had obviously been punishing himself all these years and a few words from her now would make no difference. She said nothing but squeezed his arm with her own as they approached the other picnickers. She flashed a reassuring smile as he helped her into the carriage.

On her way home that day, Jane wondered what the twenty-first century Mr. Darcy would have done had he found himself in a similar situation as the Earl. The five days they'd spent together hadn't really allowed her to know for certain how he might react to any given situation. She did believe she knew or at least understood his true character and disposition, and somehow she was certain that he would not have been so reckless as to chance a duel. She decided he would have done something far less dramatic and unobtrusive, but something just as unequivocal and irrevocable. She thought about it. *Whatever it was, he would have done it quietly and would have taken no credit. In spite of his arrogance he was not a braggart.*

Leaning back against the glove-soft leather of her brother's carriage she had decided that Elizabeth Bennet's Mr. Darcy would act above reproach; gallantly saving his own sister, Georgiana and ultimately, Lizzy's sister, Lydia from the scoundrel Wickham, and no one would have to die.

She smiled, looking forward to getting home to write.

Chapter 20

M rs. Temple had outdone herself with the most sumptuous picnic Eliza had ever seen. Fried chicken, ham, crudités, homemade bread and fresh raspberries were just the beginning. Wine and champagne were to be imbibed with the amazing feast. It was the prettiest picnic she'd ever seen, too. The housekeeper had packed it in what was very obviously an antique basket, a family heirloom, perhaps. There was china, crystal and silver for serving, as well as all the food. But the most amazing part was the cashmere stadium blanket that was to be their seating at the edge of the little lake.

As Fitz spread the luxurious blanket over the cool grass, Eliza took note of a rustic-looking swing, a wooden slat suspended from the branch of a giant old tree by two ropes. She had not seen it before in spite of having visited the lake several times in the last few days. "I don't remember seeing that swing before. Did I just miss it?"

"No. It wasn't there."

"Took it down because of the liability with all the people here over Heritage Week?"

"No, but I'll have to remember that for next year."

"And it wasn't there before?"

"Nope. As a matter of fact it hasn't been there for years. When I was nine the ropes broke, and at that age I wasn't really doing much swinging. I tended to climb the tree rather than swing, so my folks didn't bother putting it back up."

"Suddenly now you have the urge to swing?"

As he continued unpacking the basket, he shrugged. "You always sit in the rocking chair on the porch so I thought you might like the swing."

"You put it up for me?"

"Well, I asked Lucas to do it, so I can't really take much credit."

Maybe not for doing the physical labor, she thought. But his having thought about doing it at all left her more than a little surprised. "Can I try it?"

"Of course. Since Lucas did it I'm sure it's safe." Fitz continued setting out dinner.

As Eliza sat down on the wooden plank and pushed off she was confused and touched at the same time. *Is he trying to impress me or is he really that thoughtful?* Either way, it was working. She was impressed. She'd never dated anyone who was that aware of what she did and what she liked and then acted on it. She decided to continue taking her mother's advice and simply enjoy herself.

She'd read about swings like this and she'd seen them in movies, but she'd never been on one. She pumped her legs until the swing was as high as she could get it. She leaned back, her arms stretched to the limit, her legs out in front of her and closed her eyes; gravity did the rest as she glided through the evening air.

Suddenly she and the swing stopped and her eyes popped open. Fitz was standing in front of her holding the ropes, a grin on his face. The look in his eyes made her stomach jump, but she managed to say, "Thank you. I love it."

Without a word he kissed her, a kiss that made her feel like she might fall off the swing. Their lips parted and he slowly guided the swing to its original position. "Dinner is served."

The food, as always, was amazing and for hours they talked about the many different subjects people talk about when they're getting to know each other. The sun started its final descent as they dangled their feet in the obsidian water of the lake. By magic hour they were back on the cashmere blanket, and as night fell Eliza lay back, gazing into the star-filled sky. "I never understood the term 'soft summer night.' I mean, how can a time of day be soft or hard? But I think this is what it means... the way the air feels right now."

As the cicadas' song waned in the honeysuckle scented night, Fitz pulled her onto his lap and cradled her, and she sighed contentedly, luxuriating in his embrace. With a gentle touch he outlined the contours of her lovely face, then leaned down and kissed the tip of her nose, at the same time reaching over her to pick a red raspberry from the small china dish Mrs. Temple had used for the elegant picnic. He caressed her lips with the ripe berry, and just as she parted her lips to accept the luscious fruit he popped it into his own mouth, grinning mischievously.

"Hey!" Before he could finish eating the raspberry, Eliza encircled his neck with her arms, pulled herself to eye level, and kissed him with an abandon that took his breath away.

For the next several minutes much of his enjoyment came from her obvious pleasure as his hands explored her lithe frame. At the same time, she kissed his neck and around to his ear where her nibbling almost made him whimper. *God*, he thought. *I can't remember ever feeling like this.* Suddenly he pushed her into a sitting position and slid her off his lap. "I'm sorry. I can't do this."

Stunned, Eliza said, "What do you mean you can't?"

The distress on his face made her stomach turn over, and when he didn't answer, she kept saying over and over in her mind, *He can't... he can't. Why can't he?* The possibility that some horrible accident or serious illness in his youth had caused physical limitations over which he had no control was the only reason she could think of. In spite of the disappointment she felt, she asked sympathetically, "What happened?"

"What do you mean?"

"What happened that you can't?"

He looked at her rather quizzically. "Nothing happened."

"I don't understand. When you said you can't, I thought you meant you're unable to—"

Suddenly he realized what she thought and he laughed.

She frowned. "What's so funny?"

"Nothing happened to me, physically. I'm perfectly capable of... well, performing." He took her hand and kissed it. "You're cute."

She pulled her hand away and stood up.

"What are you doing?"

She turned and walked away quickly.

"You're not running away are you? You promised."

She stopped at the water's edge. She had promised. Promised to talk problems out and not run away, which had been her previous modus operandi. But right now all she wanted to do was run and hide.

Suddenly he was at her side, his arm around her waist.

She stepped to the side and pushed his arm away. Turning her back to him, she buried her face in her hands. She was completely mortified, not to mention bewildered and angry.

Gently he laid a hand on her shoulder.

She spun around, demanding, "What was all that about then? What the hell does 'I can't' mean if, in fact, you can?"

Still amused by the turn of events, he teasingly asked, "Can what?"

"Why are you doing this?"

"Why are you so upset?"

"Why? You've been here the whole time, right?"

He took her hand, leading her back to the blanket. "Sit down and talk to me."

She took a deep breath and sat down on the lovely throw, thinking about what was actually wrong. It wasn't the embarrassment of her assumption, although that didn't help. She had wanted him to undress her there in the moonlight and make mad, passionate love to her, but if she had to explain that to him, what did it say about what he wanted? And how in Heaven's name was she going to tell him any of it?

When she did look at him, she saw the question in his kind eyes. *He really didn't understand. Maybe he was just being a gentleman*, she thought. *We've only known each other for three days.* Finally she said, "You want the truth? The whole truth?"

He smiled. "And nothing but...."

"You are going to think I'm crass, uncouth and presumptuous." She wouldn't be able to say this looking at him, so she stared out at the ribbon of moonlight floating on the surface of the water. "Last night, after the Ball...." She blushed slightly. "I was really disappointed that you didn't... well, come into the Rose bedroom. I rationalized that you are a gentleman, and since you were hosting a party and still had guests in the house it would have been inappropriate. I assumed it was your southern sensibilities, and I took it as a sign that you're thoughtful and attentive to the needs of your guests. But just now when I was sure you wanted to...." She paused trying to think of a polite way to say it. "Sleep with me or make love with me or however you want to say it, I—"

"Make love to you."

She looked at him. "What?"

"You said 'however I want to say it.' How I want to say it is make love to you... and with you."

"Well, you have a very strange way of showing it. I mean, given the perfect opportunity you cast me aside and say you can't. How exactly was I supposed to react to that?"

He seemed genuinely surprised.

"I don't get an answer?"

He looked at the ground, "I'm afraid you'll think *me* uncouth." By the soft light of a full moon, he looked up with a sparkle in his eyes and grinned at her.

"Very funny."

"Eliza, I wanted nothing more than to sweep you into my arms and carry you to the bed in the Rose Bedroom last night, but you're right. I don't know whether I didn't because I'm a gentleman or because I have southern sensibilities, whatever they are, but it just seemed like the wrong time. The temporary employees, the volunteers and the regular staff were all still here. The Browns and Harringtons were still here too. There were just too many people around.

"And now?

He cleared his throat. "If all I want is sex I can have it with any number of women pretty much any time."

She flashed a skeptical look.

"I know it sounds arrogant, but it's true. Like I said earlier, that's the only kind of relationship I've had… up to now."

She never would have admitted it to him, but Eliza had little doubt that it was true, and she wondered just how many there had been.

"But with you I want it to be a product of how we feel about each other. I want it to be lovemaking in the truest sense." He hesitated. "We said we wanted to try for a real relationship this time. I know I handled it awkwardly, but it was my clumsy attempt to do things differently. One of the ways I decided to do that is to—"

"Take it slowly."

"I was going to say wait, but yes, take it slowly."

"Slow and steady wins the race?"

"Exactly. And I want to win this race, Eliza."

"Me, too." She pretended to pout. "Except…."

"What?"

She looked at him, her lower lip slightly protruding. "I really want to jump your bones."

He laughed and pulled her into his arms. "You are not alone in that, and when the time is right, you can be my guest." He kissed her again.

"Hey, you can't keep doing that if you want to take things slowly."

"You're absolutely right; perhaps we should repair to the house then."

Together they returned the china, crystal and silver as well as the remaining food to the basket, but before making their way back to the house, Eliza punched his arm.

"Hey! What was that for?"

"You can't just make a unilateral decision that affects both of us; you have to let me in on it."

He looked at the ground in mock humiliation. "Yes, Ma'am."

The two hundred year old mansion stood sentinel in the silver moonlight. The stars cast a soft veil as mist swirled in the humid summer air around the graceful façade and soaring columns that were Pemberley House. Although it was man-made, the idyllic old structure seemed to belong here, surrounded by deep woods and majestic mountains.

The grandfather clock on the second floor landing struck twelve midnight as they entered the two-story foyer. In spite of the immense size of the place it felt almost intimate. Eliza broke the quiet that had surrounded them on the walk back. "Ah, the witching hour. Time really does fly when you're having fun. I had no idea it was so late."

Setting the basket down, Fitz turned her toward him and feigned a frown. "It was just fun?"

"I'm not sure that 'just' is the adverb I'd use, but it was most definitely fun." She smiled and once more he took her in his arms and kissed her.

She pulled away, "You gotta stop that."

"You don't want me to kiss you?"

"Yeah, that's it, I don't want you to kiss me." She shook her head. "Walk me to my room. I have an early flight in the morning."

"Do you really have to leave tomorrow?"

"Absolutely. I called and told Thelma and Sotheby's to hold up doing anything, including the announcement. Now I have to go back and explain why."

Reluctantly he said, "I suppose."

At the door of the Rose Bedroom, she said, "I must tell you that was one of the sexiest dates I've ever had." She paused. "At least part of it." She grinned. "Thank you."

He slipped one arm around her and pulled her to him. "You are more than welcome. I enjoyed it too." He looked through the open door. "How long is slow do you think?"

She smiled at him. "Hey, slow was your idea so I'm afraid it has to be your call."

He visibly perked up. "You don't want to wait?"

"I believe I've already taken the mystery out of that question, but the rational part of me agrees with you that we've not dealt with relationships in the healthiest way and doing this differently might be a good thing."

"You're right... slow and steady it is." He bent down and kissed her gently. "I'll see you in the morning. Sleep well, my love."

Before he released her, she whispered, "Thank you for the swing."

He kissed her again. "Sweet dreams."

He walked to his bedroom at the other end of the hall. Sighing deeply, she didn't know how well she'd sleep tonight but she certainly knew what she would dream about, and it would be very sweet indeed.

Chapter 21

Fitz turned Eliza in his arms and kissed her, not the passionate kisses of the night before but one that told her he definitely wanted her to come back. Their lips parted and she took a step away from him. "You need to stop that or you'll never get rid of me."

He smiled. "That easy?"

"Pretty much." She opened the driver's side door.

Fitz tossed her duffle bag across to the passenger seat of the small red economy car. "When will I see you again?"

"Soon."

"Promise?"

"Promise." She gave him a quick farewell kiss and slipped in behind the wheel of the car.

Fitz and the house grew smaller in the rearview mirror as she drove through the Pemberley Farms woods and out through the wrought iron gates.

Leaning back against the dark blue velour-like seat, Eliza closed her eyes and imagined she was leaning against him with his arms around her. She sighed; it felt like the most natural place in the world to be. Did that make them soul mates?

As the 737 reached altitude and penetrated the thick cloud cover, leaving behind the green, gray and brown patchwork of the Virginia countryside, she pushed the overly romanticized thoughts aside. She was headed home to New York where a very angry Thelma Klein was waiting. She'd told Fitz that Thelma would be unhappy, but she was pretty sure anger was a more applicable emotion for how she expected the intimidating scholar to react.

She smiled. Rather than thinking about the unpleasant Austen expert Eliza decided that overly romantic or not, she preferred to think of the gratitude in Fitz Darcy's eyes when she gave him the letter. The image of that night by the lake flooded her memory. Jane Austen's letter had given him leave to fall in love with someone else. Jane hadn't just given him leave to do it; she'd actually told him to, and he had, or at least he said he had. She sighed. *If his actions were any indication, it was true.* She, Elizabeth Ann Knight, was his dearest and loveliest, or so he said, twice. Still, she had to wonder at the bond between the tall Virginian and the famed author. Could he really love both her and Jane Austen?

Eliza spent the entire cab ride from the airport steeling herself for the expected confrontation with Thelma Klein, the New York Public Library's Director of Rare Documents and self-proclaimed Jane Austen expert. She looked up at the street sign when the cab stopped for a light. She was a mere two blocks away and the thought was nerve-wracking.

Outside Thelma's third-floor apartment Eliza took a deep breath and let it out slowly, willing the strength she knew she would need to handle the volatile scholar with aplomb. She raised her hand and rapped quietly. No response. Maybe she wasn't home. With a little more confidence fueled by the idea that Thelma might not be there anyway, Eliza knocked again, a bit more loudly. The door flew open before her arm dropped back to her side.

"It's about time! What's going on? What's happened?"

Eliza stood transfixed, startled by the woman's sudden appearance.

Thelma adamantly pressed for an answer. "Well?"

Struggling to retain her composure and not allow Thelma to rattle her any further, Eliza tried to appear nonchalant. "Are you going to invite me in?"

Thelma glared at her but stepped aside, allowing the artist entrance to the apartment.

Curled up asleep in an overstuffed chair was Eliza's large gray tabby cat, Wickham. She picked him up, "How ya doin', Fat Stuff?" The cat purred and rubbed his head against her hand, then jumped out of her arms and repositioned himself in the chair.

Thelma bellowed, "Leave the damn cat alone and answer my question!"

Absently stroking the cat's head, Eliza sat on the arm of the chair. "What was your question?"

"What the hell happened with Darcy?" Eliza's heart skipped a beat. She was afraid that somehow Thelma had found out about her blossoming relationship with Fitz, but before she had a chance to respond the bombastic scholar demanded, "What did he say?"

Eliza took a quiet deep breath. "About what?"

"Don't play dumb with me. You went to Virginia for confirmation that his ancestor was the Darcy of the letters."

"No, that's why you *wanted* me to go; I went because I wanted the story behind the letters."

"Well, what did you find out?"

"He did confirm—"

"I *knew* it!" Thelma squealed, a very disconcerting sound. She was almost giddy. "I just *knew* Austen had an affair with an American! Fantastic! What a book! It'll knock the wind out of all those stuffy so-called Austen experts who think they know it all. It'll sell millions! I can't wait to start writing it!"

Thelma finally took a breath, giving Eliza the chance to finish her thought. "Well, your source had better be something other than the letters or Fitz Darcy."

"What? Why? What are you talking about?"

"He confirmed that the letter had not been meant for his ancestor. The first Fitzwilliam Darcy did not have an affair with Jane Austen."

"How is that possible?"

"According to the stories that have been handed down in the Darcy family, the first Darcy never left the United States after the revolution and from the biography I read Jane never left England, so they never met."

"What about *Pride and Prejudice*? It can't be a coincidence that she used the names!"

"Fitz told me that the farm's financial records indicate that his ancestor purchased several horses from an English breeder and used Henry Austen's bank for the transaction. It's much more logical that she heard the names from her brother, Henry, than that she had an affair with a stranger."

Thelma stared. "That can't be right! How did he explain the letters?"

"They weren't to or from his ancestor, so he had no reason to explain them."

"I just don't understand it. I was sure the letters would prove that Austen had an American lover. I mean why would she have written to an American she didn't know? It makes no sense."

Eliza shrugged and picked up Wickham, pushing the uncooperative cat into his carrier. She zipped the mesh door closed and stood up.

Thelma, after some thought, said, "I'll run some more tests on the letters. There has to be something we missed." Quietly she added, "I was so sure."

Eliza picked up the cat carrier. "Thanks for watching Wickham."

Still distracted, Thelma said, "Yeah."

As Eliza opened the apartment door, Thelma seemed to regain her composure. "Give me the letters so I can run the tests. They've already been out of the safety of the climate controlled vault too long."

Eliza, having hoped to escape before it came to this stopped in the open doorway.

She almost whispered, "I don't have them."

"Where are they?"

"Virginia."

"You left them with Darcy? Why? If they had nothing to do with his family why would you do that?"

Not wanting to lie outright, Eliza stretched the truth. "He was looking at them and slipped them into the pocket of his coat. I didn't think too much of it, and then it was time for me to leave." She shrugged. "And quite frankly I wasn't thinking about them."

"How could you not have been thinking about them when they were the reason you were there?"

"Like I said before, the letters weren't the reason I went. It was the story of the letters that I was interested in learning. Since Austen and the first Darcy never met, there was no story to learn. I didn't give them much thought after that."

"I was under the impression that you had some business savvy, some street smarts, but I'm starting to think you're a blithering idiot. Obviously he told you his family wasn't involved with Austen so you would drop it, as you did, allowing him to keep the letters. Have you any idea what's been lost by your actions? Sotheby's expects to make a small fortune, and my book will sell millions of copies. We're all going to lose a lot of money if you don't get those letters back."

Finally the artist raised her voice, "Money? Is that all you were ever interested in? What about the history, the romance the letters represented?"

"History and romance are valuable when you're talking about Jane Austen, but without the letters none of it is worth anything."

Eliza looked at her watch. "I'm meeting with Sotheby's in two hours, which gives me just enough time to take Wickham home. Thanks again for watching him." She stepped out of the apartment and closed the door, leaving a fuming Thelma behind her.

Chapter 22

Dave found Simmons in Tornado's stall talking softly to the black stallion. "Hey Simmons. What ya doin'?"

"The horse is coughing."

"Yeah, Sam's coming later." Before Simmons could respond in any way, Dave said, "Come on, everyone else has eaten and Cook says if we don't get up there we'll have to do without breakfast and I'm starving."

Feeling the need to be cautious and afraid he might say something wrong, the young groom simply nodded, patting the horse as he turned to the door.

Dave asked rather bluntly, "God, did you sleep in those clothes?"

Simmons, surprised by the question, looked down at himself, and then answered hesitantly, "Yes."

"Why?"

"I always sleep in them."

"Why?"

"I just do."

The young American shrugged. "You do know you don't have to wear the costume anymore, right? The history faire was only for the one day."

"Costume?"

Dave wasn't sure what was going on. He quietly asked, "Didn't you bring any other clothes?"

"These are all I have."

Considering the possibility that Simmons was financially strapped, he felt badly about ragging on him about it so he offered some of his own clothes.

"We can go to the cottage after we eat."

Hesitantly Simmons uttered, "Okay."

Sitting at the island in the kitchen, the two young men were served eggs, bacon, toast, some delicious crisp potatoes and coffee by the Cliftons' cook. Simmons was continually amazed at the way servants were treated here, eating the same food as the owners and in the house. His mind spun with the changes in the world as he ate the strange but wonderful food. Dave was telling him that the whole staff was invited to the annual Michaelmas party the Cliftons had before closing the house for the winter. Simmons thought about how (if he were home) he would be one of many servants relegated to the drive or stables during Lord Moore-Jeffries' Michaelmas Ball. This new world was truly amazing, and he wished Miss Jane could see it. Simmons smiled. *There's that word again: amazing.*

"Sam's coming today. You should meet him."

"Who is Sam?"

"The veterinarian, you said you want to be a horse doctor so now you can pick his brain."

"Pick brains?"

Dave chuckled. "Guess it's not an English phrase. In America it means ask him questions about his work since he is a horse doctor."

"Is that really possible?"

"Sure. He's coming to check on Tornado, the horse you were looking at when I found you this morning."

"That horse has a cold in his lungs."

"Could be. Sam will take a look."

"And the draught horse has an injury to her flank."

"Yeah, Sam's gonna look at that, too."

The two men continued with their breakfast until Simmons asked, "How did you come to work here and not with Mr. Darcy?"

Dave explained, "Well, I was here to help with the purchase of Lord Nelson, I mentioned to Linda that I really liked it here and wouldn't mind living here one day."

"The Cliftons talked with Fitz and then offered me a job. I decided to take it and do some of the stuff I've always wanted to do while I was young enough to enjoy it. I've taken trips to France, Germany, Spain and Italy; the Greek Isles are incredible. It's been great and I wanted to do it all before I get married and have kids and stuff."

"Kids?"

"Children. I wanted to do the stuff before I'm tied down." He gulped down the last of his coffee. "You finish your coffee. I'll go get the clothes and meet you in the barn."

Taking a shortcut through the garden to get to the caretaker's cottage that he shared with Mark, the barn manager, Dave surprised Linda, who was cutting flowers for the house.

"Whoa. I almost tripped over you. Sorry."

Linda stood up. "Where are you going in such a hurry?"

"To the cottage to get some clothes for Simmons."

"Why?"

"He doesn't have any clothes with him, probably doesn't even have a toothbrush."

"How do you know?"

"I told him he didn't need to wear the costume anymore and he said they were the only clothes he had. He's even been sleeping in them. I figured he must be down on his luck. I got lots of jeans and shirts, and I think they'll fit him okay."

Linda said, "That's nice of you." She paused. "Has he said anything to you?"

"Like what?"

"Where he comes from, what his plans are... that kind of thing."

"No, why?"

"Roger and I were wondering just how legitimate this plan of his is."

"It never occurred to me that it wasn't. It's the kind of thing Fitz would do, and after Simmons told me he took care of Nelson, I knew that Fitz trusted him." He shrugged. "That's all I needed to know."

"You're definitely right about that. Fitz surely wouldn't let just anyone handle Lord Nelson... and it *does* kind of fit with what I was thinking about him."

"What do you mean?"

"That maybe he's a plain-living Mennonite, which would explain the clothes and not being particularly aware of technology and modern things."

"Well, whatever he is I'm sure he's a good guy and Fitz will take care of him."

Linda chuckled. "It's just like Fitz to befriend a disadvantaged young horseman and take him in... at least I assume that's the plan, for Fitz to take him in." She paused. "I've always been surprised that he doesn't collect stray cats and dogs."

Dave smiled broadly. "He does, kind of. A lot of the animals on the farm are rescues—even some of the horses and hunting dogs—but he definitely takes in stray people, like me." He tipped his hat. "Gotta go. Sam's coming this morning."

Simmons saw the thing Dave called a truck. It looked like a lorry without a horse to Simmons and was another example of the strange horseless vehicles he had seen in his short time here.

Sam was a muscular man, older than himself but younger than Mr. Darcy. He was outside the barn talking with the Cliftons' barn manager, Mark.

Dave greeted the veterinarian. "Hey, Sam."

"Good morning, Dave." The men shook hands.

Dave turned to Simmons. "Simmons, this is Sam, our vet. Sam, meet Bob Simmons. He likes to be called Simmons not Bob."

Sam extended his hand. "Good to meet you, Simmons."

Dave added, "Simmons wants to be a vet, so he's going to follow you around and pick your brain."

"Great! We can always use good men in the field."

"I want to be a horse doctor."

"I tend to deal with all animals being a country vet, but doctoring horses is a good profession."

"Mr. Darcy has horses."

"Do you work for Fitz Darcy?"

"I hope to."

"He's a good man."

"Yes, Sir."

Inside the barn Mark stopped at the first stall. The black horse inside was wheezing.

As if on instinct Simmons approached the animal, calming Tornado with a soothing voice. He turned and said to the vet, "He has a cold in his lungs."

Sam said, "We shall see." After his examination he concurred. "And how would you treat the cold?"

Simmons didn't hesitate. "Steam, Sir."

"Steam, no antibiotics, then?"

The young groom frowned. "Anti... bi... otics?"

The three men were a bit surprised that Simmons seemed not to know what antibiotics were, but none said anything about it.

Sam explained. "Medicine to kill the bacteria causing the infection."

"We don't have such medicine at home, Sir."

He nodded. "Homeopathic medicine... interesting. Do you intend to continue that when you become a vet?"

Having no earthly idea what the man was talking about, Simmons replied in the affirmative in the hopes it wasn't another mistake. Making mistakes here had turned out to be far easier than he had imagined.

"Commendable. I think modern medicine is too much about the drugs, particularly antibiotics, and they're just not as effective as they used to be because of it."

After he gave the horse a shot in spite of his verbal sentiment, they moved on to the next animal. Jemma, the Irish draught horse, had gotten too close to an old wooden stile and a large splinter had embedded itself into her left flank. Removal of the offending sliver had left a deep laceration.

Mark said, "We did some first aid, but we were out of sterile saline and iodine." He laughed. "You'll appreciate this,

Simmons. Veronica is very much into herbs and all things 'natural.'" He gestured, creating air quotes. "She was the one riding Jemma when it happened, so when we ran out of saline she insisted we boil the water we used to flush the cut. Then she gave us some ground-up, dried kelp mixed with raw honey, which I must say smelled horrible, to put on the wound." He paused. "Jemma's her favorite horse so we did what she wanted, but it was all pretty silly, right Sam?"

Sam cocked his head and looked at the cut on the horse's hip. "Jumping to conclusions is never wise, Mark. Fact is, it looks very good. Boiling the water killed whatever microbes were in it, kelp is infused with iodine, and honey is a natural antibiotic. Veronica may have saved the Cliftons a large vet bill and the horse a nasty infection." He looked more closely, "Looks like it could use a couple of stitches, though, and I think it will heal better if it's closed."

From his bag he took out a small pair of scissors and a needle with a bright pink string attached. He sewed closed the cut on the horse, then clipped the string close to the knot he'd tied. "That should do it."

Simmons asked, "Why is the thread pink?"

Sam smiled. "Easier to find when it's time to take them out." As he put his things back in his bag he asked, "Everyone else okay?"

Mark responded, "Everyone's good. When can we exercise 'Nado and Jemma?"

"Let's wait 'til next week for Tornado and I'll check on him. We want to be sure his lungs are clear before he's ridden. And don't forget to give him his shot every day. Jemma can go out tomorrow if you're easy with her. Just watch that the cut doesn't get dirty."

"Will do."

All four young men walked to Sam's wood-sided truck. He tossed his bag onto the seat and turned to Simmons. "Good meeting you, Simmons. If you have any questions or need any help with your schooling feel free to call on me." He paused a moment. "Or are you going to study in the states?"

Unsure how to respond Simmons said, "I don't know."

"Well, good luck to you."

"Thank you, Sir," he said, bowing.

As Sam drove away, Dave poked Simmons gently in the ribs with his elbow. "You don't have to bow and call everyone sir, you know. You make the rest of us look bad. Right, Mark?"

"Indeed."

Chapter 23

Dave and Simmons fed and brushed the horses, with Simmons taking particular care to change the bandage on Jemma and inject the shot of antibiotic Sam had prescribed for Tornado.

Dave noted that the young Englishman seemed more relaxed tonight than he'd seen him since he got here. It wasn't just because he was working with the horses, because they'd been doing that for a couple of days. That first day he'd been uptight and anxious about everything. Sounds made him jump and he was afraid to talk to anyone, but now he was kind of calm and had talked almost nonstop since they'd started bedding the horses down for the night. He talked about other horses he'd taken care of, including Lord Nelson, the people he was working for when he met Fitz Darcy, and his dream of going to

America and becoming a horse doctor. The young groom was high on the possibilities of his life.

Dave came to the conclusion that Linda was right; Simmons just wasn't used to stuff but he was catching on real quick. Of course, being accepted unconditionally by the Cliftons was a huge plus for the shy horseman.

The two young men came out of the tack room with their chores almost complete.

"I'm going to turn off the steamer," Simmons said. "Don't want to start a fire."

"Good idea. I'll go lock up the feed and tack. Then we'll be all done, so we can go up to the cottage and watch some TV.

"TV?"

"You know, television."

Once again not wanting to appear completely unaware, he said, "Oh." Miss Jane had mentioned television as one of the innovations to come, but he had no idea what it was.

After securing the horses for the night the two young horsemen walked through the lush grounds of Windsong Manor.

"Want something to drink?" Dave asked as they entered the caretaker's cottage. "We have Coke and beer."

"Coke?"

"Coca-Cola. It's a soft drink." It was almost a question. *How can anyone not know what Coke was?* "Sit down; I'll get one for you."

Simmons sat in a large, plush chair that was softer and as comfortable as the bed in the barn. When Dave came back into the room he was carrying two red cans. He handed one to Simmons.

"Coca-Cola... try it."

The young groom took a tentative sip from the cold, damp can. "It's sweet."

"Yeah. Do you like it?"

Simmons took a healthier swig. "Very much."

Dave nodded. "That chair reclines you know." He pulled the lever on the side of the chair and it fell back, startling the young Englishman, who jumped to his feet. Dave laughed. "Calm down; it's supposed to do that. It's called a recliner. You stretch out and relax in it. Go ahead and sit down."

Very carefully, Simmons situated himself in the chair again and leaned back. *I could sleep this way. If everyone has these chairs, why do they use the fancy beds? Isn't one or the other enough?*

From the sofa Dave used a small black box he called a remote control and turned on the television. Simmons tried to absorb what he was seeing all around him in the room and on the glass screen hanging on the wall as Dave channel surfed. As far as Simmons could tell, "surfing" was altering what came on the television by pushing buttons on the remote control. That changed the channel, Dave said, the channel being the location of the different programs. Programs are what Dave called the different images that appeared on the television screen. He stopped on an American show called *Law and Order*, which was about lawyers and police. Continuing with his surfing through several more images that were completely unfamiliar to Simmons, Dave stopped again on another show called *Law and Order*, but this time with British people.

Then he changed the picture one last time. "The program that's coming on is one of my favorites. It's called Dr. Who. It's a science fiction show about time travel. This guy, Dr. Who, has a time machine that looks like a police box from way back in the 1960s, and it takes him everywhere and anywhere. It's really cool."

Simmons had no idea what a police box or science fiction was, but the idea of watching a story about time travel made him uncomfortable. He wondered whether Dave had somehow found out that he was a time traveler. Unwilling to stay and find out, he claimed weariness and bid his co-worker a good night.

"All right, then I'll see you in the morning, but you're missing a great show."

Simmons stepped out of the cottage and took a deep breath. *Will I ever get used to things here?* He didn't understand how people here could remember everything. Things are far simpler at home. He was halfway to the barn when he realized he'd left his bag next to the reclining chair.

At the door Dave handed him the bag.

"You know you don't have to carry it around with you. It's safe in your room."

"I'm afraid to leave it there. I've already lost a package someone gived me for Mr. Darcy."

Dave got a quizzical look on his face. "Is it wrapped in brown paper and addressed to Fitz?"

"You seen it?"

"Yeah, I found it in Jemma's stall the day of the history faire. I thought Veronica had left it there since she was the last person to ride Jemma, so I gave it to her."

"Who is Veronica?"

"Linda's secretary. Don't worry; I'll get it from her tomorrow."

Simmons sighed. "Thank you." He was more than pleased that he wouldn't have to explain to Miss Jane why he had been unable to give Mr. Darcy her package. He returned to his room in the barn and his cloud-like bed.

Breakfast, like the past three days, was in the kitchen of the manor house, today with Mark and Dave. The main topic

of conversation was the planned chores for the day which included exercising Jemma, something Simmons volunteered
to do, as well as looking after Tornado, who did seem to be
improving.

Mark and Dave continued the discussion but Simmons'
mind wandered to other things. He'd watched people using
the telephone and was confident that soon he would be able to
figure out which characters on Mr. Darcy's card were the ones
that were the American's telephone number. On the small window of the telephone in Mark's office, Simmons had watched
as Dave tapped out 001540 and a series of numbers after that
to call his mother, who lived very near Pemberley Farms, Mr.
Darcy's estate. Checking later he discovered that Mr. Darcy's
card had 540 and seven additional numbers on it, most likely
the number for his telephone.

Cook pouring more coffee into Simmons cup roused him,
and he smiled and thanked her. Mark and Dave were talking
about a movie, which seemed to be very like television as far
as he could figure out from the conversation. He was mostly
fascinated that the two young men seemed such good friends
since Mark, as Windsong's barn manager, was Dave's boss. He
thought about William Johnson, Master Edward's steward and
his boss, who only ever deigned speak to Simmons if it was absolutely necessary. The rest of the time he treated Simmons no
better than he treated the hunting dogs, and often he treated
the dogs better. The young servant smiled at the thought of
Miss Jane's kindness to him.

"Morning all," said a very pretty young woman as she entered the kitchen.

Simmons perked up considerably. *Who is she?* He'd never
seen her before. He thought her the prettiest girl he'd ever seen,
and when she smiled at him her eyes sparkled.

Dave, as usual, was first to speak, "Hey, V, welcome back. How was Dublin?"

"Great. Trinity is such a beautiful old school. On the tour they told us that in the middle of the 1800s, to build the library's inventory, they started receiving a copy of every book published in the British Isles! Now there are so many books, you almost can't see the walls. It's amazing."

"That's great!" Dave said and then turned to Simmons. "Veronica has been in Dublin for a few days getting ready to go to medical school there. She's going to be a doctor." He paused a moment. "Hey you don't know her, do you?"

Simmons shook his head.

"Well, Veronica Holquin meet Bob Simmons."

Simmons immediately slid off the stool and bowed. "Miss Veronica."

"How cute. No one's ever bowed to me before. I love it." She extended her hand to him. "Nice to meet you, Bob." She made a small curtsey.

Dave corrected her "He prefers Simmons to Bob."

"Okay, Simmons," she said and turned to leave. "Must be off, lads. Have loads of work."

Simmons looked at Dave and cleared his throat. Dave smiled.

"Right. Hey V."

Veronica turned back to the three young men.

"Turns out that package I gave you the other day belongs to Simmons here and he'd like it back."

Her lovely face registered concern. "Oh."

"What?"

"Well, I sent it to Fitz. Linda made a cake for him the day before I left and I was getting ready to send it when you gave

me the package. Since it was addressed to him I just put it in
with the cake."

"Can you get it out?" Dave asked.

"I posted it before I left for Dublin. It's probably already in
Virginia." She turned to Simmons. "I'm so sorry. I had no idea
it was yours."

"You sent it by post to Mr. Darcy?" Simmons inquired.

"Yes. It did have his name and address on it, so I just assumed that Linda meant for him to have it." Veronica gave him
a pouty smile. "Do you hate me?"

"As long as Mr. Darcy gets it, I suppose it makes no
difference."

"Oh, good! And again, I am sorry." She left the kitchen.

Simmons sat down; he wasn't sure how he felt about it. He
was relieved that Mr. Darcy would be receiving it and that he
had not lost it, but he had hoped to deliver it in person. Since
there was nothing he could do about it, he finished his coffee
and started his chores of caring for the injured horses.

Chapter 24

Pemberley Farms ~ Virginia, USA
Summer, Now

The Lipizzaner filly trotted around the bullpen at the end of a loose longe line while Fitz observed her movements. The newly acquired horse, the color of freshly churned buttermilk, moved with such grace it was hard to believe she'd been rejected by The Spanish Riding School as a brood mare. Her gait was steady and smooth; he looked forward to seeing how she handled jumps. That, however, would have to wait. After a transatlantic flight she had arrived just in time for Heritage Week, and Jake felt she needed a bit more time to get acclimated to her new home. In spite of his eagerness to ride her, Fitz agreed that the commotion of the last week very likely made Corazón a tad nervous, although at present she seemed to be adjusting pretty well. Pleased with the progress the horse was making and the gentle workout, he walked her back to the barn, the longe line folded on itself and laying on his shoulder. Picking up two small apples on the way past the feed bins, he led the spirited animal into her stall.

The tall Virginian removed the cavesson and hung it along with the longe line on a hook inside the closet where some of her tack was kept. Standing with his back to her it took only a moment before she was directly behind him, nuzzling his shoulder. He chuckled; she was as smart as she was beautiful. She'd seen him pick up the apples and she wanted them. He turned, one of the small fruits in the center of his open hand. He secured the lower part of the Dutch door after giving her the second apple.

Coming out of one of the newer wings of the barn, Jake saw Fitz exit the little filly's stall. "How's she doing?"

"Good. She should be ready to ride in a few days."

"Outstanding. With all the people milling around here last week and especially over the weekend I was afraid she'd be skittish."

"Nope, she's fine. She's going to be a great addition to the farm." He paused as they neared Jake's office. "Mrs. Temple usually puts coffee on at this time of day. Care to join me?"

"Sounds great. At my age I need an afternoon break."

"Then come on, old man."

"Looky here, y'young whippersnapper; I can say I'm old, but you're not allowed."

Fitz gave him a jaunty salute. "Yes, Sir!"

The banter continued on the walk to the house, and they were still laughing and joking with each other when they went into the mud room right off the kitchen. While the two men washed up and brushed their boots free of dirt and scraps of things you definitely do not want tracked into the kitchen, Fitz thought about how grateful he was for his barn manager. Jake was as close to a father as he had after his own father died. He'd stayed on at the farm even though he'd gotten more than one lucrative offer to work elsewhere. His strength and loyalty had helped Fitz and his mother through several rough times, and he was often Fitz' voice of reason—and not just where horses were concerned.

Mrs. Temple did, in fact, have a fresh pot of coffee brewing and a cake displayed on a pedestal milk glass cake stand.

While Jake made his compliments to the housekeeper, Fitz went over and smelled the cake. Periodically Linda Clifton, the wife of one of his closest friends, made a moist, dense, delicious cake and sent it to him. She called them her care packages as he had no wife to bake for him. She'd found the recipe in *The Jane Austen Cookbook* and had made it for him several years ago when he was celebrating his birthday in England. He had proclaimed the fragrant Madeira spiked pound cake to be his favorite of all desserts.

A small package wrapped in brown paper and tied with twine caught his eye. His name and address were written in a hand he did not instantly recognize. He picked it up and turned to Mrs. Temple, "What is this?"

His housekeeper stopped her conversation with Jake. "I don't know it. It was in the box with the cake."

Mrs. Temple went back to her task and conversation. Fitz looked more closely at the handwriting. He was pretty sure it wasn't Linda's. Using his pocket knife, he cut the twine and unwrapped the parcel. *Odd,* he thought. *No tape or anything else securing the ends of the paper.* The three small books inside were covered in what appeared to be simple white cotton fabric with tiny black dots, and in the middle of the cover of the topmost volume were three letters beautifully rendered in black silk embroidery. He looked at the spine, nothing; so he was more than a little surprised to find that it was *Pride and Prejudice*, the title page said. *Written by the author of Sense and Sensibility*. He looked up, staring across the kitchen at nothing in particular. Then he looked down again at the book. *A novel in three volumes. Volume One, London, printed for T. Egerton, Military Library, Whitehall.* At the bottom of the page, below everything else it read, *1813*. He closed it. An intricate D flanked by F and J created his monogram. He smiled. He had been unaware that Linda did such ornate embroidery. In fact, he hadn't realized she did embroidery at all, but this was a gorgeous example of the art. *Why would she do such a thing?* "Was there a note or anything with this?"

"No, just the package. Why, what is it?"

"A book."

"Maybe she wrote inside. That's what I do when I give someone a book."

Fitz flipped it open just past the title page, fully expecting to find a note from Linda, but he was greeted with *My Dear Mr. Darcy. That's not how Linda would start a note to me.* He scanned the page, finally landing on the end of the inscription: *Yours affectionately, Jane Austen* left him speechless.

Fitz put the book on the counter and leaned heavily on the granite surface, his heart racing. He looked again at the monogram and then the inscription; it was obviously meant for him, but if Jane had embroidered and covered the books, how had she gotten them to this century? His head was spinning with the possibilities.

"My God, Fitz, what's wrong? You're white as a sheet!" Jake reached for the book. "What is it?"

"It's nothing... nothing at all." Fitz hurriedly closed and gathered up the three volumes and the paper in which they were wrapped. "I need to call Linda and thank her." He headed for the door.

"What about our cake and coffee?"

He turned. "What?"

"Cake, coffee. Afternoon break."

"Oh... yes.... Go ahead without me."

Mrs. Temple and Jake looked at each other as Fitz rushed out of the kitchen. Finally Jake shrugged. "He said to go ahead. Shall we?"

Agreeing with the barn manager the housekeeper poured the coffee while he served the cake.

Fitz sat at his desk, the three books on the blotter in front of him. He leaned back in the chair and closed his eyes. *How did this happen? Where did Linda get them?* He sat up and picked up the phone, he had to find out. He put it down again. What if he was over-reacting and this was just a silly joke? It didn't feel silly. Still, that was a far more logical explanation than the only other one he could think of.

He picked up the first volume and read the inscription again, then went to the file cabinet and removed the two letters he had from Jane. He laid the one Eliza had given him next to the page in the book. He wasn't an expert but it looked the same to him so it probably wasn't a hoax.

Even if it wasn't a joke perpetrated by his English friends, surely they would know why it was in the package with the cake. Not hesitating this time Fitz picked up the phone and dialed the Cliftons' number. The phone rang six times before Bobby, their houseman, answered. In a brief conversation he learned that Linda and Roger were gone and were not expected to return until late tomorrow.

Fitz slowly hung up. He tried their cell phones but both went directly to voice mail. They were either somewhere with no reception or had the things turned off.

He stood up. There was no way to guess what was going on so he would just have to wait and talk with Linda when they returned. It was, after all, only a day and he could certainly wait for twenty-four hours. He rewrapped the three small volumes in the brown paper and slipped the package into the lower right drawer of his desk.

A restless night was followed by a day that kept him busy enough to keep him from obsessing about the source of the book. Unfortunately, with the coming evening and another un-productive phone call to Windsong Manor, he did begin to obsess about it. Linda and Roger had decided to extend their trip to Brighton by a day, so they wouldn't be back until tomorrow sometime.

Unable to concentrate on anything he gave up and found himself walking the halls of his home. He ended up in his mother's office. He had lived here alone for more than twenty years, but suddenly the house seemed empty. Even in this room where the memory of his mother usually comforted him, the emptiness persisted. Standing in the middle of the perfectly appointed room, all he wanted to do was run to wherever Eliza was and tell her about it, show her the book, and explain his fears. She was the only one who would understand but she wasn't answering her phone either.

The blue Jeep rolled down the drive toward Pemberley woods and the wrought iron gates of Darcy's estate. In the rearview mirror fireflies were dancing in the pale light of the new moon. The scene reminded Fitz of a story he'd heard as a child about Martin Luther seeing stars shining through the trees in the forest. Unable to describe it to his family adequately Luther had put candles on the branches of an evergreen tree and lit them. Legend held that was how lights came to be on Christmas trees. He doubted the veracity of the myth, but that was exactly how the woods looked, like tiny white Christmas lights were twinkling on every tree.

He turned on to the highway. He would be in the city by ten thirty if Pete was right about the flight time from Roanoke to Newark. His friend Pete Dohr was a doctor who used his own Mooney Acclaim to fly into rural areas that had no medical services. Tonight, however, he was flying Fitz into Newark airport. Fitz' anxiety level had been much too high for him to just sit at home, so he decided to head for New York. If his worst fears were realized after he spoke to Linda, he would need to get to England in a hurry, and leaving from New York was much faster than leaving from Roanoke. Besides, now he could see Eliza if she was home. Several attempts to call her had failed and he hadn't bothered to leave a message. He would try again when he got to the city. It would only take a half an hour to get from Newark Airport to his apartment, and he hoped against hope that Eliza would be there this time.

Chapter 25

New York City
Summer, Now

The streetlight outside cast an ethereal glow over the patina of the centuries-old rosewood in Jane Austen's vanity. Warm to the touch, Eliza ran her hand over the satiny surface; she never had wanted to sell it. The excitement of the find and the reactions of Thelma Klein and the experts from Sotheby's had overwhelmed her, and she'd found herself agreeing to things she never would have considered under ordinary circumstances. It was that realization that had triggered her decision to go to Pemberley Farms. She looked into the depths of the old mirror. *How would things have been different if I hadn't gone?*

Meeting Fitz was certainly the most important difference but after seeing how the folks at Sotheby's had reacted when she'd told them about Fitz' business card being in the sealed letter, Eliza acknowledged that she could easily have been accused of fraud if the auction had gone forward. She was grateful that she would never have to find out, and the representatives of the famed auction house had been more than happy to vacate the agreement before any promotional money had been spent. Eliza had breathed a huge sigh of relief. None of what she told them was a lie. It wasn't the whole truth, but she had been able to keep Fitz' involvement to a minimum, preserving his privacy and his story.

The delivery that afternoon of the eighteenth-century dressing table had brought to an end the machinations of Thelma Klein and her push to prove that Willie Darcy of Pemberley Farms, Virginia was Jane Austen's lover. Eliza was just glad it was all over. Fitz had the letters and she had the vanity; all was right with the world.

Although the agents from Sotheby's were more than willing to end their contract, the lawyers couldn't simply write 'void' across the face of the document, so their team of barristers had found it necessary to generate a whole new batch of legal documents, to justify their existence she supposed. And of course that couldn't happen in a day.

Eliza had shifted many of her mundane, day-to-day chores to the back burner in the wake of discovering the letters. With the three days the lawyers needed to create the new paperwork she had been able to get caught up with cleaning and laundry. She'd even made a batch of date-nut bread, a piece of which she was enjoying with her evening tea.

After slipping on her nightgown she sat down on the small upholstered stool she'd purchased in anticipation of the vanity's return. The reflection of the flickering flame from the candle on her nightstand stopped her from brushing her hair. Lightly she touched the cool, silvered glass and wondered how many times Jane Austen had gazed into it.

Jane.... Does Fitz really only admire her? Does he just love the idea of her, as he claimed? Is it really possible that I am his happily ever after? Is he mine? When she was with him, everything seemed possible. Her mother always told her that she analyzed things too much and that she should take life in stride. She wished it was that easy.

She glanced at the small framed needlepoint her mother had done for her when she was twelve. It was her father's favorite quote and strangely enough it was from Jane Austen: *It isn't what we say or think that defines us, but what we do.* That was what her father said and his example was always, 'You can tell someone you love them 'til you're blue in the face, but if you don't act like it then it simply isn't true.' On that basis, Fitz definitely liked her; maybe even loved her.

But was it really possible? Why would he prefer her to Jane Austen? By his own account Jane was selfless, sweet, kind and gentle. And she probably loved horses. *Whereas I am a cynical, volatile and contrary, so Mom says, New Yorker who's terrified of horses.*

She leaned back slightly, then stood up. *Enough! I've known him less than a week and I've been away from him for only three days. This is ridiculous. I'm obsessing.* On the other hand he'd never been very far from her thoughts. She had purposely not called him, even though the idea had presented itself more than once, particularly after she'd found herself daydreaming about him, wondering what he was doing or when they'd be together again. She hadn't wanted to seem desperate or anxious by calling him, but he hadn't called her either. Did he feel the same way or did he just not care whether he talked with her? Eliza had barely finished the thought when the phone rang.

He began simply enough. "Hi."

"I was just thinking about you."

"I knew there had to be a reason my ears were burning."

"I'm pretty sure that's talking about, not thinking about."

He chuckled nervously. In spite of his agitation he didn't want to seem nervous, so he calmly asked, "So how did the auction house handle your news? Have you been able to get all your work done?"

After going into some detail about her meeting with Thelma and the arrangement with Sotheby's, she said, "My work is on-going. It's never really done, which is why I can't let it slide for long."

He mumbled his understanding, but made no comment on any of it. Something wasn't quite right. She asked, "Is everything okay?" He was breathing but he didn't say anything. "Fitz?"

"Yeah."

"What's wrong?"

"Can I see you?"

"When?"

"Now."

"Where are you?"

"My New York apartment."

"You never said anything about having a place here."

"It never came up. I'm not a big fan of hotels." He paused. "So can I see you?"

"You don't have to ask. Just come over." Again he didn't respond. "Fitz?"

"I'm still here... sorry."

"What's going on?"

"Something really bizarre happened yesterday and... I need to... I want to..."

Eliza waited, then asked, "You want to what?"

He seemed to steady himself, pulling himself together. He took a deep breath. "I want to see you. I'll be there in a few minutes." He hung up.

Eliza went into her bedroom and slipped on a comfortable summer dress and sat at the vanity table. She ran the brush through her hair a few times, then looked into the mirror as though she was trying to see something. *What did he say? Something bizarre happened?* Leaning closer to the mirror she whispered, "So Jane, what's up with your Mr. Darcy?"

She watched him get out of the cab in front of her building. When the phone rang, she just buzzed Fitz in. She was waiting for him with a glass of brandy as he stepped off the elevator. "Hi, stranger," she said cheerfully.

He had wanted to see her. It was, after all, the reason he was in the city, but he hadn't expected an actual physical reaction. Just seeing her seemed to relax him. He slipped his arm around her waist, leaned down and kissed her lightly.

She opened the door all the way. "Come in." Slowly she closed the door and locked it, watching him all the while as he stood silently in the middle of her living room. She stepped in front of him. "So... bizarre?"

He seemed to come out of a mental fog. "What?"

"You said something bizarre happened. What was it?"

He handed her a package. She looked into his sea-green eyes and saw fear and confusion. Offering him the brandy, she said, "Trade?"

He took the snifter.

"Why don't you sit down? Relax."

He turned and looked at the couch, then sat down. He stared at the brandy, swirling it around in the glass.

Lowering her drafting table so it was flat, Eliza set the awkwardly wrapped package down. His name was on it and his address in the kind of cursive they no longer even taught in school. She smiled. "It looks like Jane's handwriting," she said innocently. Casually she glanced over her shoulder and was amazed at the stricken look on his face. "What's wrong, Fitz? What's happened?"

"Open the package."

Concerned by his behavior, she slowly unfolded the stiff wrapper and found the three small fabric-covered books. She picked up the one on top, taking in the beautiful hand work that had created his monogram.

"I've never seen a book with this kind of cover."

"I'm pretty sure it was handmade." He paused. "Look inside."

She did. "My God! It's a first edition of *Pride and Prejudice*! Where did you get it?"

"Linda sent it to me, I think."

"She really is a good friend."

"Yes."

She looked at Fitz. "Is this what you're so upset about?"

"Yes."

"But it's so beautiful and such a generous gift... why does it upset you?"

"Turn the page."

She looked at him after reading the inscription. "I guess I was right about the handwriting."

He raised one eyebrow but said nothing.

Eliza put the small volume on top of the other two, then sat down opposite him.

"I don't understand why you're so upset."

"If Linda actually sent it to me—"

"What do you mean 'if' she sent it?

"She makes a cake that I particularly like and occasionally sends me one. This was inside the box with the cake she sent a few days ago. She didn't include a note so I don't know that it's from her."

"It does seem likely, though, doesn't it?"

"Not really. Where would she have gotten it?"

Eliza leaned back in the chair and tried to posit an explanation that might ease his agitation. After a few moments she said, "Maybe Jane put it somewhere in the hopes that someone would find it and get it to you."

He looked at her over the edge of the brandy snifter. "What do you mean?"

"She put the letters behind the mirror. Maybe she put the book somewhere like that. You told her your friends lived near Chawton; maybe she found a way to hide it in the house."

"The house wasn't built until the early twentieth century."

"Oh. Well, then maybe she put it in a piece of furniture."

He sipped the brandy. "I suppose that's possible, but it begs coincidence that it ended up with the Cliftons."

A realization suddenly struck Eliza. "You're afraid Jane's come through the portal, aren't you?"

Leaning his head back Fitz sighed, the snifter cradled in his hand. "Yes, I can think of no other explanation, and if she did, it will change everything."

Eliza hated to admit it, but she was jealous of Jane; she'd been able to control it because the iconic author was dead and buried. What would it mean if she was here in this time? *His first love... maybe his only true love.*

Her throat tightened. She got up and walked to the window, staring out at nothing in particular. *He's right; it would change everything. I'll be eliminated from his life.* She bit back tears.

This certainly explained his reception of her, or the lack thereof. She'd fully expected him to take her in his arms and kiss her. Only three days ago he couldn't keep his hands off her. The little buss he gave her when he arrived was not much different than doing nothing at all. Since then he almost hadn't looked at her.

Fitz watched as she stood at the window, backlit by the street light. *What is it about her? Being with her is like, like... it's just where I want to be.* He looked around Eliza's apartment, finding it odd that he felt more comfortable here in a room he'd never seen than he had in his mother's writing room, and all because of the woman standing at the window. He heaved a deep sigh. He didn't want to leave, but he knew himself well enough to know if they were going to do things the right way he had to leave. He stood up, walked to the window and put his arms around her.

She leaned back against him.

He kissed the top of her head. "It's late, I should go."

She bit her lip and swallowed hard to keep her tears at bay, but failed miserably. She quivered, crying.

He turned her to face him, tears streaking her cheeks. "Good God, what's the matter?"

Eliza just shook her head.

Concern for her drove all other thoughts from his mind. He pulled her closer. "Come on Lizzy, what's this about?"

Startled, she looked up at him and asked, "Why did you call me that?"

"What?"

"Lizzy."

"I don't know; it just came out."

"No one's called me that since daddy died."

"I won't call you that again if it bothers you."

Sadly she said, "Actually I kind of like it."

He gave her a light kiss.

In spite of the hot summer night, Eliza shivered.

"All right," Fitz said. "What's going on?"

She shook her head and swallowed the tears. "Nothing." She couldn't look at him.

He tipped her face up to him. "You don't hide your emotions, so you can't keep saying nothing. Tell me what's wrong."

She sniffed, "What does Jane's being here do to us?"

"Nothing, she has no impact on *us* other than she's the reason we met."

"But you love her."

"As I've said before, I love the *idea* of her."

"But you said everything will change if she came through the portal."

"It will, but for *her*. It's 1813 there. Only two of her books have been published, so if she did come and stays, *Mansfield Park* and *Emma* will never get published or possibly even written. For her everything would change, if it hasn't already."

Eliza cleared her throat. She'd been thinking only of herself and what it would mean to her, with no thought at all to what it would mean for Jane and the literary world. She put her arms around Fitz' neck and they kissed each other, deeply, passionately.

Fitz finally pulled away and withdrew her arms. Holding her hands, he said, "I really do need to go."

"You don't have to."

He smiled, "Yes, I do. We're going to do things the right way this time." He bent down and kissed her lightly. "Besides, I left a message for Linda that I'd be at the apartment and I really need to talk to her."

She smiled up at him. "Right, because you don't use cell phones."

"I may start," he said with a big smile.

With tears still in her voice, she offered the suggestion that he could call England and leave her number as his call back. It took all his will power to not give in to the temptation and accept the invitation.

"There are rules about taking advantage of emotional situations," he said, bringing her hand to his lips. "So, my love, I bid you good night and wish you sweet dreams." He brushed her hand with a kiss. "Thank you for letting me come over. It's been an immense help."

"You're welcome... I guess. I didn't really do anything."

"Just being you is enough." After one last kiss she watched him get on the elevator. As the doors closed, she quickly locked her door and ran to the window to wave as he hailed a cab.

Before turning the lights off in the living room, she picked up the small volume decorated with his monogram and read the inscription. *It really isn't much of a mash note; maybe Jane doesn't love him.* The thought somehow made her feel better.

It was fifteen minutes to two when she slipped in between her freshly washed sheets, but before she turned off the light Eliza reached under her nightstand and withdrew her worn copy of *Pride and Prejudice*, published in the early 1990s. It had been a gift from her mother when she was a teenager, and she'd read it at least once every year since. As she quickly thumbed through it, the book seemed to be intact which, it seemed to her, meant that as far as the books were concerned, Jane's coming here had changed nothing. She drifted off to sleep remembering Fitz' kisses.

Chapter 26

Eliza's pleasant slumber was rudely interrupted by the incessant ringing of her phone. She looked at the clock as she picked up the phone. The digital numbers glowed 5:57. *Who could possibly be calling at six o'clock in the morning? Fitz must have talked with Linda.* Even half asleep she was happy he wanted to tell her about it.

Not bothering to focus her sleepy eyes on the caller ID, she answered. "Hello?"

The woman's voice was raspy, "Good, you're up."

"Who is this?"

A colleague had reminded Thelma that you catch more flies with honey than you do with vinegar, so as pleasantly as she was able to muster, she said, "It's your friendly neighborhood document expert. Let me in, please."

"Thelma? What are you doing here?"

"Buzz me in... please."

"Why?"

Through clenched teeth, Thelma said, "Please, just let me in."

Afraid the bombastic woman would make a scene and wake her neighbors, Eliza stumbled out of bed and deactivated the lock on the security door. By the time she had slipped on her robe and slippers, Thelma was knocking loudly on her apartment door. She ran through the living room and threw the door open.

"My neighbors are sleeping, or trying to!"

Any semblance of a pleasant demeanor was gone and the big woman pushed past Eliza into the apartment, saying with an unpleasant grin, "Sorry."

"Why are you here?"

Thelma turned and looked at her hostess. "I talked with Bill Christopher at Sotheby's."

"So?"

"So what is this BS about a business card?"

"Not that it's any of your business, but when Fitz and I opened the sealed letter we found his business card inside it."

"You're lying. I authenticated those letters myself; there is no possible way his business card was inside the letter."

Eliza walked to the door. "I'd like you to leave. Now."

"I'm not going anywhere until you've told me what's going on."

"That's easy. What's going on is that I decided not to sell the letters or the vanity. Now it's over, so go home."

Trying desperately to control her anger, Thelma said, "Look, my professional reputation is on the line here. I authenticated those letters, which in turn authenticated the vanity, and now Sotheby's thinks they're all fakes."

"I think you're overstating it just a bit. Sotheby's experts authenticated them, too. It doesn't seem to be bothering them, so what is this really about?"

The older woman paced, crushing the short pile of the Berber carpet under her blocky oxford shoes. Still trying to stay calm, she admitted, "I couldn't believe I'd made such a huge error authenticating the letters. When you brought them to me I was certain they were fake but my testing proved beyond any reasonable doubt that both letters were real. Particularly the one in Austen's own hand, which we matched to known examples of her handwriting.

"Of course, Darcy's letter was more difficult because we had nothing to compare it to, but the paper and ink matched the Austen letter, leaving very little doubt that it too was real. After I talked with Bill I went over and over the results of those tests, hoping to find some miniscule amount of any chemical unknown in the early nineteenth century. There was nothing. Still, I had to be sure so I had a handwriting expert, who had never seen the letters, examine them. Well, he examined the copies and he says that unquestionably Jane Austen wrote the sealed letter."

Eliza only shrugged.

"There was one thing I hadn't caught before; the letter had been sealed twice."

Eliza said, "Well, there you have it: a hoax. Someone opened the letter, put the card in and resealed it."

The scholar quickly said, "I'm afraid not. The tests showed that the two seals were identical in chemical makeup."

"What does that mean?"

"It means that Jane Austen herself did the sealing and re-sealing, which is further proof that the letters are authentic." She paused for dramatic effect, certain she had Eliza over a barrel. "What do you have to say now?"

"Nothing."

"Come on, you know as well as I do that the letter was written by Jane Austen, plain and simple."

Eliza yawned. "You're absolutely right, it is plain and simple. Whether they were written by Austen or not, the letters were mine and now they belong to Fitz Darcy. End of story."

Angrily, Thelma shouted, "It isn't the end of anything! You have to tell me what he told you! Why you left the letters with him and when I can get them back!"

"I don't have to tell you anything, and I don't intend to get into a screaming match with you about any of it. It's done. Over. Deal with it." Before Thelma could respond the phone rang. Eliza looked at the black instrument and back at Thelma. *What if this time it* is *Fitz?* "I'm going to take this in the bedroom."

The barrel-chested woman was seething with anger, but she could do nothing until the uncooperative artist returned.

In the bedroom Eliza picked up the phone, disappointed that caller-id read *Jerry. What does he want at the crack of dawn?* It only took a few minutes for Eliza to realize just how drunk he was and cut off his crying and pleading for a reconciliation with a stern, "Go sleep it off."

She hung up the phone, quivering. She was annoyed with Jerry, but she was suddenly outraged at Thelma's uninvited visit, and she didn't intend to put up with the woman's antics any longer. Incensed, she stormed into the living room, intent on demanding that Thelma leave immediately. The room was empty.

Quickly Eliza checked the kitchen and powder room, both empty. Thelma was nowhere to be seen. She noticed the chain lock on her door was undone even though she'd carefully locked the door after Thelma had invited herself in. She went to the living room window and was surprised to see how fast the over-weight woman could move as she hurried down the street, away from the building.

She didn't know why Thelma had left in such a hurry, but her sudden departure was perfectly in character for the woman's generally rude behavior. She sighed with relief, just glad Thelma was gone.

On a corner, a block away from Eliza's condominium Thelma clutched the package she had found in the young woman's apartment, a smug smile twisting her mouth. She was safe for the moment, certain that Eliza would just be happy that her early morning visitor had left. She would have to hurry now because it wouldn't be long before the artist would realize what Thelma had done. She didn't care, by then she'd have the unequivocal proof that Fitzwilliam Darcy the first had enjoyed an affair with Jane Austen.

Hailing a cab, she looked down at the crinkled brown paper in her stubby hands and laughed out loud. The letters didn't matter anymore. Clutching the stolen package, she now had all the proof she needed.

Chapter 27

Chawton, England
Summer, 1813

Jane used a hand-embroidered handkerchief to mop the perspiration from her forehead and the back of her neck. The weather had been so dreadfully hot that it kept her in a continual state of inelegance, and she was more than glad to be home after an ill-advised walk to Alton.

Waiting for her was a letter from James Edward, eldest son of her eldest brother. She went to her bedroom, dropping her bonnet and gloves on the dressing table. From the glass pitcher on her bedside table she poured herself a glass of water and sat on the wide sill of her window where she opened the envelope. Within, the entire letter was in the form of a poem.

To Miss J. Austen:
No words can express, my dear Aunt, my surprise
Or make you conceive how I opened my eyes,
Like a pig Butcher Pile has just struck with his knife,
When I heard for the very first time in my life
That I have the honour to have a relation
Whose works are dispersed through the whole of the nation.
I assure you, however I'm terribly glad;
Oh, dear! just to think (and the thought drives me mad)
That dear Mrs. Jennings good-natured strain
Was really the produce of your witty brain.
That you made the Middletons, Dashwoods and all
And that you (not young Ferras) found out that a ball
May be given in a cottage, never so small.
And though Mr. Collins, so grateful for all,
Will Lady de Bourgh his dear Patroness call,
'Tis to your ingenuity really he owed
His living, his wife and his humble abode.
Now if you will take your poor nephew's advice,
Your works to Sir William pray send in a trice,
If he'll undertake to some grandees show it,
By whose means at last the Prince Regent might know it,
For I'm sure if he did, in reward for your tale,
He'd make you a countess at least, without fail,
And indeed if the Princess should lose her dear life
You might have a good chance of becoming his wife.

Jane laughed out loud at the final words for they were a tease from her brother's son in acknowledgement of her disapproval of the Prince Regent's dissolute lifestyle, a position she had never tried to hide even from the younger generations of the Austen clan.

She leaned back against the casement. She had attempted to retain some anonymity as the lady who had written *Sense and Sensibility* and *Pride and Prejudice*. It was her brothers who had a difficult time keeping her secret. As far as she could tell Henry told anyone and everyone. Edward told a story from his last trip to London that he and Henry had been advised by a gentleman celebrated for his literary attainments that they should read *Pride and Prejudice*. The man considered it one of the cleverest things he had ever read, and added without much gallantry that he should like very much to know who the author is, for it was much too clever to have actually been written by a woman. Jane had no doubt that Henry and Edward were pleased to tell the man just who had written the book.

Jane went to her vanity and withdrew the letter she had started the day before to her sister and not very humbly told Cassandra about James Edwards' poem. After copying it for her she went on with a description of Fanny's tea party and how horribly wet she had been because of the summer storm and about the green dress.

Jane stretched her neck by bending her head forward then backward and side to side. She closed her eyes and sighed; she was home and it was quiet. She told her sister that she had been all alive for several days in a row but now it was over for a while and she was not sorry it was so for there was nothing like staying home for real comfort.

Two days were soon gone and Jane was visiting at Chawton Great House. Inside Fanny's bedroom, Jane and her niece were sharing secrets as friends are wont to do.

Jane asked her niece, "Did you know that Mrs. Knight has offered me the gift of her spinning wheel so that I might have one of my own?"

"Spinning wheel?" asked an incredulous Fanny. "What did she think you would do with a spinning wheel?"

Jane laughed. "If I were able to spin straw into gold I might have accepted it, but as it was I probably would only have spun a rope to hang myself rather than use it to spin wool."

Fanny giggled. "What did you do?"

"I thanked her for her kind offer and changed the subject." The two women giggled like school girls.

Fanny began complaining about what she perceived as a dearth of eligible young men even though she had recently received an offer of marriage. "Oh but he is so serious-minded that he is often very dull. However, I do wonder whether his strong attachment might not be the best thing for a marriage partner."

Jane admonished her niece. "It must be affection on both sides, for marriage should be a partnership. If you do not feel the same regard for him as he does for you, then it is best to not prolong the affiliation."

"I do not want to marry him and have already told him no but I have met no one else I would consider marrying. Why can I find no one?"

"Perhaps you are looking for the kind of excellence that is difficult to find in people. You seem to want a kind of perfection in which grace, spirit and worth are united with manners, heart and understanding; however, even should you find such a man he may not belong to your country."

Fanny smiled. "You mean like Mr. Darcy?

"I made him up, Fanny."

"He did not look made up to me and Mr. Darcy of Virginia was, most definitely, not of our country." Fanny looked slyly at her aunt. "While he was staying here I was sure I observed affection on both sides and he was very real. Was there no attachment there?"

A tiny smile curved Jane's mouth. "There might have been, given the opportunity, but it was not to be."

"And do you not regret that?"

"Regret serves no useful purpose and past experience is what makes us who we are so we should regret as little as possible."

"What about Tom LeFroy? Cousin Anna says you were much in love with him but he treated you very ill."

Jane shook her head. Everyone seemed to make much more of that connection than either she or he ever imagined. "He went away at his family's urging, which could hardly be considered ill treatment. However, even if he had left because he simply wanted to, he never imposed upon me and never injured me, and we were never attached to each other. It was a flirtation of very short duration."

"Truly?"

"Yes."

"So there has never been anyone you would have married?"

Jane thought for a moment and Fanny took her aunt's hesitation as confirmation that there was someone. She giggled. "Tell me! Who was he?"

Jane chuckled. "It was many years ago and I cannot say absolutely that I would have married him, but he was one of the most amiable men of my acquaintance. He died before I was able to know him well. So in answer to all of your questions, there has been nothing out of the common way... no attachment that has overclouded happiness."

Jane then read excerpts from *Pride and Prejudice*, mostly the ones involving Mr. Collins and his fawning, unctuous behavior, which both women found exceedingly funny. It was gratifying, for Jane, that Fanny enjoyed it so much since she had written the character as a comic figure.

Marianne and Louisa were sitting atop the first step of the stairs, finishing off the cake they had procured from Cook when Fanny's bedroom door opened and their sister and Aunt Jane came out. Dusting their hands of cake crumbs, the girls jumped up. Their aunt smiled and took their hands in hers.

"Come along, girls. To the garden we go."

As the three Austen females skipped down the stairs together and out into the garden, Fanny went to check on the other Austen-Knight children.

Jane and her young nieces ran through the garden, tumbling onto the soft grass under a large beech tree.

Marianne begged, "Tell us a story, Aunt Jane."

"Yes, so I shall." Their aunt thought for a moment, then began. "Once upon a time there was a young farmer who vanished two days before his wedding, his bride swore to the heavens that she would stop at nothing to find him. She pleaded with the fairies of the garden for their help."

After keeping her young charges enthralled for some time Jane ended the story. "The fairy queen brought the farmer back to his bride just in time for the wedding. In their joy the farmer and his new wife set out a great feast for all the fairies, and in appreciation for saving the groom from the ogre who kidnapped him the couple left tokens, gifts and food for the fairies every night. For the rest of their lives they lived in peace and harmony, always watched over by the fairies in their garden." With a verbal flourish Jane said, "Finis!"

The young girls clapped and Louisa said, "Tell us another, Aunt Jane."

"Another time, dear."

Relinquishing the shade of the tree and the comfort of the cool grass, Jane, Marianne and Louisa returned to The Great House after taking a turn through the fruit orchard. Their aunt reached up and plucked apricots for each of them from the lowest branches on one of the trees.

When they reached the courtyard the small cadre of Austen females found Fanny speaking with James, the groom.

Seeing her aunt over the stableman's shoulder, Fanny said, "James here has asked whether you would like him to bring the curricle around when you are ready to return home."

Jane smiled at the young man "I thank you, James, but I have been sitting so much today that I believe some exercise is what I need. I will walk across the far meadow on my way home. I do appreciate your thoughtfulness."

As Jane bade farewell to the Austen-Knight clan with a promise to join them for luncheon the next day, Fanny wondered at her Aunt's unnatural familiarity with the servants. Knowing there was nothing to be done, she ushered the little girls into the house.

Chapter 28

Steam filled the stillroom from the great copper kettle boiling in the corner. Maggie glanced up from her task of peeling ginger for ginger beer. Jane was in the doorway.

"Are you off to the Manor now?"

Jane nodded. "Yes." Casually she turned and walked the rest of the way through the garden and onto the road to Chawton Great House where she was expected for a planned luncheon.

A solitary walk was just what Jane wanted. After the routine activities of the morning, including a time at the piano forte, finishing her letter to Cassandra and a visit with a neighbor, she had not thought much about Simmons and his journey into the unknown.

It had been several days since he had gone over the wall, and she couldn't help wondering whether her brother's groom had made it to the twenty-first century and contact with

Mr. Darcy. Her concern for whether Mr. Darcy had made a safe return to his own time was now compounded by having no way of knowing whether Simmons also had made the trip in safety. Was Simmons still in England or had he gone to America? Was Mr. Darcy in England? Were they together? Were they just on the other side of the stone wall but two hundred years away?

With so many unanswerable questions about the young horseman and the tall American spinning in her head, Jane was optimistic that the company of her family and friends would take her mind in a more agreeable direction.

The party for lunch was made up of Edward (finally back from Kent) and his children, her brother Henry, the Benns and the amiable young lady who had been spending the summer with them, Miss Lee. All four of the Rodgers were there as well, along with a Mr. Taylor who was visiting with them from London and, of course, Lord Moore-Jeffries. The assembly sat around the dining table, partaking of a luncheon of fish and fowl, cooked vegetables and salads, soups and sweets. Tea and cake would follow later.

In the second-floor drawing room Jane sat in a corner with the children gathered around her, telling the story she had promised the day before. The children listened with rapt attention, spellbound by the tale she spun as her sweet voice rose and fell with emotion during the progression of the yarn. After half an hour, Edward came to recruit his sister for the adult gathering near the fireplace. The story would have to await its finale for another time. Grumbling from her youthful audience followed Jane as she took her brother's arm, moving to the other side of the room.

She had an agreeable visit with the Benns, then went on to spend time with Annabelle Rodgers and her brother Tom, a charming and amiable man with whom, it turned out, Jane had much in common. Although Annabelle was accomplished in the girlish occupations of sewing, embroidery, painting and music, her mind did not lend itself to more intellectual pursuits, and since she had little knowledge of the subject her friend and brother were discussing and even less interest, she went off to join Miss Benn and Miss Lee. Jane and Tom continued with talk of the Navy, a favorite subject for her. As he was a sailor, he was eager and willing to have a conversation on the topic. Discussion of the ships on which Jane's brothers, Frank and Charles, as well as Tom had served were included in the energetic telling of her brother's exploits and Tom's. It was, all in all, a most enjoyable time. Annabelle finally came to have her brother join them at the whist table; he bowed to Jane and thanked her for a delightful afternoon.

Jane had taken the opportunity for a bit of a breather from the party and walked to one of the large windows that overlooked Edward's estate. The southern prospect with the vast lawn framed by trees, sheep and cows grazing in the near distance, on the other side of the ha-ha, was an idyllic picture. At the edge of the lawn the wilderness began, and stands of trees and underbrush left to nature created muted shades of green in the late-afternoon light. As she considered the serenity of the woodland, Jane's reverie was interrupted by Mr. Taylor, the Rodgers' house guest.

The man bowed. "Miss Austen."

She curtsied in return. "Mr. Taylor."

"Your brother tells me that you write novels."

"Yes Sir, I do."

"I understand that *Pride and Prejudice* is of your making."

"It is."

"Do you not think that some other activity might be more suitable for a woman of your age and situation in life?"

"More suitable, Sir?"

"Writing novels is hardly a thing a lady does. It is only the most wicked part of our society that takes novels as entertainment. I believe that novels should be banned entirely as they lead to a wanton state of affairs."

Jane's back stiffened with a defiance her family would have recognized immediately but that went unnoticed by Mr. Taylor. However, Lord Moore-Jeffries had seen the change in her demeanor and moved closer.

In a strong voice Jane said, "Mr. Taylor, I am not in the habit of defending my activities to strangers, nor will your behavior compel me to do so. I am sorry you feel as you do but it has no effect on me. I do not consider novels wicked nor evil, and neither do I believe they are responsible for the ills of society."

Shocked he said, "I am astonished at your disrespectful and cavalier attitude, Miss Austen."

"And I am astonished at your offensive attack on my character when you know nothing of me."

"This is an outrage! I cannot understand why your brothers encourage you in what they consider to be your talent!"

To Jane's great relief, Lord Moore-Jeffries joined them. "The real outrage, Sir is that you behave so abhorrently while a guest in Miss Austen's brother's home. And I will tell you that it is not only her brothers who are proud of her. The pride I feel for what you derisively call her talent could only be greater if I was her father. Her talent is God-given, Sir, for Miss Austen is able to evoke everyday life and make it entertaining for all who read her work. Is it not the greatest of sins to waste a God-given gift?" The Earl bowed and offered Jane his arm. "Now, if you will excuse us we are expected elsewhere." Jane, her head high and on the arm of her father's best friend, left the man speechless.

Patting Jane's hand, his Lordship said, still in the man's hearing, "Unfortunately, my dear, money does not buy good manners. Some men, no matter how high-born they are or how wealthy, are boorish oafs, all crass and crudeness."

Jane squeezed the Earl's arm. "Thank you."

"You owe me no thanks, my dear; I was expressing only the truth."

Almost whispering, Jane said, "I only wish I had been brave enough to say that I think a person who does not take pleasure in a good novel must be intolerably stupid."

The Earl smiled sadly. "It is better you did not. I can tell you from experience, as you well know, that getting what you want by way of an unchristian word or deed is in no way satisfying."

Jane was slightly ashamed, although she truly felt it would not have been worse than his Lordship calling the man a boorish oaf. However, she did know that coming from a man of the Earl's stature, the comments had much more impact than anything a mere woman might say, particularly to a man like that.

With Jane's arm still linked in his as they walked farther into the room his Lordship said, "Let us move on to more agreeable endeavors. Shall we go to Edward and Henry who are most likely speaking of business matters, or perhaps you would like to take a seat at the whist table?" He knew full well Jane did not like card games.

She smiled at his small joke.

"No, I am sure you would prefer to join the young ladies who are, no doubt, talking of the latest fashions."

"In truth, your Lordship I would prefer a walk."

Squeezing her hand, he said, "Lovely. Then will you join me in a turn through the wilderness? It seems so peaceful today."

"I would like nothing more." Jane smiled.

The dropped leaves and needles at the base of the woodland trees crunched under foot as the Earl and Jane strolled in the cool shade afforded by the canopy of criss-crossed branches in the upper reaches of the forest.

"Henry tells me you are to have another book published."

"Henry is too quick. He has not finished reading it, so he has not taken it to the publisher. However, I am hoping on the credit of *Sense and Sensibility* and *Pride and Prejudice* that it will be published."

"And what is this one about?"

"My heroine is a poor relation brought up by a rich uncle. His children treat her with disdain except for the second son, Edmund, with whom she falls in love. She grows into a pretty, virtuous girl, unlike her cousins, and ultimately marries Edmund after much drama and scandal in the family." She giggled. "It's nothing like the others... not nearly as entertaining but Henry seems to like it." She blushed slightly. "Of course, Henry likes everything I write."

"As well he should." He smiled at her. "I look forward to reading it. I understand James' son fancies himself something of a writer."

"It is not just a fancy, your Lordship."

"Uncle Jeff, please, when we are alone."

She flashed a shy smile. "James Edward found out recently that I was the authoress of *Sense and Sensibility* as well as *Pride and Prejudice* and wrote me the most astonishing poem. His writing is strong and manly, spirited sketches full of variety and glow. Indeed, it is much more than a fancy."

The Earl smiled. "Your writing is strong and spirited and has much variety, Jane."

"Oh, your Lord—"

The Earl cleared his throat.

"Uncle Jeff... in comparison mine is but a little bit of ivory on which I work with so fine a brush as to produce little effect after much labour."

"Your modesty is most becoming, Jane, but do not belittle what you do. You are, as I told that boor Taylor, exceedingly gifted."

She blushed slightly at the compliment.

They walked in quiet for a while, enjoying the peace and serenity of the place, arm in arm, winding their way through the Chawton wood. His Lordship broke the silence. "I went to the stable on my arrival this afternoon seeking that young man who seems to know horses so well. Alas, he was not there. Your brother's steward tells me he has gone and may not return for some time... something about his mother being unwell and a young sister who is in need of his help."

Jane had wondered what Simmons had told those at the Great House about where he was going when he decided to attempt his excursion into another century. Saying he was going to take care of his ailing mother and his young sister was very like Simmons who, she had no doubt, would do just that if the circumstances had actually warranted it. And it was a very good reason for him to give Edward, for her brother would certainly understand and accept family obligations. "I was unaware that his mother was ill."

"I am sorry to hear that. Edward thought you might have more information about him as he often drove you. He thought the boy may have confided in you of his problems and when he expected to return." He paused, then added in an almost conspiratorial tone, "Your brother seems to think you have an uncommon intimacy with some of the servants, including... I am sorry, what is his name?"

"Simmons. And yes my family does believe that I have a disdain for people of the upper classes, and that to show it I commune with the lower classes."

"Is it true?"

"No. I simply believe we are all the same and should be treated so, that there should be no class distinction. Prejudice of a person's birthright or lack of same should have no bearing on what he or she might make of their life, rich or poor."

The Earl laughed. "I should have known! It is, after all, the story of your books."

Jane changed the subject. "Why were you looking for Simmons?"

"I bought a racehorse and need someone to look after him; I had thought to ask your brother whether I could borrow Simmons for a time. I want someone who particularly likes and knows horses, and your description of the young man impressed me. If I recall correctly, he took care of that magnificent horse Darcy had here a few years ago." The Earl thought a moment. "The beast's name was—"

"Lord Nelson," Jane said.

"Right you are. I remember our amazement at his audacity, naming the animal after our Naval hero, but then what can one expect from an impudent American?"

Jane smiled, remembering her own outrage until she learned the truth, that the English breeder had named the horse two hundred years from now.

The Earl continued. "It seems to me that Darcy was impressed with the young man."

Jane confirmed. "Yes, he was. You want him to care only for the racehorse?"

"Indeed. He is a very expensive animal and I need someone to care only for him. My steward suggested the possibility of sending whomever I hire for special training in doctoring race horses as they tend to frailty and I want the stallion kept as healthy as possible."

She smiled and thought that the opportunity for which Simmons was traveling through time would today be his, if he was here. "If he was here I am quite sure he would be more than happy to accept your kind offer. What did my brother say?"

"Well, as Simmons is not here we did not explore it further, but I did not sense any objection to the idea."

"Perhaps his mother will recover quickly and he will return soon."

"Perhaps."

They continued out of the wilderness and across the lawn, returning to the house as all the guests were departing. His Lordship saw Jane home and went on his way.

Chapter 29

After being startled awake and then harangued by the overbearing Austen scholar, there was no way Eliza could sleep anymore. Besides, it was almost seven, time to start the day. In the kitchen she put coffee on, and as the dark caffeine-rich liquid filled the pot, the phone rang again. Leaving the coffee maker to continue its appointed task she went into the living room.

Fitz' voice was cheerful, a far cry from last night. "Good morning."

"You, too."

"I didn't wake you did I?"

"No."

There was something in the single word answer that made him think she'd had a rough night. "Didn't sleep well?"

Surprised it was that obvious after she'd said only three words, she said, "Can't say I did."

"Too hot, huh?"

She saw no real advantage in telling him the story of Thelma's disruptive visit or Jerry's maudlin phone call, so agreed that the weather was very unpleasant.

"England will be cooler."

Disappointed, she said, "Are you going to England?"

"Yes."

"You didn't say anything about it last night. Did something happen?"

"I talked with Linda this morning; she doesn't know why the book was with the cake but will look into it. Not that it matters... seems I have a visitor staying with them."

A small knot formed in her stomach, "So Jane did come?"

"No, Simmons. I'm assuming he brought the book, so I need to go to England."

"Simmons. Should I know who that is?"

"He's Jane's brother's groom, and he took very good care of Lord Nelson while I was there."

Hesitantly she asked, "The portal is definitely open, then?"

"I assumed it was because of the book."

"I assumed there was a more... normal explanation."

"You mean logical and rational."

"Well, yeah." There was an exaggerated pause. "Are you still there?"

"You don't actually believe it happened do you?"

"Yes, I do... absolutely. It's... it's just that I thought it was a one-time fluky kind of a thing. It never occurred to me that it might happen again. Or maybe I just hoped it wouldn't."

"Well, it has."

"Has the portal been open the whole time?"

"I don't know. I never looked."

"What are you going to do?"

"Obviously Jane told him about it, but I can't imagine why. Whatever the reason, I need to get him to go back."

"Why does he have to go back?"

"He's an integral part of Jane's life; his being gone might affect her destiny. If he doesn't go back, who knows how that might change things."

"For Jane."

"For everyone. We don't know how time travel affects anything or anyone. In this particular instance we do know how it's supposed to be since we know Jane's history. I need to exert every effort to make sure it stays that way."

"When are you going?"

"Today some time. I want to get there as soon as possible, but I haven't even started to make arrangements yet."

"Too bad the Concord was grounded; you could have been there in a couple of hours."

"I'm sorry I never got around to flying on it."

There was a somewhat pregnant pause before Eliza asked, "Fitz, are you still there?"

"I am."

"Is something wrong?"

"No." After a short pause he said, "Will you go to England with me?"

Eliza agreed to go and he said he'd call with the travel particulars.

After a light breakfast of coffee and toast and catching up on orders from her website, Eliza began to lay out what she would pack for the trip. Her grandmother told her that when you travel you should lay out all the clothes, sundries and cash you think you'll need; then put away half the clothes and double the amount of money. She didn't actually lay out the money since she used ATM and credit cards but laying out what she intended to take before packing had become a habit. She then went into the depths of her closet and dragged out the luggage her mother had gotten for her when she graduated from college. The set had three Pullman cases in graduated sizes, a hanging bag and a train case, and there was a pink hat box that didn't match the others but her mother thought it so cute she couldn't resist buying it, too.

Trying to decide which Pullman to use, she wondered how long they would stay in England. Would they be at a hotel or staying with the Cliftons? Did she need dressy-type clothes for any reason or just jeans? *Guess I need to call and ask.*

As she picked up the phone she realized that she didn't have his phone numbers, land or cell, she didn't have his address either, at least not the one in the city. She hit the CID button on the phone, his number was there but why hadn't he given it to her? She'd given him her business card, with all of her information on it, before she left Pemberley Farms, but he had not reciprocated. Why? Was he keeping his contact information from her on purpose? She looked at all the things she'd laid out on the bed and was deciding whether she should call him to ask about the trip or to tell him she couldn't go when the phone in her hand rang. Caller ID told her it was Fitz.

Eliza answered with a tentative greeting.

He said, "I just realized I never gave you my phone number, so I thought I'd better in case you need to get in touch. I'll even give you the cell phone number."

She smiled, "Yeah, but will you turn it on?"

"For you I will."

She went to her night stand for paper and pen and wrote down all the information he gave her, then thanked him. After an awkward pause, he said, "You've changed your mind about going, haven't you?"

"I was thinking about it."

His voice was tinged with disappointment. "It's all right. I mean, I understand your hesitation. I suspect you were wondering whether it was a good idea since we've known each other for such a short time."

"How'd you know?"

"'Cause I thought about it too."

"What do you mean?"

"Well, any other time and with anyone else I would have left without saying anything at all. I would have just gotten on a plane and gone." He paused. "But because I'm trying to do things differently I decided to call to tell you I was leaving. As we talked, I realized I wanted you to be with me."

Eliza didn't say it out loud, but she wanted to be with him too. That's why she'd said yes in the first place. And he was right—the agreement was to do things differently and that meant she needed to be more open to possibilities and be willing to take a risk, or so her mother would say.

"So what's your decision?"

"I want to be with you too. I want to go."

"I'm glad. I'll call soon with the arrangements."

Putting the phone back in the base, Eliza was almost giddy with her decision, then suddenly realized she still hadn't asked how long they'd be gone or what kind of clothes to pack. *Oh well, I'll pack enough for a few days and add my little black dress and Grandma's Eisenberg Ice necklace and earrings, just in case.*

With Wickham safely at Annalise's, her across-the-hall neighbor, Eliza set about gathering her drawing supplies. She couldn't go to England and not capture the landscape.

Her pencil box was full and her pastels complete, so she set them all on the drafting table along with her portfolio and a sketch pad. Yawning, she hoped she would be able to sleep on the plane.

Where's Fitz' book? She was sure she'd left it on the drafting table last night. She tried, but could not remember moving it. Still, just to be sure, she looked all over the apartment; she couldn't find it anywhere. Where could it be? Maybe he took it with him. She went back over the events of the previous evening, and realized she had even looked at it after watching him get into a cab. Then she had turned off the lights and slept soundly until Thelma—*Thelma! That's why she left in such a hurry! She stole the book!*

Thelma's home phone rang unanswered. *Doesn't the woman have voice mail?* A technician at the lab told her that Dr. Klein had stepped out for a while and he wasn't sure when she would be back.

The marble floor of the library echoed with her footfalls as she ran up the stairs to confront the brazen scholar. After waiting for over two hours Eliza left, exasperated, angry and aggravated.

The elevator in Eliza's apartment building seemed to crawl up the cables, not that she was in a particular hurry since the day had already spun out of control, but she wanted to be home. She'd managed to avoid Fitz' persistent phone calls but she wasn't going to be able to hold him off forever. How was she going to tell him that she lost his signed first edition of *Pride and Prejudice*? Her head throbbed.

The doors of the elevator finally opened on her floor and there he was, Fitz was leaning against the wall next to her door. *No way to avoid him now.* She took a deep breath and stepped into the hall.

"Where have you been?"

Guilt fueling her anger, she snapped, "What business is it of yours?"

"I've been trying to get in touch with you for hours. It was like you vanished. I was getting concerned."

"Well, as you can see I didn't vanish."

"What's going on?"

"Nothing's going on!" she snapped.

He hadn't taken his eyes off her since she'd gotten off the elevator and it was making her very self-conscious. She made a point of not looking at him while she unlocked the door. He remained in the hall after she went in.

She turned to him. "Are you coming in?"

She could actually see concern in his eyes, intensifying the guilt. Out of the blue he asked if she'd had lunch. She took a deep breath. Grateful for the change in subject, she said no.

He reached for her hand. "Come on, I'm buying."

Chapter 30

In spite of the pleasant and innocuous talk over the shared deli sandwich, Eliza's head was still throbbing; of course she knew lack of food was not the cause of the headache. Fitz' continuing cheerful patter about the wonderful sites in the Hampshire countryside that she would be able to incorporate into her drawings wasn't helping. She loved that he was taking a sincere interest in her work, but it just made her feel worse.

In front of her building she kissed him goodbye and got out of the cab. She was surprised when he got out of the cab, too.

As the taxi drove away he asked, "You don't mind if I come up, do you?"

What was she going to say, 'yeah I mind'? Of course, technically she didn't but she really had hoped that he would go home so she could sort out this mess. She looked away from his eyes, which seemed to be boring into her. "What about your flight?"

"It can wait."

"What do you mean it can wait?"

He gave her half a smile, and then gestured to the door. There it was again, his uncanny ability to get his own way without saying anything. Defeated, Eliza walked into the building; Fitz followed closely, fully intent on finding out what she was hiding. Inside the apartment she put her purse down and turned to him. "Make yourself comfortable."

He stepped across the short distance that separated them and took both her hands in his. She glanced up at him, then away. Continuing to hold one hand he turned her face to him.

"Tell me."

"Tell you what?"

"Why you've decided not to go the England with me."

"I didn't say—how did you—"

He lifted a single eyebrow. "Does it have something to do with an old boyfriend or something?"

"*No!*"

"I don't understand why you think you can't tell me, then."

"It isn't that I can't. I don't want to."

"Why?"

She broke free and walked to the window. "I just don't."

Fitz watched her. After a few minutes of excruciating silence, he said, "I thought we were going to be open with each other in this relationship."

She turned toward him. "It doesn't have anything to do with our relationship."

"Eliza, if we keep secrets from each other, it can and probably will affect the relationship." She turned back to the window without comment.

After several more minutes of quiet Fitz sat on the couch, "Tell you what, I just won't go until you can."

"What about your travel plans?"

"They're your travel plans too, and like I said, they can wait."

"What does that mean, they can wait?"

Very calmly he said, "I'm not going to let you change the subject. I'm staying until you're willing to go with me."

"But you were in such a hurry."

"There is some urgency, but I don't imagine Simmons is going anywhere."

Why is he doing this? All I wanted was the opportunity to get the book back from Thelma. What am I going to do now that he's refusing to leave? She continued staring at the river, getting dizzy watching the sun's kaleidoscopic effect on the fast-moving water. She glanced over her shoulder at him.

He was watching her, silently.

"You're just going to sit there?"

He shrugged.

The silence finally got to her. In guilt and utter frustration she blurted out, "Thelma took the book!"

Startled, he said, "I beg your pardon?"

"Thelma Klein, the Jane Austen expert from the library. She came over early this morning. She found out from Sotheby's that they'd canceled the contract because I told them the letter was a fake. She showed up here and barged in to tell me she didn't believe it and demanded that I tell her the truth. When I left the room for a minute she took the book and ran out. I spent most of the morning on the phone and then went to her apartment and the library. I either got no answer or people who claimed not to know where she was or when she'd be back." She paused and looked at the floor. "Well, there it is. I don't know what to do."

"She took the book?"

Eliza nodded. "Yes."

"Jane's book?"

"Yes."

"My God! Why did you leave her alone with it?"

Eliza had asked herself that same question a thousand times, but his asking made her angry. "Hey! She woke me up and I—why did you leave it here?"

He held up both hands. "You're right. I'm sorry. It's not your fault."

Her fault or not, the guilt was made worse when he became disturbingly quiet again. She stepped away from the window and sat on the chair at her drafting table, waiting for him to say something, but he remained quiet.

Finally she asked, "Are you really angry?"

He shook his head. "Not at you."

Somehow that didn't make her feel any better. After an excruciatingly long few minutes he asked, "Do you have the number at the library?"

"She's not there."

"She might be. Obviously she knew what you wanted so she would have avoided you."

"Won't she assume it's why you're calling, too?"

"Possibly, but she's been trying to talk to me for two years, ever since I acquired the first letter; she just might take the call."

From the kitchen she could hear him on the phone, and it sounded as though Thelma was talking with him. She was astonished and angry that the woman had been avoiding her. He hung up as she came back in with a tray of coffee.

"You got her?"

"Yes."

"That ticks me off."

"I'm not defending her, but apparently she really wasn't there when you were. She was out, having the book air-freighted to the British Library for authentication."

"She didn't waste any time."

"She probably wanted to get it off before you realized it was gone."

"Now what do we do?"

"We go to England and pick it up while we're there. She gave me the woman's name and phone number at the Library. Klein is supposed to call and tell her it's mine, but I'll call from Hampshire to make sure they know and that it doesn't get sent back to *that* woman. We can pick it up when we're in London."

"We're going to London, too?"

He grinned. "Can't go to England and not go to London."

"I thought it was just a quickie trip to Chawton."

"It doesn't have to be but if you would prefer that—"

"No, I *love* London!"

"Then London it is."

They sat quietly for a moment. As the resolution of the situation sunk in Eliza finally asked, "How did you get her to cooperate so quickly?"

"I threatened to have her arrested for theft."

"Would you really have had her arrested?"

"In a heartbeat."

"I thought about calling the police, but I was afraid of the publicity... you know, public records and all."

"I'm glad I didn't have to." He paused. "I just hope the authentication brings an end to all of it."

"You're going to let them authenticate it?"

"My initial reaction was to demand she have them return it immediately, but it occurred to me that if it's authenticated by someone she respects, maybe she'll leave me alone."

"It might also give her more reason to harass you. She planned on writing a book based solely on the letter. I'm sure she sees the book as proof of her theory. That's why she took it."

"But deep inside she's a scientist,"

"Maybe, but it's very deep."

"Yes, very deep. Still, she can't publish without evidence and that would take my cooperation and access to the book and letters, but the authentication might at least give her the proof of her personal conviction. I hope after that she'll leave me alone."

"I'm pretty sure she'll see it as an impetus to push harder."

"Well, I'm pretty strong-willed, especially when it comes to my private life. Eventually she'll have to give up."

Eliza decided not to argue with him, but she had her doubts that the tenacious, pugnacious scholar would ever give up.

As he sipped his coffee from the steaming mug, she said, "Guess there's no point worrying about it."

Agreeing with her he finished his coffee and stood up.

"You're leaving?"

"I'd like to get going. So you've decided not to go with me, right?"

"Did you really think I wouldn't?"

"It occurred to me."

She stood on tip toe and put her arms around his neck. "You can't get rid of me that easily."

"Darn." He kissed her pouty mouth. "I don't ever want to get rid of you."

"We'll see about that," she said smiling up at him. The kiss radiated warmth through both of them.

He stepped back and breathed deeply. "When can you be ready?"

"All I have to do is put the stuff in my suitcase."

She walked to the door with him. "I really am sorry about all of this."

He slipped an arm around her. "Will you please stop saying that? It wasn't your fault and we've taken care of it."

"You've taken care of it."

"*We* did it, because *we* talked about it, so no more secrets." He kissed her goodbye and she stood in the doorway until he was on the elevator and the door closed.

Chapter 31

Private Jet
Summer, Now

It wasn't until they arrived at the private terminal that she realized they weren't flying commercial; his saying that the travel plans could wait finally made sense.

The plane sat on the tarmac, gleaming in the summer sun. The blue stripe against the white fuselage and tail made the plane look fast even on the ground. Winglets, the up-turned extension on the end of the wings, reduced drag and improved fuel efficiency and almost made the beautiful plane look cute. The Citation X, the fastest private jet made, reaching a cruising speed of nearly Mach 1, the speed of sound. She smiled; the CX had been her father's pipe dream. He had been a private pilot for as long as she could remember and had even invented a game for them to play when she was a small child; she had to identify airplanes they saw. She still looked up when she heard an aircraft and attempted to determine its make and model. Of course, without her father to share the game and tell her whether she was right or wrong made it a bittersweet exercise. But she never stopped looking up when she heard a light aircraft overhead.

The inside of the Citation was even better than the outside. The pale blue executive chairs rocked and reclined, and the buttery soft leather felt like kid gloves. She didn't know whether the paneling was real burled wood, but it was warm and elegant. Eliza laughed when she looked in the lavatory; it was much nicer than her bathroom at home, and the hanging closest was twice as big as hers. It really was an amazing plane with video screens and BluRay and CD players, as well as an iPod dock. There was a phone and a fully stocked bar and galley. She suspected there was a computer somewhere too, or at the very least Internet connections.

Eliza watched Fitz lean back in the chair, his seatbelt secure. "These are great seats," he said with his eyes closed, enjoying the luxury of the Recaro chair.

She said. "You act like you've never been in one of these."

"I haven't."

She looked around the beautifully appointed cabin. "I guess you can't move a horse in one of these."

He chuckled. "No. Transport planes are not designed for the comfort of people."

"So you usually travel commercial?"

"Yeah, why?" A touch of suspicion graced the question.

"Since you travel to and from Europe with some frequency I'm surprised you've never chartered a jet or flown on the Concord. Seems like you would have at least once, if for no other reason than to say you had."

"When I charter a jet it's only to move horses, and I didn't expect the Concord to get grounded." He shrugged. "Figured I had time."

"Why aren't we flying commercial tonight?"

"None of the airlines go directly into Southampton; they all require changing planes and inordinately long layovers, adding many hours of travel time. I want to get there as soon as possible." He leaned back again and closed his eyes.

She looked around the plane. "Well, a Citation Ten is definitely the way to go. It's the fastest private jet made."

"Citation Ten?"

She gestured to the elegant surroundings. "This plane is a Cessna Citation Ten, CX... very fast and very expensive."

"Why do you know that?"

"Daddy was a pilot and this was his dream plane."

"I thought he was a graphic designer."

"He was but he was also a weekend pilot. He had a Grumman Tiger that we used for day trips and vacations. I used to help with the hundred hour check and the annual. I got pretty good with a rivet press for relining brake pads. And of course he insisted Mom and I learn to take off and land in case something happened to him in the air."

"Rivet press, huh?"

She smiled and nodded.

Fitz reached over and squeezed her hand "You really are something else."

"I know." She winked at him. "You just haven't figured out what that is yet, right?"

The plane started to taxi, and as she leaned back into the chair the jet lifted off. They were on their way to England.

The luxury aircraft continued its ascent to altitude, which the pilot said would be 45,000 feet. Eliza told Fitz that at that altitude they shouldn't have to deal with much turbulence. When the pilot said they could move around the cabin, Fitz got up and made coffee. He brought back two steaming cups and set them on the shiny wooden table that separated the two chairs. "Have you been to England?"

"Yes. My mother and I did the whole European tourist thing after I graduated from college. We only went to London though. Hampton Court was as far out of the city as we got. I've never been to Chawton or Southampton."

"Well, once I get the Simmons thing sorted out we can do the tourist thing too."

"Tell me about Simmons."

"I don't really know much about him; he was a stable boy who took very good care of Lord Nelson while I was unconscious at the cottage."

She grinned. "You mean while you pretended to be unconscious."

"I actually was part of the time."

"Uh-huh."

"I never should have told you that; you're never going to let me forget it are you?"

She gave him a very pretty smile. "Probably not."

"Well anyway, Simmons arranged for the paper, pen and ink, and sealing wax so I could let Jane know I was going into hiding. Then, risking his own job and possibly his life, he found a place for me to hide and wait for sunrise away from the probing eyes of the Austen men. Of course, I ultimately returned at sunset when Captain Frank Austen came after me, but because of the hiding place I saw them before they saw me so I was able to make my escape." He shook his head. "If I'd been caught I would have been hanged as a spy and he could have been too, as a conspirator." He took a breath. "I owe him my life."

Eliza put her hand on his. "I'm exceedingly grateful to him."

Fitz smiled at her and put his other hand on top of hers. "So am I."

"Even though it's Simmons and not Jane who came through, you still seem pretty upset or are you still angry about Thelma?"

"I've been angry about Thelma for two years, since the first time she called and tried to wedge herself into my private business." After a protracted pause, he said, "While I was there I was in constant fear that I might do something that would alter the future, particularly Jane's. Luckily we know that my being there had no effect on her."

Eliza couldn't help but giggle. "Right. No affect at all."

"What's that supposed to mean?"

She reached across the small table and cupped his face in her hands. "You pleased a woman worthy of being pleased, Mr. Darcy."

He rolled his eyes. "Come on, it's just my name, it isn't me."

"Right. She sent you a copy of the book because you *aren't* that Darcy."

He shook his head. "She sent the book because it was the one she was working on while I was there." He sighed. "The point is, my having been there doesn't seem to have altered her legacy in anyway. I'm concerned that Simmons just vanishing from her life might. He's been with her for so long that I can't believe his being gone won't cause some kind of ripple. I don't know why he came, but I hope I can convince him to go back."

"You said he's been there so long, but you called him a boy. How old is he?"

"He was eighteen or nineteen when I was there, so I guess he's twenty-one or so now."

"At that age how long could he possibly have been there?"

"He told me he'd been with the Austen-Knights since he was nine. He was there before Jane moved to Chawton."

"Nine? What did he do at nine?"

"Worked in the stables."

"So he didn't go to school?"

"Most people didn't back then."

"It really wasn't a great time was it? No school, no medicine, no plumbing—I'd always thought of it as a romantic era—"

"Thanks to Jane."

"Yes, but how did she do that? There wasn't very much that was romantic about it."

"No, there wasn't, but Jane was an eternal optimist. Besides, it wasn't romance for her. It was simply the way it should be: relationships based on mutual respect and love."

"Instead of money and land."

"Exactly."

"So you really think his being here will affect her somehow?"

"It definitely could, but I'd like to protect his legacy as well."

"You know what happens to him, too?"

"While I was researching to see whether I could find proof that I'd been there I found out he becomes a famous horse trainer and doctor."

"How do you know it's him?"

"Obviously I can't know for certain, but I think it begs coincidence that Lord Moore-Jeffries was the owner of the race horse trained by the Simmons I read about and the same Lord Moore-Jeffries was Jane's father's best friend. The Earl had a summer home in Hampshire and was often a guest at the Great House and Cottage. I even met him that night at dinner."

"Wow."

He smiled at her and got up. "If you'll excuse me."

Something in his demeanor made her imagine that he bowed before he made his exit. She smiled. He really was Mr. Darcy.

She watched him walk the length of the plane, ruggedly handsome in a royal blue polo shirt and button fly Levis; she blushed slightly for having noticed. Wanting to control her embarrassment before he returned, she busied herself by pulling out her drawing of Chawton Cottage. She would see the real thing soon. Part of her was excited by the prospect, but there was the fear she just couldn't shake that being there would somehow make him want to return to Jane now that he knew he could.

"That's the one I saw at the farm, isn't it?" He was leaning over the back of her chair.

She looked up at him. "Yes, it's a preliminary sketch for one of my paintings."

"You sketch in color?"

"Yeah, I have kind of a peculiar technique. I sketch with colored pencils and fill in with pastels. It gives me a clearer idea of how something will look as a painting. It makes the final process a bit faster since I know exactly how I want the finished piece to look."

"I envy your ability and talent. I have absolutely no artistic ability at all. Even in school when we were required to take a semester of music and art, the art teacher suggested that if I wanted to make a living with art I should take up art history."

"That wasn't very nice."

"Maybe, but it was true. I can't draw a straight line with a ruler or a circle with a compass." He took in the details of the drawing. "Do you paint the originals in oil?"

"Sometimes. I prefer water colours though. One year for Christmas Mom and Dad made paper out of junk mail and stuff from the rag bag and they had it all bound into a book and gave it to me along with my first really good set of water colours: all natural pigments that had to be mixed with gum arabic and water. Because of that my favorites are the ones I do on natural paper with natural pigments."

"So your folks were eco-friendly, huh?"

"Yeah, they were. Mom still is but it was really more about the history. How people used to paint, what it took to create the great masterpieces. Daddy wanted me to have a good foundation in the craft as well as the art. He said that talent wasn't enough."

He came around and took the drawing from her, then sat down next to her rather than across from her.

"It's very good." He chuckled. "It reminds me of the afternoon I visited Chawton Cottage after I'd recovered and gone to her brother's." He paused a moment. "Jane had sent a note to the Great House inviting me after she discovered the location of my fall. Not wanting to hang out with her brother any more than I had to, particularly since he wanted me to go shooting with him, I got to the Cottage early. She was kneeling down on the ground, planting lavender next to the kitchen door. I surprised her and she was embarrassed that I saw her like that, but she was enchanting. Her dirt-smudged face was flushed with the work, her eyes sparkled in the afternoon sun... she looked amazing. I offered her my hand to help her up; it was so small and soft."

"Did you tell her that?"

"I did. She kept apologizing for her appearance. I wanted her to know that I thought she looked great."

A silly grin brightened Eliza's face.

He looked at her through squinty eyes. "What?"

She giggled. "Jane wrote Mr. Darcy saying that about Elizabeth Bennet."

"No she didn't."

"Not in those words. She has him say that Elizabeth's eyes were brightened by the exercise of walking to Netherfield when Bingley's sisters were deriding her for having done it."

He rolled his eyes but made no comment. Instead he seemed to drift off into his own world or maybe Jane's. A stab of jealousy grabbed Eliza's heart. Would she ever be able to accept Austen as simply a part of his past? Once again she wondered how she could compete with—how had he described Jane? the eternal optimist? the ultimate romantic?

He came back to the present and smiled at her.

Her half-smile did not go unnoticed but he said nothing, and when he left to refresh their coffee Eliza took the pastels out of her bag and made an addition to the cottage drawing. After he served the hot beverage and sat down she handed him the picture again.

"You did this while I was getting coffee?"

She nodded.

"Amazing." He flashed a smile of admiration.

She blushed slightly.

He said, "The fact that you can't see her face is perfect. Jane didn't like to sit for portraits. I think that's why there's only the one picture of her, and I can tell you it's not a very good one. No offense to Cassandra but it really doesn't look anything like Jane except for the basic shape of her face."

"People are really hard to do, particularly faces and hands. It's why I don't draw them very often."

"There was one other painting Cassandra did of her but Jane refused to turn around so it's only of her back."

"Her back?"

"Well, she's sitting outside under a tree or near a bush or something. Basically it's a painting of Jane looking out at the landscape." He handed the sketch back to Eliza and looked out the window. "The pilot says that you get a great view of the aurora borealis in this area in September."

She leaned over him and looked out the window too. "I bet that's a spectacular sight."

Without comment he took her hand, smiled, leaned back and closed his eyes.

He seemed so vulnerable, she wanted to gather him to her and never let him go. Lifting their clasped hands to her lips she kissed the back of his, then kissed each finger. Gently she opened his hand, running her finger along the lines in his palm, she kissed a small scar. "How did you get this?"

"Nail."

She remembered the summer she'd stepped on a rusty nail at the beach. "You fell on it?"

"No, I was using a nail gun and it got away from me."

"Is carpentry a hobby?"

"No. I was helping a friend."

"Do what?"

He hesitated, and she took the hesitancy to mean it had something to do with a woman. After a few seconds she asked, "Was the friend Faith?"

He looked at her and chuckled. "God, no."

"Was it some other woman?"

"Why do you assume it was a woman?"

"Because you're avoiding answering the question."

" Well, it wasn't a woman. I have a friend who volunteers with Habitat for Humanity as a foreman on building projects. He told me I shouldn't use the nail gun as I had no experience with it and it could be tricky and dangerous. Of course I knew better; I mean, how hard could it be?" After another slight pause, he added, "I'm just grateful that I hurt myself and not someone else."

"So you were helping build a house for Habitat for Humanity?"

His affirmative answer was accompanied by an embarrassed shrug.

Eliza couldn't help but smile. *He really does just get better and better.*

Fitz suggested, "The pilot says we're still about three hours out. Would you like to watch a movie or something?"

Playfully Eliza asked, "Or something?"

With a roguish grin he reached over and took her wrist, pulling her out of her chair and onto his lap. He held her firmly with one arm around her waist the other at the back of her neck and kissed her, a hard, very passionate kiss that literally took her breath away.

"Well, *that* was something," she gasped when he released her.

"Not what you had in mind?"

"Oh, it's *exactly* what I had in mind." She punctuated the statement with a kiss of her own.

Chapter 32

Windsong Manor ~ Hampshire, England
Summer, Now

As soon as the wheels touched down Fitz was up and out of his chair. Typically, not expecting to be waited on he helped offload the luggage and carried it to the waiting rental car himself, leaving her with only her portfolio and train case.

Eliza smelled the ocean as they disembarked the plane but they were twenty miles north of the ocean according to the pilot. So was it just her imagination?

The big SUV sped along the four-lane highway and the landscape around them faded into dark as late evening turned into night. There were hills but no mountains, and the countryside was very open. It went on for miles.

They'd been on the road about a half-hour when Fitz turned off the highway onto a driveway, past two stone posts, one carved with the words, *Windsong Manor*.

"Windsong Manor?"

"The Cliftons' summer home."

"Isn't that the name of your horse?"

He nodded. "Windy was a gift from the Cliftons and the estate is named after the sailboat on which they had their honeymoon."

The house was big, although not nearly as large as Pemberley House. Fitz stopped the car in front and walked around to the passenger side while Eliza gawked at the Edwardian manse. He opened her car door and escorted her up the front steps. Without bothering to knock or ring the bell, he opened the door and walked in.

The immense entry hall was split by a curved staircase that swept in an arc from the second-floor landing. The stairs were covered in plush eggshell carpet, and floral upholstered chairs stood sentry against the walls. The space was lit by bronze sconces made to look like flowers and leaves.

Fitz' voice echoed off the walls. "Linda? Uncle Rog? We're here."

"Uncle? I thought he was a friend."

"It's a nickname."

Eliza turned as a wide and obviously heavy wooden door to the right opened and a woman in her late thirties or early forties ran to Fitz and threw her arms around his neck. Fitz picked her up and whirled her around, then kissed her full on the mouth. Following very closely behind, a man in his mid-forties came through the same door.

"Watch it, Kid; that's my wife you're kissing."

Fitz put Linda Clifton down and shook hands, then embraced Roger Clifton.

"Great to see you," Roger said, then turned to Eliza. "Fitzwilliam, who **is** this lovely creature?"

Fitz introduced everyone, and without hesitation Linda and Roger hugged Eliza, who hugged them back rather hesitantly, being unused to physical intimacy with strangers.

"Luggage?" Roger asked.

"In the car," Fitz replied. "I can get them."

"Not to worry." Roger turned and in a voice slightly louder than normal said, "Bobby?"

A young man in his early twenties came into the entry hall through a door at the far end, seemingly from under the stairs. Fitz gave him an enthusiastic greeting which was returned in kind.

"Bobby, can you get Fitz' luggage out of the car and take it up to his room, please? Thanks."

Linda linked arms with the American couple and led them into what she referred to as the sitting room. "I have the coffee ready, and I made another cake since you didn't get any of the one I sent."

"Thank you, dear." Fitz leaned down and kissed Linda on the cheek.

Roger, following along behind, said, "Would you please stop kissing my wife?"

Linda leaned toward Eliza and in a stage whisper said, "Fitz loves to kiss."

Eliza blushed slightly.

Linda grinned. "But I see you've already found that out."

Linda and Roger sat in matching pale green wing chairs, leaving Eliza and Fitz to sit on the floral covered love seat opposite them. The Eastlake table in the middle held a silver coffee service, china cups and plates. The Bundt cake sat on a crystal plate.

Roger started the conversation. "You guys made great time."

Fitz looked at the cake and coffee, which as Linda poured it, was steaming. "How did you know when we were going to get here?"

"I asked Jim at the terminal to call when your plane landed, and knowing you with your lead foot, it was pretty easy to guess from there."

Fitz wasted no more time. "Where is Simmons?"

Linda flashed a strange smile. "The barn. We offered him the room next to yours, but he insisted he belonged in the stable. He's been working with Mark and Dave, seems to have a real knack with the horses. Bit of a strange young man, though. He never says much and he's so polite."

Roger added, "The lads were teasing him about it, saying he was making them look bad with his bowing and calling everyone Sir and Ma'am." He paused. "You met him when you bought Nelson?"

An enigmatic smile and singular, "Yes," was his only response.

Linda and Roger looked at each other. Considering the fact that news of the young man's appearance had instantly brought Darcy to the UK, they had expected more of an explanation. But they knew there was no coaxing Fitz to say anything he didn't want to say.

After a bit more small talk, Linda stood up and Roger followed suit. "Well, we must be off to bed. We're leaving first thing in the morning. Rog is in a golf tournament in Scotland. We'll be back on Monday. Will you still be here?"

Fitz stood up, "I'm not sure. We'll try to be. I'd kind of like to do the tourist thing with Eliza."

Before they left the room Roger shook Fitz' hand and hugged Eliza, and Linda kissed them both. Linda said good night, but Roger said goodbye as he expected to be off before either of his guests were up.

Sitting down again, Fitz and Eliza sipped their coffee and Eliza ate small bites of cake with her fingers while Fitz devoured his in two or three mouthfuls.

"The cake is really good," she said.

"It's my favorite."

After another bite of cake and sip of her coffee, Eliza asked, "They said 'your' room. Do you actually have your own room here?"

"Yes. I'm here enough that they let me have the same room every time."

"And did I hear right? Simmons is staying in the barn?"

Fitz chuckled as he finished off his piece of cake. "He'd probably be more comfortable in one of the stalls, but I'm sure he's in the apartment out there."

"Why is there an apartment in the barn?"

"When the Cliftons modernized the barn some years ago they added an apartment for their barn manager, but Mark lives in the caretaker's cottage now so I imagine the apartment was empty."

Fitz stood up and offered her his hand. "Come on. I'll show you our living quarters."

"Living quarters? Is it an apartment, too?"

"It's certainly big enough and the bathroom alone needs a guided tour. You'll love it though; it's spectacular."

"Good, I could use a bath."

He smiled. "That won't be a problem here."

Fitz gave her the tour and then kissed her, promising to return soon.

Leaning down to retrieve her Pullman case, Eliza ran her hand over the edge of Fitz' suitcase. Did his leaving it here mean their go slow plan would end tonight? Part of her hoped so. Their make-out sessions were fun but it was getting more and more difficult not to take it to the next step, and she was ready. As she took a pale-pink handkerchief-linen nightgown from her Pullman case she hoped he was too.

Spectacular was hardly the word that Eliza would have used to describe Fitz' bathroom. In fact palatial was more appropriate. Switching on the lights was a treat in itself. The halogen fixtures gave off a clear white light instead of a blue florescent glare or yellow incandescent haze. There were also lights that flickered like candles, and some even looked like candles. The wood wainscoting was teak, and the walls above were painted a calming pale blue-green. In the far corner was a shower like she'd never seen before—Fitz had called it a vertical spa—with multiple stationary showerheads as well as a hand-held shower head. There was a steam apparatus that turned the whole thing into a steam bath with a teak bench that pulled down, big enough for two. Teak steps led down into a soaking tub that was two feet deep and also big enough for two. The two sinks were lapis-colored funnels with simple but gorgeous faucets that turned on when you touched them. She found a control panel that said the floor and towel racks were heated. She opened what she assumed was a linen closet but turned out to be a sauna. Near the door that led to the bedroom was a fainting couch similar to the one in Fitz' Rose bedroom. She was having a hard time deciding whether to take a long, soaking bath or a massaging shower with steam or a sauna and then a bath or shower. She laughed at the choices. It wasn't so much a bathroom as a mini-spa.

She opted for a long, soaking bath. Bath salts from an antique etched-glass apothecary jar filled the room with a light, fresh scent of lemons. Breathing deeply, she was able to unwind from a very hectic day.

As she walked into the bedroom she scanned the space. It was reminiscent of romance novel bedrooms belonging to Dukes and Earls, and she imagined a coronet suspended above a massive four-poster bed surrounded by red velvet drapes. However, the pale moss-green walls and damask bedspread on the delicately carved bedstead were far more inviting.

Climbing into the king-size bed, she reveled in the sheets that were so finely woven they felt like silk. *Do they make thousand thread count sheets?* She lay down, her head cradled by an outrageously soft down pillow.

A contented smile curved her lips as she drifted off to sleep, hoping Fitz would wake her with a kiss.

Chapter 33

Simmons was in the first stall when Fitz walked into the barn. The young man was intent on his task and unaware that he was not alone. Fitz stepped back out of sight and watched as Simmons changed the bandage on the injured horse. The groom was wearing jeans and a t-shirt and looked as though he belonged here. Still, seeing Edward Austen-Knight's stableman stirred the memory of that fateful gray English morning when he'd made his trip through time. He could almost feel Nelson's muscles tensing under him as horse and rider flew over the low stone wall and into the early nineteenth century.

He shook off the memory and moved to the door of the stall. Remembering how Jane's kind eyes and sweet voice had somehow made what was happening to him not so terrifying, he hoped seeing a familiar face might make Simmons feel more at ease, although he didn't appear to be very far out of his element. He leaned against the door jamb and quietly said, "Simmons."

The young man spun around. "Mr. Darcy! How did you know? Where did you—When did you—"

"It's all right; the Cliftons told me you were here. I thought you might like to see a familiar face." Fitz put his hands on the boy's shoulders. "How are you, Simmons?"

His mind stumbling for words, he was finally able to say, "I am well, Sir."

"Why are you working so late?"

"Sam said we should keep the bandage clean, and she seemed a bit anxious, probably because of the pain. I wanted to calm her."

"I see."

Finally able to grasp the situation, Simmons said, "It's good to see you, Sir."

"And you, Simmons. But why are you here? Is Jane all right?"

"Miss Jane is okay."

Fitz grinned at the young man's use of modern American colloquialism. "So why did you come?"

He looked up at Fitz. "I want to work for you, Sir."

"You came through… you came here to work for *me*?"

"Yes Sir."

All the things that could have gone wrong rushed through his mind. *Why would he take such a risk? There was no way he could possibly have known for sure that he would arrive here safely. What did Jane tell him?* More than a little surprised, Fitz said, "But you have work at home."

Hesitantly Simmons said, "Master Edward is a good and generous man but I will never be more than a groom to him. I want to make something of myself."

Fitz put his arm around Simmons' shoulders. "If you're finished here, let's go to the house. I could use some coffee."

With only a new moon in the night sky, their way was dark until the first of the motion sensor lights turned on. In spite of having been here for several days, Simmons was still startled each time they passed a lamp post that instantly flooded the dirt path with yellow light. Looking up at the tall American it occurred to Simmons that he could now ask all the questions that had been whirling in his brain since he'd arrived here and without fear of revealing his circumstances. But there were so many questions he couldn't pick just one. Finally he admitted, "I wasn't sure you would remember me."

"Of course I remember you."

"I never felt like I was somebody to be remembered."

"I don't forget people who take good care of my horses."

"How is Lord Nelson, Sir?"

"He's just fine. I'm surprised you remembered him."

"I never seen a horse like him before. Even Master Edward talks about him some times... calls him a magnificent beast."

Fitz patted the boy's back. "He is that."

Fearing the American's presence meant he'd made some egregious mistake, Simmons asked, "Why did his Lordship tell you I was here?"

"Roger didn't tell me; Linda did." In response to a quizzical look, Darcy added, "I called her to find out about the book." There was still a questioning look on the boy's face. "The package from Miss Jane."

"Oh! I was afeared I'd lost it; then Miss Veronica said she posted it but I couldn't be sure and it would have been a great disappointment to Miss Jane."

"You needn't worry. I did get it."

In the main entry of the manor house Fitz led Simmons toward the sitting room, but Edward Austen-Knight's groom stayed back. "I don't belong in the drawing room, Sir."

"That isn't the case anymore, Simmons. You are welcome anywhere, and it's perfectly acceptable."

"It don't feel right, Sir."

The boy's reaction forced Fitz to remember that Simmons was a servant and as such had limitations that were so ingrained he couldn't bring himself to ignore them. The extreme class distinctions of the lad's era was one of the things Fitz had disliked about it. If Jane told Simmons how he had arrived in nineteenth-century Chawton she probably had told him what Darcy had told her of the changes in society. Suddenly the risk of the boy's excursion into this century made sense. Freedom and equality—Simmons wasn't the first to risk it all.

Having Simmons' comfort in mind, he suggested the kitchen. The island in the large country-style room had been constructed from old general store cabinetry. A nine-drawer bean counter was backed by a seed cabinet with five-inch square drawers, an apothecary cabinet with twenty drawers with brass pulls, and a bread display case with open slat shelving and glass doors. The four individual pieces were joined by a single red oak, walnut and cherry wood butcher block top. Chrome bar stools, upholstered in 1950s style oil cloth, sat on either side. It was all very American for an English country home.

"Sit down, Simmons." Fitz poured himself a cup of lukewarm coffee left over from earlier in the evening and put it in the microwave.

"Yes, Sir."

As the microwave whirred in the background Simmons stared at the glass plate turning slowly inside. There was one of those machines in his room but he had no idea what it did or what it was for. Now he watched in wonder as the mug turned round and round.

"Do me a favor, will you Simmons? Don't call me Sir. Fitz is fine."

"I couldn't, Sir."

Fitz grinned. "Mr. Darcy, then. Please."

"Yes, Mr. Darcy."

"Would you like something to eat?"

"I am a bit hungry."

"When was the last time you ate?"

"Oh, Lady Clifton had Cook make a plate for me when I arrived and I've eaten with the staff ever since. His lordship and his wife have been very good to me."

Fitz laughed, that was the second time Simmons had referred to Roger as Lord. "They aren't Lord and Lady. Roger has no title."

"I'm sorry, I thought...." He didn't finish the statement, ashamed of having made a mistake.

"Don't worry about it. They'd be thrilled by the elevation."

The microwave bell chimed and Fitz removed his steaming coffee. Intrigued, Simmons asked, "Did it get hot in there, Sir?"

Fitz grinned. "Yes. It's a microwave oven. It cooks food very fast."

He turned to the refrigerator for milk and at the same time got out a roasted turkey, condiments, bread and a bottle of Theakston's Old Peculiar. While spreading mayonnaise and mustard on the bread, Fitz casually asked, "You couldn't have known, when you came, that you'd meet people who were friends of mine, and I'm only here because Linda was under the impression that your being here was planned by both of us. How did you intend to contact me?"

From the pocket of the jeans Dave had given him, Simmons produced Fitz' business card. "Miss Jane gave me this and said that some of the numbers were for your telephone. She thought it was how I could contact you. She believed that the telephone was an instrument of communication. Since I been here I seen Dave use the phone, calling his mum in Virginia so I hoped I would be able to figure out which numbers would work."

Fitz chuckled. He supposed it seemed like a logical and practical plan when Simmons had left 1813, but he was glad the young man had found the Cliftons or vice versa. He finished making the snack for the time traveler and returned everything to the ice box, then cut another piece of Linda's cake for himself. As he set the food in front of Simmons, the young horseman offered the card back to Fitz.

After pointing out his telephone number, he said, "You can keep it."

The young man looked up at him. "I thank you for it, Sir, and for the food."

Fitz grinned at Simmons' use of "Sir." *Old habits die hard.* "You're welcome, Simmons." He watched the stableman take several bites of the sandwich and swigs of the dark Yorkshire ale before he asked, "You're sure Jane is all right?"

Simmons swallowed and said, "Miss Jane is very well indeed and sends you best wishes, Sir." Realizing his mistake, he quickly added, "Sorry."

"How did she come to tell you about me?"

Finishing the snack and sipping the beer, Simmons said, "A few days ago I come across her—" He blushed slightly. "Sorry, Miss Jane, in the meadow at the stone wall. I was riding and the horse surprised her. She fell trying to move away."

"She wasn't hurt was she?"

"No, but I asked her if she was okay. She thought I'd seen you because she hadn't heard the word since you went away." He looked down, a bit embarrassed. "So we talked about you. I told her I been thinkin' of goin' to Portsmouth to hire on to a ship and go to America so I could work for you and learn about horses. She said it wouldn't be possible and then she told me how you'd arrived there."

"How did you know the portal was still open?"

The young man smiled and gazed off as though he was re-membering. "It opened while we was there. We saw a plough with no horses, and we saw a car."

"Jane must have told you how dangerous it might be. What made you decide to try to come anyway?"

"I want to be a horse doctor." He paused, then quietly add-ed, "I was never schooled but Miss Jane taught me to read and write, Sir and what she said about you and your time made me sure I could learn horse doctoring here... with you. She thought you would help me if I came here, and when we saw the gateway still opened I knew it was my only chance."

There it was again—the class distinction. He was of the servant class so he deserved no such considerations, even from men as open minded and liberal as Edward Austen-Knight. *Jane probably taught the boy to read surreptitiously, and she must have agreed with Simmons that her brother wouldn't educate him, to have given him the wherewithal to make this journey.* Neither of them could have known that somewhere along the way Lord Moore-Jeffries had given him the very opportunity for which he had jumped through time. Now Fitz had to figure out a way to get him to go back so he could fulfill his own destiny and not jeopardize Jane's.

Fitz rubbed his eyes and looked at the old school clock on the wall; it had been a long and tiring day. "Look, it's late;

we'll talk about all of this tomorrow. Right now we both need sleep."

Simmons rose and bowed, then turned toward the back door.

"You don't have to stay in the barn, you know." Fitz said.

"It's best I'm in the barn, Sir. Dave and me are going to work the horses tomorrow morning."

"All right. Can you find your way back or would you like me to come with you?"

"With the lights along the path I'll have no trouble. Good night, Mr. Darcy."

"Good night, Simmons."

Fitz sat alone, remembering how terrified and then bewildered he'd been when he'd first realized he was in another time and place, and he was amazed by Simmons' calm demeanor. Roger had said that Simmons and Dave hit it off right from the start so that the young stranger had already become one of the Windsong family. Simmons was in a place where he was accepted as an equal, where his desire for an education was considered commendable and possible. Fitz feared that it would take more than a few well phrased sentences to persuade him to return to a life of subservience.

He watched as the young man walked through the pools of light from the automated standards and smiled at Simmons' original plan to try to figure out what numbers on the business card would enable him to phone Virginia.

The last of the lights along the path went out and a strange thought surfaced. Only a week ago he had opened the letter from Jane that Eliza had found and his business card had fallen out. *Now, though, Simmons is carrying that very card, meaning it wasn't in the letter. Does that mean Jane didn't bother to hide the letter?* After all, she had written it and he hadn't seen it until recently, so it had no intrinsic sentiment attached to it for her. If she didn't hide it behind the mirror of her vanity, then Eliza would never find it and ultimately find him. He might never have met her. *I might never have met her! Does Simmons having the card mean none of this ever happened and she isn't upstairs in my bed?*

Fear gripped him. Suddenly the possibility that Simmons' entrance into this century could alter his and Eliza's life and not just Jane's was very real. In spite of their short acquaintance he could not imagine his life without her. He ran from the kitchen, took the stairs two at a time and burst through the bedroom door. He almost shouted her name but stopped short. His raven-haired beauty was asleep in the massive bed, her hair fanned out on the silk-like cotton pillowcase.

He sat on the edge of the bed and took off his shoes. Rolling his shoulders and rubbing the back of his neck he turned and looked at Eliza, and his heart went to his throat. Simmons having the card hadn't changed his meeting with her but he had to wonder what would happen now. If Simmons did or did not return to his own time would their history be revised or nonexistent? He'd read about the paradox of going back to the past and causing alterations in the time yet to come but he'd never seen anything about a paradox created by someone who went forward. What alterations might be wrought?

The thought was troubling but he was much too tired to think clearly about anything. He leaned over and gently kissed Eliza's cheek, more than grateful she was still there. He smiled at her contented sigh, then stretched out next to her and closed his eyes.

The sun was shining through the space between the drapes at Fitz' bedroom window. Eliza stretched and rolled on to her back, surprised to find Fitz asleep beside her, on his back on top of the covers, fully dressed. She sat up and looked at him. *He must have been exhausted... all he took off was his shoes.* She leaned over and kissed him.

A small, sweet smile curved his lip. "Jane," he whispered, then rolled over onto his side.

Eliza stared at him, feeling as though she'd been punched in the stomach. *Jane... I knew it! I knew we couldn't come to England with him knowing the portal was open and not want to see her, not want to be with her.* She jumped out of bed and ran into the bathroom, collapsing onto the fainting couch in tears.

Chapter 34

As the tears waned she slowly got dressed. At the mirror she brushed her hair, staring at her image without really seeing herself. She clutched the brush with both hands and began crying again. All she wanted was to be away from here, away from him. Gathering her belongings, she stuffed them into her suitcase. After pulling the zipper closed she leaned heavily on it. *This is what comes from listening to my heart and not my head.*

She stood in the bathroom doorway and watched him sleep. *What was I thinking, traveling to Europe with a man I barely knew? Is this the kind of risk my mother said I should take? To what end?* Slowly she walked out of the bedroom, glancing back at him as she walked out through the door.

Bobby, the Cliftons' houseboy, came in through the front door just as she stepped off the last stair. "Good morning, Miss."

"Good morning. Are the Cliftons gone?"

"Oh yes, Miss, they left a good two hours ago." He paused. "There's coffee there on the sideboard." He pointed to a lovely setting with silver and china but also heavy crockery mugs. "Can I get some for you?"

She forced a smile. "No, thank you. I can do it."

Taking a mug of coffee with her, Eliza walked out through the front door and down the porch steps into the formal garden to the left of the circular drive. The fragrance of the roses in the warm summer air reminded her that one of Fitz Darcy's strongest memories of his time in Regency Hampshire was the faint scent of roses in Jane Austen's bed. *Is that what happened? Did the perfumed air of the rose garden remind him of Jane so he couldn't sleep without thinking of her?* After wandering through the entire garden, she sat down on a wrought-iron bench.

She was surrounded by beautiful flowering plants, topiaries in the form of animals, and precisely trimmed shrubs that Jane Austen would call hedgerows, but she was unable to appreciate any of it. Under normal circumstances she would have been sketching everything in sight but right now drawing was the farthest thing from her mind.

Wiping away the final remnant of tears, she wanted it to not hurt so much. To her great consternation she felt no anger. She understood anger; she could handle anger, but the deepseated ache was completely alien to her.

She turned her head at the sound of the gravel crunching. Fitz was beaming as he walked toward her, his smile bright in the morning sun. She forced a smile.

"Bobby said you've been out here for a while so I figured you could use some fresh coffee." He handed her a mug.

She glanced up at him. "Thanks."

He leaned down to kiss her but she turned her head so he could only kiss her cheek.

"What's wrong?"

She glanced up at him, then away. "What makes you think something's wrong?"

"No secrets, that was our agreement."

"Secrets?"

He sat down, took her chin in his hand and turned her face to him. "Tell me what's wrong."

She pulled away and stood up, took a few steps away, and then turned toward him.

He rose.

She put her hand up. "No. Please, stay there."

He sat again.

She told him about waking up and being thrilled to find him in bed with her, that she had kissed him, hoping to awaken him gently and end their go-slow plan.

He smiled because he had hoped for the same thing.

Her tears started again in earnest. "But you whispered Jane's name after I kissed you."

"But I—"

She put her hand up again. "I don't blame you. She's Jane Austen. I'd probably love her too." She took a deep breath. "I knew you loved her going in, but I thought since she was dead that maybe we had a chance—maybe *I* had a chance—but she isn't dead for you, is she?" She swallowed the lump in her throat. "I can't compete with her Fitz, alive or dead."

"You aren't competing with her."

She shrugged. "Maybe this is fate's way of getting you guys together again."

"I don't want to get together with her again."

"So you say."

Fitz buried his face in his hands. After a few moments, he said, "I don't know what you want me to say. I've told you I don't love Jane but you refuse to believe me."

"I did believe you—that's why I'm here—but then this morning...."

"I didn't mean—"

"I know, but it hurt. I can't even tell you how much it hurt. It was like I'd been punched in the stomach and had the wind knocked out of me."

"I can't explain calling you by her name other than to say that this whole thing with the book and Simmons has made me think about her. She is, after all, the reason any of this happened, including our meeting. I can only assume that she's on my mind because of it. But I assure you, it *is not* because I love her."

A sad smile was her only response as she returned to the bench and sat down.

"God, Eliza, I didn't mean to hurt you."

She tried to smile. "I'm glad it wasn't intentional." She paused. "But I keep hearing it in my head, over and over—you saying her name—and it hurts every time." When he said nothing, she asked, "How often when you kiss me are you wishing I was Jane?"

"Never!"

Eliza raised an eyebrow but said nothing.

Fitz stood and took a few steps away from the bench. With his back to her, he said, "I've been alone a long time, partly because of the loss of my family and partly because it was the way I wanted it. There have always been people who wanted to be close to me, but only because of who I am. When you come from old money, everyone seems to want something." He turned to face her. "I know you don't believe me, but the truth is that Jane was the first woman who loved me or at least cared about me for me, not because I'm a Virginia Darcy and not for what she thought she could get from me, but for *me*, the man. She took me into her home, a perfect stranger, having no idea who or what I was, when she could as easily have sent me off to her brother's house where I would have been tended to by servants at no inconvenience to anyone in the family." He paused. "And I admit that she meant more to me than anyone else had up to now, but I've *never* wanted to spend my life with her even if I could, and I don't want to go back to her."

He returned to the bench and sat down. The hurt he saw in her eyes made his throat tighten. He gently kissed her tear streaked cheeks and then kissed her lips and was encouraged that she kissed him back.

They sat quietly, each sipping the rapidly cooling coffee. After a few minutes of silence Fitz asked, "Is everything okay now?"

She looked over at him and giggled. *A strange reaction,* he thought, considering the intensity of the preceding conversation.

"I guess so. I just don't understand."

"Understand what?"

"Why, in Heaven's name, when you can have Jane Austen would you want anything to do with me?"

He cocked his head as he thought a few moments. "You really aren't that different. Maybe that's why you are the two women who mean the most to me."

"What do you mean? She's Jane Austen. I'm nothing like Jane Austen."

"I disagree. You're both gifted artists and relatively humble about those gifts. You're both intelligent, strong and independent, stubborn, opinionated and quick-tempered. You're both passionate." He paused. "You're both sweet with compassionate hearts."

Incredulous, she said, "Sweet? You would describe me as sweet?"

"When you're not on the defensive or being irrational, you're one of the sweetest people I know." He smiled.

He turned her toward him, cupping her face in his hands. "You both have beautiful eyes that delve the very depths of my soul." He kissed her.

Their lips parted and he whispered, "But I love *you*, Lizzy, not Jane."

She saw the truth in his sea-green eyes and threw her arms around his neck. He held her in the embrace for several minutes.

Leaving their coffee cups behind, Fitz took her hand and they walked farther into the garden. Droplets of cool water splashed them as they walked past a marble fountain.

Eliza looked at him out of the corner of her eyes and smiled. She took a deep breath in an attempt to contain her giddiness. She really did believe he loved her. It was just hard to wrap her head around the idea that he would rather be here with her when all he had to do was step over the wall and he could be with Jane. But he was here, now, with her and that's all she needed to know. In her continued giddiness she squeezed his hand.

Reacting to her sigh and the sudden squeezing of his hand, Fitz asked, "You okay?"

"I am, thanks," she said cheerfully.

Leading her to the farthest corner of the garden and what appeared to be a simple hedge, he said, "You're going to love this. Linda and Roger planted a small version of the Hampton Court maze."

As they started their way through the labyrinth, she asked, "How long have you known them?"

"I've known Roger most of my life; he's like my big brother."

"Schoolmates?"

"No. When I was thirteen I entered my first international competition—"

"Competition?"

"Horse show."

"Oh." She thought about all the ribbons and trophies in the Pemberley Farms barn. She'd seen the equestrian events during the Olympics and assumed that was the kind of competition he meant.

"It was the Royal Windsor Horse Show."

"Like Windsor Castle?"

"Yes. Most of the events actually take place on the castle grounds."

"Was the queen there?"

He nodded. "And Prince Phillip. Until a few years ago they both competed."

"Did you meet her?"

He chuckled. "No."

Eliza shook her head. "You live in an amazing world."

"Same world you live in."

"No it isn't. I can't even imagine living the way you do." After a few moments she prompted him. "So you met Roger at the Windsor Horse Show...."

"Yes. After the show his father invited my folks and me to their estate in Basingstoke. It's not far from here."

They hit a dead end so turned back.

"You said his family estate is near here?" Fitz nodded. "So why does he have the manor?"

"Roger's parents are still alive so they live there. He and Linda bought Windsong to be close but have a home of their own."

"Is his parent's house as big as his?"

"Actually, Parkwood Abbey is immense and very old."

Eliza giggled. "Queens, princes, Windsor Castle, Parkwood Abbey, Windsong Manor, Basingstoke. I feel like I've fallen into a romance novel."

Fitz smiled, pleased that she was enjoying herself.

She continued. "So you knew him before your parents died."

"Yes. He and his family were a godsend after my dad passed. My mother was in a world of her own for the first year or so, and I ended up spending a lot of time with the Cliftons. When she died they were my saviors. I've known Harv and Faith longer but I'm much closer to Roger and his sister."

"It really helps when you have someone in times like that. My mom and I only had each other. If she had lost it I'm not sure what I would have done. It would have been like losing both of them."

He squeezed her hand. "That's exactly what it's like, losing both parents."

Pain was evident on his face even after all these years, and she squeezed his hand back as they made their way out of the maze. He smiled sadly and asked, "What about your grandparents? Weren't they around?"

"They all live on the west coast. After the funeral they went home so they weren't around for the day-to-day stuff."

"You seem to have made it through fairly well."

"Yeah, I guess." She paused. "It's been a long time, but sometimes it doesn't feel like it."

"I know exactly what you mean."

As they entered the part of the garden that was in back of the house Eliza saw the barn in the near distance.

"Don't you need to talk with Simmons?"

"Yes, I do." Leading the way out of the garden, he said, "You'll like him, he's a really nice kid."

Chapter 35

Unlike the barn at Pemberley Farms, this one looked and smelled like a barn, dirt and straw and the unmistakable smell of large animal manure. A young man Eliza had not seen before came out of the office as the pair walked past.

"Fitz!"

The American stopped. "Mark, how are you?" Fitz let go of Eliza's hand and shook the offered hand of the young manager.

"Great... just great."

"Mark, I'd like you to meet Eliza Knight. Eliza this is Mark Valenzuela, the barn manager here."

Eliza smiled at the young Englishman.

Mark smiled in return, then turned to Fitz. "I had no idea you were here. When did you get in?"

"Last night."

Dave appeared from the shadows. "Fitz!" Dave and Fitz embraced. "It's good to see you, man."

"And you. So, it looks like England agrees with you."

"It's great here."

Fitz said to Eliza, "Dave used to be Nelson's groom, but he liked the Cliftons better than me so I left him here."

"I never said I liked them better, I just thought it was cool here and—oh, why am I explaining it to you? You know why I did it." He turned to Eliza. "Did I hear Fitz say your name is Eliza?"

She nodded and extended her hand to the two young men. "Yes. Nice meeting both of you."

Dave asked Fitz, "Here to see Simmons, are you?"

The American nodded. "Either of you know where I can find him?"

Mark nodded. "In one of the stalls, probably Tornado's. Sam said he could try his steam treatment so we showed him how to set up the humidifier."

Fitz asked, "What do you mean *his* steam treatment?"

Dave jumped in. "While Sam was here—" He turned to Eliza. "Sam is the veterinarian." He continued. "Anyway Simmons listened to 'Nado's breathing and told Sam the horse had a cold in his lungs. After his examination Sam agreed and gave him a shot of antibiotics—by the way, the kid had never heard of antibiotics. He also asked Simmons how he'd treat the horse and Simmons said with steam, so Sam told him it was okay for him to do it, that it might actually help the horse heal faster."

Mark added, "Simmons seems to have a natural knack with the horses."

Dave nodded. "Yeah, he's a real horse whisperer."

They all agreed. Mark asked, "Where did you find him?"

Fitz smiled, "Right here." He took Eliza's elbow. "Later, guys." He led her farther into the barn.

"Horse whisperer, huh?" she asked.

Fitz grinned at her. "He might be the original."

Steam was seeping from under the door of one of the stalls. Fitz opened it and looked inside. "Simmons?"

From behind them, Simmons said, "Hello, Mr. Darcy." He was across the barn in the stall with Jemma.

Fitz closed Tornado's stall door and he and Eliza walked across the barn.

She wasn't sure why, but she'd expected a large strapping man, probably having to do with the fact that he'd saved Fitz' life and she assumed he'd look heroic. She didn't know what heroic looked like but she certainly hadn't expected the excited young man who was standing before her dressed in jeans and a chambray shirt. He was rather small, not as tall as she was, with dark hair, long but not excessively so. Heroic or not, he looked like he belonged here.

"Good morning, Simmons. How has your day been?"

"I've been working with the sick horses this morning, doing some of the things Sam and Miss Veronica showed me."

"What did Veronica show you?"

"Sam called it hom-e-o—"

Fitz helped. "Homeopathic?"

"Yes. Miss Veronica showed me how to use honey and boiled water on open sores. She used sea weed too, but I never heard of that. She gived me some though. I'm learning so much here."

A stilted silence fell over the trio. Simmons kept glancing at Eliza but said nothing to her, and when she asked him if he was enjoying his time here, he just looked at her and then at Fitz, who suddenly was aware that he had not introduced them.

The nineteenth-century stableman couldn't speak to her without a formal introduction.

He was slightly flustered by his own breach of etiquette but mostly because he realized the boy's eagerness was going to make sending him back very difficult. Fitz rushed the introduction. "You guys don't know each other... sorry. Eliza, Simmons. Simmons, Eliza."

The young horseman bowed.

"Nice to meet you, Simmons. Well, I guess you guys have stuff to talk about, so I'll leave you to it." She smiled at both of them and started to go, but Fitz stopped her.

She looked up at him and he gently caressed her cheek then kissed her lightly. "I'll see you later."

The two men watched as she left the barn. Fitz turned back to Simmons. "Are you through here?"

The boy nodded.

"Let's go outside then."

At the paddock Fitz leaned against the railing. "So you want to stay?"

"Oh, yes Sir. Everyone here is so kind and no one laughs at my wanting to be a horse doctor. At home they think I'm trying to be high by wanting to better myself. The men here treat me as an equal and His Lord—" He stopped and bowed his head. "Sorry, I forgot. Mr. Clifton and Mrs. Clifton acted as though I was a friend." He lowered his voice. "They even said I could stay in the house when I first met them."

"What if you're missing opportunities at home?"

"There is no opportunity for me there. All I would do is to keep working for Master Edward. And as good a man as he is, I'm sure that I have not been missed."

"Certainly you could achieve your goals at home."

"I have no reason to think that possible, Mr. Darcy."

Fitz couldn't think of a reason to give the young man that would compel him to return to his own time. He was beginning to think that no reason or explanation would convince him.

"Excuse me, Mr. Darcy, but I need to look after the steamer."

Fitz nodded his assent and followed the would-be horse doctor back inside the barn. He stood in the doorway as Simmons petted the animal, talking to him quietly. Fitz grinned; he believed the lad really was a horse whisperer. He watched as the youngster added more water to the humidifier, amazed that Simmons had managed to work with twenty-first-century technology so quickly and easily. He didn't appear at all overwhelmed by any of it and thought, *You're a better man than I am, Simmons; I was terrified and unaccepting of everything in your world.*

From the door of the barn, Dave hollered, "Simmons, Mark and me are going into town to get something to eat. Want to come?"

Simmons looked at Fitz, who nodded, but as the groom started to leave the stall Fitz stopped him. "Wait a minute, Simmons. You'll be going to a restaurant, a place where food is prepared and served."

"I've heard tell of them, Sir, but ain't never seen one."

"Well, they're common now and you will be expected to pay for the food you order. So you'll need money."

Simmons reached into his pocket, showing the American a coin in the open palm of his hand. "Miss Jane gave it to me."

Removing the wallet from the back pocket of his jeans, Fitz said, "I'm afraid you can't use that here." In answer to the quizzical look on the lad's face, he added, "Money is different now. It's mostly paper." He put a few rumpled bills on top of the coin in Simmons' hand.

"This is money, Sir?"

"Yes. See? The picture is of the current monarch, Queen Elizabeth. Your coin has King George on it and might attract attention because of it." He didn't mention that a gold crown would definitely raise eyebrows.

Before Simmons could respond, Dave hollered again, "Simmons, are you coming?"

Fitz answered for the time traveler. "He's coming." He closed Simmons' fingers around the money he'd put in the young man's hand.

Simmons looked up at Fitz and slipped the crumpled bills into the pocket of his jeans. "Thank you, Sir."

Fitz patted him on the back and walked out with him, then stood and watched as the three young horsemen got into Mark's truck, the tires kicking up dirt as they drove off the property.

Chapter 36

Fitz marveled at the young nineteenth-century horseman's ability to fit in so well in this century. Simmons was so happy. How was he ever going to get Edward Austen-Knight's groom to return to his own time? Part of him wanted Simmons to stay. He wouldn't be able to go to veterinary school since he had no formal education, but he certainly could be taught what he wanted to know. He wondered whether Simmons wanted to stay here in England or go to the U.S. He knew the boy's original plan was to go to Virginia but that was to find him. Maybe he'd really rather stay close to home. Then again there was no real reason to do that since all the people he knew were long gone.

Forcing himself to return to the present he went to the tack room. Riding always helped clear his mind. He found Dave's western saddle; he usually sat English but decided it might be fun to ride western for a change. He went to the stall of one of the Irish Draught horses and prepared him for a ride. He led the horse out into the early afternoon sun, which had just crossed its zenith. He swung into the saddle and trotted out to an open field where he would be able to gallop. He hoped the wind racing around him would help him find a solution to his dilemma.

Fitz and Josiah—Dave called the horse Jed, after the character in West Wing—rode hard for a good half hour. The jumble of thoughts had shifted into place, but he still had no earthly idea how he could resolve the situation. Horse and rider arrived at the woodlands area of the estate and slowed to a walk, entering under the canopy of branches from trees hundreds of years old, trees that had probably seen Jane and Simmons.

Eliza was walking in what Bobby had called a wilderness. It was basically a small forest as far as she could tell. Unable to focus well enough to sketch, her original plan when she left Fitz and Simmons, she took a walk instead. The shade of the old trees was comfortable in the humid summer air. She didn't realize it got so warm here. She'd always thought of English weather as cool and foggy.

As she wound her way through the underbrush she wondered whether Fitz had succeeded in convincing Simmons to return to his own time. He seemed a nice boy and obviously worshiped the American. What would he do if the young man refused? From behind she heard a horse and rider approaching so moved quickly off the path.

Fitz reined Jed to a stop and jumped down. "Sorry, didn't mean to frighten you."

She smiled up at him. "It's okay. For a minute it was déjà vous all over again."

"Luckily there was no mud this time." He smiled back. "May I walk with you?"

"Of course."

Fitz held the horse's reins in one hand and took Eliza's with the other.

"So how did it go with Simmons?" Eliza asked.

"He likes it here so much that even if I told him exactly what will happen to him in his own time I don't think it would convince him."

"Wouldn't he go back just because you told him to?"

"Probably. But for how long? He knows the portal is open and that he can get along fine here and he doesn't want to stay there. I have to find a reason for him to stay."

"Just tell him about the Earl and that if he waits he'll get what he wants."

"And if his excursion here has already altered that in some way and it doesn't happen, what's to stop him from coming back? And I'm pretty sure that would screw up Jane's life. From what I've read it's very easy to create a paradox that can cause major repercussions in the near and distant future."

"Paradox?"

"A time travel paradox is something that happens in the past that didn't happen before so it causes a change in the future. The most common and extreme example is called the grandfather paradox. It's when you go back in time and kill your own grandfather before your father was conceived."

"Wow! How is that even possible? If you're father wasn't conceived then you wouldn't exist and therefore couldn't kill anyone, could you?"

Fitz nodded. "Hence the paradox. It was the thing I was most concerned about while I was there, that something I did would change Jane's life and her books wouldn't get published."

Fitz paused. "All of this is made even more difficult because Simmons isn't interested in being rich or famous. He just wants to work with horses and better himself, and he's convinced he can only do that here, he has no real reason to go back. And he can easily get along here unlike my inability to get along there."

"There's a big difference between you being there and him coming here, though. He sees this as a better time, and for him it probably is. But for you... why am I telling you? You know what the differences are."

He smiled at her attempt to make him feel better and the embarrassed blush that spread across her lovely face. He really did love her. He ran his hand through his hair and rubbed the back of his neck. His heavy sigh made her look up at him.

"What's wrong?"

"I didn't really try very hard to convince him. I'm not sure I want him to go back."

Surprised, Eliza asked, "Why?"

"One of those paradoxes may have already happened. Even small paradoxes can change things in unimaginable ways, so none are trivial."

"What are you talking about?"

"Simmons is carrying my business card with him. Jane gave it to him so he would be able to contact me."

Eliza looked at him. "What does that mean?"

"I'm not sure but it was strange seeing it in his hand when just a week ago it fell out of the letter you found. It made me wonder what would happen if he stays here because Jane won't have it to put in the letter. If he goes back and doesn't return the card to Jane, the same thing could happen. Basically she would have no reason to hide the letter behind the mirror."

As soon as he said "mirror," she realized what he meant. *If Jane doesn't hide the letters there, I won't find them, research them and meet Fitz.* "Why wouldn't Jane still hide them?"

"I'm pretty sure she hid that one because of the card. She would have been concerned about someone finding it. Since she wrote the letter, she would have no reason to keep it or hide it unless the card was inside."

"She wouldn't have wanted anyone to know she'd been writing to you, so she still might have hidden it," Eliza said.

"Without needing a hiding place for the card, it would have been much safer for her if she just destroyed it."

"So if he stays will things remain as they are?"

"I don't know. I'm assuming the reason nothing has changed for us is because she gave him the card after you gave me the letter. But does that mean nothing will change because it already happened or has whatever the change is not happened yet?" After a moment of thought he added, "The paradoxes I've read about are always when time travel is to the past. I don't know whether it holds for travel into the future. I'm afraid if he doesn't go back it might affect Jane, but now if he goes back and does anything differently...." He didn't even want to think about what it would mean, never mind saying it out loud.

Tentatively Eliza asked, "If any of this does cause changes for Jane will her books just suddenly vanish? You and I won't know each other?"

"In the grandfather paradox you no longer exist... never existed. So I suppose all of that is possible."

They continued to walk, silently. As they moved through the cool shade of old growth forest, Eliza asked, "If Simmons stays, it's possible nothing will happen to us?"

He nodded.

She stopped and stared at the dirt path. "But if he doesn't go back it might destroy Jane's legacy." She looked up at him. "And we would knowingly be a party to that."

Fitz just nodded again.

The humid summer air felt heavy as they walked in subdued silence. Eliza finally said, without as much conviction as she would have liked, "I'm not sure I could live with myself... or with you."

Fitz swallowed the lump in his throat.

Her eyes brimming with tears she looked up at him, biting her lower lip to keep the tears at bay. "You have to convince him to go back, whatever the risk to *us*."

"I don't know if I can."

"You mean convince him?"

"I don't know if I can knowingly do something that might destroy us." His voice caught. "I don't want *us* to end."

In an attempt to find the silver lining, Eliza said with a sad smile, "I suppose *we* won't end. *We* will never have happened in the first place." She swallowed hard. "So we'll never know what we missed." Almost whispering, she said, "We'll be strangers."

Close to tears himself, Fitz reluctantly agreed that he would try to convince the young stableman to return to his own time. They would have to hope against hope that whatever he did would still allow Eliza to find the letters.

Fitz broke the despondent silence by saying suddenly and loudly, "Jane! Jane is the answer! I don't know why I didn't see it sooner!"

Confused by his sudden outburst, Eliza asked, "See what sooner?"

"I'll tell him about Jane and the books. He might not go back for himself but I'm sure he will do it for Jane."

"But mightn't there be repercussions if he knows about her?"

"I don't know. I don't know anything, but I think he'd keep a secret for her benefit, to protect her, where he might not for himself. After all, he almost lost his life and certainly his job by keeping quiet about her connection to me."

"I thought he did it for you."

"He didn't know me; it had to have been in large part for her. Anyway I hope it was. And I think it's the only way he'll stay there."

They stopped at the edge of the wood and looked out at the meadow beyond. Finally Fitz said, "I don't imagine avoiding talking with him will make it any easier." He slipped an arm around her waist and leaned down to give her a light parting kiss. To his surprise and her own Eliza put her arms around his neck and kissed him. A deep and passionate kiss.

Their lips parted and she released him.

He smiled at her and said he'd see her later, then swung into the saddle once again.

She stood at the edge of the wilderness as he cantered out of the woods and into the open field.

If Simmons stayed because he hadn't done everything in his power to insist that the young Englishman return to his own time, then any life he and Eliza had would be forever tainted. Still, the thought of losing her caused physical pain as his chest tightened.

He thought about Eliza's selfless words, insisting he do whatever he had to do to convince Simmons, risking their relationship to protect Jane. As he spurred Jed to an all-out gallop and the horse's hooves crushed the soft grass of the English meadow, Fitz said a silent prayer: *Please God, don't let me lose Eliza.*

Chapter 37

In the barn Fitz handed Josiah's reins to Dave. "Do you know where Simmons is?"

"He's out in the paddock exercising Jemma."

"Thanks."

Fitz stood at the paddock gate and watched Simmons walk Jemma through her paces. When the young man saw him, he and the horse walked over to the American. Simmons was petting the animal.

"When you're done here I have something I want to show you."

"We can do it now, Sir. I can finish with Jemma later."

"Fine."

After returning Jemma to her stall the two men walked quietly to the house. Inside Simmons became nervous and uncomfortable, and Fitz could see it. "Sorry, I know you would prefer not to be in the house but what I want to show you is here." They walked past the staircase and down a short hall, then through a hand-carved door. Simmons kept looking around. he'd never been this far into a manor house. Even when he went to the Great House to get pen, ink and paper for Mr. Darcy, the maid had him wait in the kitchen.

The library, as Mr. Darcy called it, was a large room with very high ceilings, there was a table and chairs and a desk, but mostly it was shelves and shelves of books. He'd never seen so many books. Fitz went to the desk and opened a small box, removing a key. Then from a drawer in the table he removed a pair of white gloves and put them on. Unlocking the glass doors of one of the book cases, Darcy took out two books. He opened each of the books and pointed out to Simmons that they were both written by Jane Austen and published in 1833. Leaving them on the table for the young man to see he went to one of the open shelves and removed six more books and brought them to the table, opening them to the title pages as well.

"As you can see these two are the same book, both written by Jane. These were published in 2009. For more than two hundred years people have been buying and reading her books."

Simmons looked at all the books and then at Fitz. "I don't understand, Mr. Darcy."

"You know that Miss Jane writes books, don't you?" He pointed to both copies of *Sense and Sensibility*. "This was the first. It was published in 1811. *Pride and Prejudice* was published in 1813. There'll be four more." He picked up copies of *Mansfield Park* and *Emma* and then *Northanger Abbey* and *Persuasion*. "They were all written by Jane."

Simmons looked closely at all the books as Fitz contin-ued. "What I'm trying to show you is that even today her books are being published and read all over the world. She is famous." He paused. "In fact, she's more than famous; she's world renowned. Her books have been published in almost every language in the world." Carefully he replaced all the copies of the books, locked the bookcase and returned the key to its hiding place.

At the far end of the room was a sitting area that included a television and DVD player as well as a collection of movies on DVD. Fitz took one of several versions of *Sense and Sensibility* and slipped it into the player. Simmons stood amazed as images of things that seemed familiar moved across the screen.

Fitz said, "This is a movie. It's pictures and sound that have been made from the story in one of her books. There have been a lot of movies made from all of her books. This is just one."

Simmons was confused. He watched as the feature played on, but he didn't understand what any of it meant or why Mr. Darcy was showing it to him.

"Come on," Fitz said. "We're going for a drive."

"Yes Sir."

In the car Simmons said nothing.

Fitz prodded. "Did you understand what I was showing you?"

"I'm not sure. I know Miss Jane writes stories. I've heard Master Edward talk of them, and Mr. Henry, and even the Captain. But I never seen them."

"Well, those books I showed you were what they were talking about."

Simmons watched as Darcy turned the black SUV at a sign that said *Chawton*. He parked the car on a street that did not look at all familiar to Simmons, but as they rounded the corner Chawton Cottage was sitting on the other side of a paved road. He looked at the American. "The pond is gone."

"Among other things, but the house is now a museum in Jane's honor."

"Museum, Sir?"

"A place where people honor her memory. Come, we'll go see it."

They passed through the gate. "This isn't where the gate should be," the groom said. In the garden Simmons pointed at several things. "That's where the donkey is kept, and the still-room should be over there." A small smile brightened his face.

Fitz asked what he was thinking about.

"Maggie didn't like it when I spoke with Miss Jane. I saw her in the garden some days ago and we were talking. Maggie was very angry."

"She didn't like me being around Jane either." Fitz patted him on the back. "Shall we go inside?"

Simmons took a step back. "Truly, Sir?"

"I believe Jane would want you to see it."

"If you think it best, Sir."

Inside the Cottage Simmons was in awe. Only ever having been as far as the entry, he looked around each room as they made their way through the house, taking particular interest in many of the historical items. Looking at a framed portrait of the novelist created by her sister, Cassandra, the young horseman whispered, "It doesn't look like Miss Jane, Sir."

"I know."

"Why is this here?"

"It's the only portrait of her that lasted until now."

"Don't they know she's pretty?"

"The people now don't know what she looked like."

In the garden again Simmons wandered around the outside of the house alone, reading the plaques and signs. Waiting for the young groom, Fitz made a leisurely circuit of the house.

Walking past the kitchen door he smiled, remembering Eliza's sketch of Jane planting lavender. He was surprised to see a lavender plant still by the door. He looked around to be sure no one saw him, then bent down and plucked a few stems of the bush and quickly slipped them into his pocket. Attempting to act as casual as possible he continued his own tour of the garden. He found Simmons by the sign at the garden gate.

The young man looked up at Fitz and back to the sign. "It was only a few days ago that I stood here and talked with Miss Jane." He paused a moment. "It is hard to believe that Master Edward's youngest sister means so much to the world. I think you want me to understand that this world has much love and respect for Miss Jane."

"Yes, that's exactly it... but I'm afraid if you stay here something might happen to change that."

"I cannot believe that anything I do would make a difference in anyone's life."

"No matter how inconsequential we think something is, it can affect things around us and ultimately history as well."

"How is that possible, Mr. Darcy?"

Standing outside the back of the house and looking up at what Fitz knew was Jane's bedroom, he said, "What I'm saying is that you are so connected to Jane that if you do not go back all of this might not happen."

"I don't understand what my being here or there has to do with it."

The only example Fitz could come up with quickly was, "You drive Miss Jane."

Simmons nodded. "And Mrs. Austen and Miss Austen."

"Yes and what if you don't go back and someone else is driving them and something happens, like the carriage overturns and kills her or even hurts her badly. We know because of history that while you were there everything was fine. But if we change that, it is possible that all of this would be lost and the world would not have her books, nor even remember her." He paused. "It is her destiny to write the books and to have all of this happen in her memory. If you do not go back it could alter that history."

Simmons accepted the explanation without comment, but still found it difficult to believe that his existence would matter to anyone or anything at any time.

Not wanting to harp on the situation, Fitz asked, "Would you like to see the Great House?"

"Is it a museum, too?"

"Kind of."

"Is Master Edward famous as well?"

Fitz smiled. "Only as Jane's brother."

Simmons was quiet as they returned to the car. On the way back to Windsong Manor, Simmons finally said, "Miss Jane said you were mightily afeared of how your being there might affect her life. Is this what she meant?

"Yes. I was very concerned that I might do something that would change what is meant to happen for her."

Simmons nodded, apparently in thought. "And she was concerned how my coming here would affect you, but I thought myself much too low to matter to anyone's history but my own. I don't suppose either of us thought my being here would affect her history." He paused. "And you're sure that if I don't go back it will change Miss Jane's history?"

"The history you see here is what happened when you were there. We can't know for certain what might happen if you are not there, but it is possible that everything could change."

They drove the rest of the way in silence. Fitz parked the car, but they remained inside. Simmons spoke first, "Tell me what to do Mr. Darcy."

"I can't do that, but I can tell you that in July of 1817, Jane's legacy will be secured. If you still want to come after that you are more than welcome."

Simmons sat quietly for a few minutes. "Well, I need to check the horses." He got out of the car. Fitz watched the confused and disappointed young man walk dejectedly to the barn.

Chapter 38

Fitz pushed open the car door but didn't get out. He felt drained. He turned his head from side to side and back and forth to try to ease the tension in his neck. He lifted his shoulders in an attempt to stretch his back a bit, and finally dragged himself out of the car.

In the kitchen Bobby told him that Eliza had come in a while before and after having a snack had gone upstairs to rest. Fitz plucked a peach from the basket on the island for a snack of his own and, in spite of his weariness, rushed up the stairs, anxious to see her. He burst through the bedroom door. She wasn't there. The bathroom was empty as well. Her pencil case on the night stand was open. Several pencils and her portfolio and sketchpad were missing. He went to the window and looked out at the vast estate. *She could be anywhere. It would be foolish to go out looking for her.*

In the bathroom he turned on the shower, he hoped a shower and steam would ease some of the tension in his neck and shoulders.

The shower had helped. He was sitting on the edge of the bed tying his shoes as the clock struck the hour. It was getting late. He needed to find Simmons and get him to go back if he hadn't already made the decision himself.

The lavender he'd pilfered from Chawton Cottage lay on the bedside table among the keys and loose change from his jeans pocket. He picked up the fragile stems and crushed the purple buds between his thumb and forefinger, releasing the essential oils. It was a lovely fragrance and one he would forever associate with Eliza. He gently slipped them back into his pocket.

Heading down the stairs Fitz realized that he would be sorry to see the young groom go home to what he thought was a continuing life of subservience. Hopefully it would only be temporary.

The possible loss of Eliza preyed far more heavily on his mind. In what could only be deemed a last-ditch effort, he'd slipped a note into the watch pocket of his riding waistcoat that would enable him to reconnect with the New York artist if something caused a reversal of their meeting. He took a deep breath and stepped out the front door. Even if there was no way to ensure his future with Eliza, he did need to do whatever was necessary to ensure Jane's.

If Windsong Manor was a small estate compared to Parkwood Abbey, Eliza couldn't even imagine how big *it* must be. She had wandered all over the place, stopping only to render sketches of different views of the Hampshire countryside. Fitz was right; it was very much like Virginia, except that the northern light somehow softened the way everything looked.

Halfway across one of the far meadows Eliza saw a figure walking toward her, coming from the general direction of the barns. At first she thought it was Fitz come looking for her but as the two got closer she realized the figure was a good deal shorter than Fitz. He was wearing strangely baggy clothes and a hat with a low crown and somewhat wide brim. When they met in the grass he immediately doffed his hat and bowed. Simmons was no longer in the jeans and chambray shirt she'd seen him in earlier. He was wearing the clothes of his own time. He put his hat back on but said nothing, waiting for the lady to speak first.

"I didn't expect to see anyone out here. Where are you headed?"

"Home, Ma'am."

"Home. Home to 18—"

"To 1813, yes, Ma'am" He'd wondered whether she knew, but now it seemed obvious that Mr. Darcy would have told her. "Excuse me, Ma'am, but I must keep to the path to reach the wall before the sun sets."

"May I walk with you, Simmons?"

The young man shrugged, amazed that she would even ask. He wondered whether he would ever have gotten used to the idea of everyone being the same.

They began their walk together. After a hundred feet or so she asked, "Why are you going home?"

"Mr. Darcy is fearful my staying here might change Miss Jane's history."

They walked on. "Fitz says you want to be a vet."

"Pardon, Ma'am?"

"You want to be a veterinarian."

"I'd like to be a horse doctor."

Simmons explained how Miss Jane had told him what the future was like, how everyone had the opportunity to better themselves. "And I wanted to work for Mr. Darcy, and Miss Jane felt sure he would help me."

"In spite of all of that, you're going back because he asked you to?"

"Mr. Darcy is the best of men, Ma'am. He wouldn't tell me those things about Miss Jane if they wasn't true. I can't be the cause of making all that go away."

"So you're going back for Miss Jane?"

"Yes, Ma'am."

Eliza chuckled. She certainly would like to know what it was that Jane Austen did to instill such fierce loyalty in the men in her life. They walked on a bit further. "What will you do now?"

"Mr. Darcy said he would help me if the portal was still open in 1817 and I wanted to come then."

"What happens in 1817?"

"I don't know, Ma'am, but Mr. Darcy says that Miss Jane's history will be secure. I don't know what that means but he said I could come back then if I still want to."

The low stone wall over which Fitz and Lord Nelson had sailed, landing in 1810, was just ahead of them. The trees were just as she had imagined them when she'd drawn the picture of horse and rider leaping over the wall in a blaze of light.

Simmons looked out at the horizon. "It shouldn't be long now."

Eliza couldn't resist asking a question she wasn't really sure she wanted the answer to but asked anyway. "Did you and Miss Jane talk a lot about Mr. Darcy?"

"No, Ma'am."

"How did you know about the portal?"

"I told her I was going to go to America to work for Mr. Darcy. She told me why I couldn't do that."

"Oh."

After a moment of thought, he said, "Miss Jane regretted most that she had no way of knowing if Mr. Darcy arrived safely in his own time. I am glad to be able to give her comfort in that."

A soft mist started to swirl in the space under the arching branches of the trees. Something was there. They both stepped close to the wall and peered into the rising fog. As the thickening mist started to dissipate, the faint image of a person slowly became a solid entity.

Simmons gasped. "Miss Jane!"

"Miss Jane?" In her surprise Eliza dropped her portfolio.

Simmons immediately removed his hat and in a most gentlemanly manner introduced the two women.

"Miss Jane, this is Mrs. Darcy."

"Mrs. Darcy? No... no, I'm not married to him. I'm just a friend... we're just friends."

"I'm sorry. I thought... I'm sorry." The groom shuffled his feet in embarrassment.

"Eliza Knight... my name is Eliza Knight."

"How do you do, Miss Knight?" Jane asked as she assisted the startled artist in retrieving the drawings that were scattered on top of and on either side of the wall.

"F-fine," Eliza stammered. "I can't believe I'm talking to you."

"Amazing, is it not, speaking across the centuries?" Jane said as she picked up the drawings on her side of the wall. "Did you do these?"

Eliza nodded rather than answering, still stunned that she was in the presence of Jane Austen.

Jane smiled. "I recognize the house in this one, but the mountains are unfamiliar to me."

Finally able to control her awe, Eliza said, "They're the Smoky Mountains of Virginia. I draw what I imagine things might be like so I surrounded your house with Fitz Darcy's Pemberley Farms."

"It is lovely."

"Thank you."

Jane looked closely at the sketches of Fitz. The one with the American on Lord Nelson she handed back to the artist, but lingered on one of him at the foot of a staircase with his arm outstretched. "What captured his attention in this one?"

"He was waiting for me to come down the stairs during his annual Rose Ball."

"Indeed?" There was an unasked question in the word but she continued. "It is an excellent likeness. You are quite gifted, Miss Knight."

Eliza blushed and demurely said, "Thank you." She began to gather the rest of her fallen pictures and slip them into her portfolio. Jane was still holding several of the drawings, including the small watercolour portrait of Fitz. She studied it, tracing the contours of his face with her index finger.

Still kneeling, Eliza asked, "May I ask a question?"

Jane smiled down at her. "Of course."

"With the portal open all this time, didn't you ever think about coming to our time... to see Fitz again?"

"Until Simmons and I saw it a few days ago, I was unaware that it was open." She paused. "I have wondered over the years what it would be like to step through to another time and there are things in your world that intrigue me, that I would very much like to experience, but I am not brave or adventurous. Much of what Mr. Darcy told me about what is there and how things are frightens me."

Returning another of the drawings, Jane continued. "Some would call it prudent that I fear the unknown, but prudent or cowardly, my curiosity and keen interest in your world must be satisfied by my experience with Mr. Darcy... three years ago."

A look of mild disbelief crossed the American woman's face.

"You are not jealous of me are you, Miss Knight?"

"Jealous? No. No, I'm not jealous."

Jane smiled at her then glanced away. *If Miss Knight is jealous, he must still think of me with affection.* The thought caused her heart to beat a bit faster. Still there was no reason for Miss Knight to be concerned.

"I am sure any affection he feels for me arises out of his appreciation of my caring for him when he was injured. And I was, at times, pleasant to him in a very alien environment."

"You aren't in love with him?"

"There are things I love about him, but no, Miss Knight I am not in love with *your* Mr. Darcy. I love that he accepted me as his equal, his high regard for my ability to write and—" She cast her gaze down and blushed. "I love that he made me feel pretty, even desirable." She paused for a moment. "I believe it is the *idea* of him that I love. He accepted me for exactly who and what I am. Yes, it is definitely the idea I love. Mr. Darcy is simply the embodiment of that idea."

Eliza gathered the remaining sketches and her portfolio and stood up. "When I read *Pride and Prejudice* I had the impression that you are Elizabeth Bennet. Are you?"

"Good heavens, no!" She added conspiratorially, "Although I would very much like to be as independent and brave as Elizabeth, I fear I am not. Lizzy Bennet and Mr. Darcy are imaginary characters in a trifling work of fiction. There are similarities, of course. Elizabeth frequently voices my opinion, which I would never do in polite society, and often while I was writing it, I imagined how Mr. Darcy of Virginia might react or do things, but be assured, Mr. Darcy and Elizabeth Bennet of *Pride and Prejudice* are not real."

She paused and looked once again at the portraits in her hand. "You are in love with him, are you not?"

Eliza's heart skipped a beat and she blushed, wondering that it was so obvious.

Taking her silence as an affirmative reply, Jane smiled. "And I would say that from the look on his face in this portrait he loves you as well." She handed the large format picture back to the flustered artist.

Embarrassed, Eliza said. "We haven't really known each other very long."

In an understanding tone, Jane said, "Time does not determine intimacy, Miss Knight, it is disposition. Many years would be insufficient to make some people well-acquainted, for others a few days are more than enough." She paused. "His nature is changeable, I know, but there is no charm equal to tenderness of heart, and I can assure you of his tender heart."

Simmons stepped up to the wall. "It is almost time."

With a sad smile Jane handed Eliza the small portrait of the American horseman.

"Would you like to keep it?"

Jane once again ran her finger over the rendering and then smiled at Eliza. "Truly?"

"I'd be honored for you to have it."

Jane pressed it to her heart. "Thank you."

As the sun started its final descent, the space between wall and branches, past and present started filling with mist. All three visitors turned suddenly when Fitz said, "Simmons." He reached the wall just as Simmons climbed atop. Stunned to see her, all he could say was, "Jane."

She smiled radiantly. "Mr. Darcy."

The mist started to thicken and turn to fog, and from atop the wall Simmons said, "Goodbye, Mr. Darcy. Thank you." He turned and made a slight bow. "Miss Eliza."

Fitz turned his eyes to the young horseman and extended his hand in farewell. "It was good to see you again, Simmons." The Englishman shook the hand of the American, then nodded and stepped off the wall.

Jane stretched her hand out. "Happiness to you both."

Through the thickening fog Fitz stretched out his hand, too. As the Regency couple began to fade, Fitz said, "Goodbye, Jane." Their fingertips just touched as the brilliant light flared. The dazzling light of the sunset radiated across the centuries. Jane and Simmons were gone.

Eliza and Fitz waited for their vision to return. When it did the meadow was empty, and in the distance they heard the sound of a jet. The portal was closed.

After a few minutes of trying to absorb what had happened, Fitz finally said, "So you met Jane."

She looked up at him and smiled. "I'm not sure I believe it but yeah, I guess I did."

"Please note," he said, gesturing to the space between the arched branches of the trees. "The portal was open, and I saw Jane but I'm still here. Any lingering doubts should now be gone."

Eliza raised an eyebrow. "Bet you were tempted."

"There's only one thing tempting me at present," he said with a wicked grin. "And I can state unequivocally that it has nothing whatever to do with Jane Austen." He grabbed her, picked her up and whirled around with her in his arms. Setting her down softly he kept his arms around her and gave her a gentle, long and lingering kiss that made her spine tingle and her knees weak.

Their lips parted and without a word he took her hand and led the way back to the manor house.

Chapter 39

Chawton, England
Summer, 1813

Jane and Simmons waved farewell to the Americans through the fog as the final burst of light left nothing but the empty field beyond. Jane slowly pulled her hand back as the blinding light started to fade and the mist in the archway dissipated.

Her brother's groom turned at the sound of the donkey snuffling and pawing at the ground. He went to the animal and rubbed his head and patted his neck.

"How is Mr. Darcy?" Jane asked.

"He is well, Miss." No more information was forthcoming.

"Why did you come back?"

Keeping his eyes on the donkey as he continued to pet it, he said, "Mr. Darcy was fearful that my staying there would change history."

"Yes, that was always a concern for him." She paused. "What did you see while you were there?"

Finally he turned to her, his excitement pushing away the disappointment of having to return. "Oh Miss Jane, there was so many things! I know not where to start." He paused, wondering whether it would be all right to tell her of some things that might be considered indelicate to bring up to a lady, but it was all too amazing to keep to himself. "There was privies *inside* the buildings, Miss, and not just the house but the barn too. They call them loos."

"Like the card game?"

"Yes, except these are rooms for the privy. They also call them bathrooms because some have bathtubs in them. They even have a thing called a shower, where water runs out of a spigot that makes rain. Other spigots that they call faucets allow water to be in many different places: in the barn, outside in the garden and the kitchen. And the water, it runs hot and cold, Miss. There is a box in the kitchen that stays cold to keep food fresh and another one that makes things hot in less than a minute. There are lights everywhere that turn on and off with small switches, some that turn on when you just walk under them. It was truly wondrous, Miss Jane."

"And did you see the jets and automobiles Mr. Darcy told me about?"

"Oh yes. I even rode in them. Not the jet, but I saw one in the sky. The coming time is amazing, Miss."

Jane looked around at the gathering dusk. "I want to hear all about it, but it will be dark soon and I must be home; however, I shall be walking here tomorrow afternoon."

Simmons made a small bow in acknowledgment. "Shall I drive you home, Miss?"

"That would be very nice, Simmons."

He helped her into the little cart and then jumped up beside her, clucking to the donkey to move along. On the short ride to Chawton Cottage, Simmons told Jane about the soft bed in his room in the barn, the fabric-covered chairs there and the reclining chair at Dave's. And he told her of the cold sweet drink in a red can. Jane was sorry when they arrived at the house and the young man's excited description of the future had to end. Simmons stayed in the cart and watched Jane enter the front door. When he was certain of her safety he led the donkey into the yard and handed off the reins to Browning.

After a cold supper that she ate alone, Jane asked Sally to help her wash her hair, the length making it more than difficult to do by herself. As her maid poured cool water over her head she shivered and it made her think of the room Simmons had mentioned that had a rain-like spigot and hot water. It seemed as if such a convenience would make washing hair much easier than it was tonight. Jane sat in the kitchen near the fireplace to allow the heat to remove most of the moisture from her hair.

Still slightly damp a couple of hours later, Jane's hair fell in soft waves down her back, the sable tresses in stark contrast to the white of her nightgown. The only other person in the house was Browning and he was asleep in the attic. Her nightgown skimmed the top of her bare feet as she went deep into the recesses of her closet where she recovered a box her brother Frank had brought back from some exotic port. From behind the mirror of her vanity she took the small portrait Miss Knight had given her and looked intently at Darcy's face. He looked as he had when he lay in her bed three years before. She smiled realizing that she had hoped, somewhere in the far reaches of her mind, that he might come back to be with her.

What she had told Miss Knight was true; there were things she loved about him, but she was not in love with him. She was pleased that he had found his true love, as she had predicted, and while she was happy for him, she knew that it also meant she would never see him again. She looked down at Eliza's drawing, laid an open hand on top of it and closed her eyes. *At least I have this, created by the woman he loves and who loves him.*

Jane slipped the portrait into the box where it would stay hidden as one of her special treasures. Unfortunately, putting the picture on display was out of the question. The family knew Jane was not adept enough to have painted it, so there would be many questions and no explanation for the portrait's sudden appearance.

No, she would keep it for herself along with the flowers they'd picked on their last afternoon together, long since dried out, and the chain he had given her for her brother Charles' topaz cross. Once he was gone she had not worn it again because her brothers would have known it had been Darcy's. These things were her connection to him and a future she would never know, so carefully she hid the box behind a loose board in her closet.

As she got into bed she thought about her conversation with Eliza Knight. Mr. Darcy had told her that the books still existed in his time but she had not believed him. But Miss Knight said she had read *Pride and Prejudice*... no, it was too ridiculous to imagine. Miss Knight must have read it at Mr. Darcy's urging. What other reason could she have had?

Jane lay awake for a long time. She had suggested that Miss Knight was jealous of the time she and Mr. Darcy had spent together, but the truth was that *she* was jealous of Miss Knight.

At the very least she was envious; envious of the options available to the American woman to do and be anything she wanted. Tears filled her eyes, she *was* jealous. Had Miss Knight and Mr. Darcy engaged in the intimate relations he had told her were common practice even in casual relationships? Had Miss Knight felt his tender and gentle touch on her bare skin? Had Miss Knight touched his lean, strong body? He was one of the kindest and most considerate men of her acquaintance, and she had often wondered whether he loved the same way. Swallowing the lump in her throat and brushing away the tears she was finally able to drift off, remembering his kisses and thankful that she would always have the memories.

The sun was warm but not with the oppressive heat of recent days. A gentle breeze helped keep the air comfortable as Jane began her walk toward the meadow. She was only a short distance along the path when Simmons appeared from behind a tree. His hat in hand he bowed and asked to walk with her.

"My brother must be pleased that you have returned."

"I haven't seen Master Edward, but Miss Fanny asked about my mother and sister."

"That was a very clever excuse. No one would have been surprised had you not returned." Sensing that he was eager to tell her of his time in the future, she asked, "So what other wondrous things did you see and do?"

Since Miss Jane was the only person with whom he could share his experience, he was more than a little grateful that she didn't make him wait.

He told her of going over the wall and finding the closest house and that it had turned out to be the home of Mr. Darcy's friends, the Cliftons. Clifton was a name she remembered the American saying when she'd thought he was delirious. He was talking about a house that was only a mile away but did not exist in her time.

"They were so kind, Miss Jane. They told me I could stay in the house, a room right next to Mr. Darcy's. I couldn't imagine staying in the house, so I told them that the barn was good enough for me. And you will find this hard to believe, Miss Jane, but Mr. Darcy made me a meal when he first arrived from America, then sat and ate with me. I never imagined it, Miss... sitting and breaking bread with someone like Mr. Darcy."

Her brother's excited stableman told her of one of the Cliftons' grooms, also an American, named Dave who had found Simmons walking away from the wall the morning of his arrival. As luck would have it Dave was very friendly, making it much easier for the Regency horseman to make the transition. "Dave used to work for Mr. Darcy in Virginia. And that very night the Cliftons had a party for the neighbors and even some of the servants. I mean, the servants were actually invited to attend!

There was nothing like it, Miss Jane. Cook makes the same food for the servants as for Mr. and Mrs. Clifton, and Dave told me that the Cliftons have a Michaelmas party before they close up the house for the winter, and the servants, all the people who work for them, are invited as guests. Can you imagine that? It was amazing, Miss. They treat everyone the same. I couldn't help but wonder if it's that way everywhere, if everyone is like that."

"I envy you having that experience, Simmons. It is the part of the future that most intrigues me." She experienced a slight stab of regret that she would never see it.

He rushed on to tell her about how the veterinarian had allowed him to help treat the horses and how they had coloured thread to sew gashes. He told her about the medicine called antibiotic that killed the things that cause infections in animals and people. Tiny bugs, Sam had told him.

"And Miss Veronica, Mrs. Clifton's maid, they called her a secretary, she showed me how to make medicine with plants and herbs, things I can do here for the horses."

By this time they had reached the fence that separated the path from the meadow, and Simmons helped Jane step carefully onto the stile. Then he jumped over the fence and helped her down the other side, so she could step on to the soft ground with ease.

"Since we are talking about taking care of horses, Lord Moore-Jeffries wants you to take care of a race horse he has purchased recently. He has already talked with my brother. His steward has suggested that they send you to school to learn horse doctoring. We will need to talk with Edward first, but I will go with you to Rosemont Hall to talk with the Earl if you would like. I have already taken the liberty of communicating with him that you have returned, and he is expecting us this afternoon." She paused, more for dramatic effect than anything else. "If you want to."

"Oh, yes, Miss!" Reaching the stone wall he sat down and stared at the ground. Jane assumed he was just too astonished to say anything more, so she was surprised when he said, "Do you suppose Mr. Darcy could have known about this?"

"I cannot say."

"When he was telling me why I couldn't stay there he said I might be missing out on opportunities that were waiting for me here. I thought sure he was just saying it to force my return." He continued to stare at the ground.

Jane said, "He must have known something to say it. Is that the real reason you came back?"

"No. I couldn't believe there was anything for me here."

"Did Darcy refuse to help you?"

"Oh no, Miss. Like I said yesterday, he was afeared that my staying there might affect your history."

Jane thought about it; perhaps that was the cause of Miss Knight's jealousy—Darcy's concern for her future. He had been concerned that the ripple in time he had already created was going to be made larger if he did not leave quickly. She was hugely gratified that Simmons had returned more for her future than his own. It made her all the more keen to help his situation with the Earl.

Simmons had not said much about Mr. Darcy and she had an intense curiosity about how he was in his time and, of course, his relationship with Miss Knight. "Simmons, why did you think Miss Knight and Mr. Darcy were married?"

He smiled. "It was the way he looked at her, Miss, when she left the barn after I met her." He lowered his voice. "And he kissed her, Miss Jane, in front of me. I was sure they was married. I never saw a man and woman kiss before, even me mum and dad."

Jane smiled. "I see." She paused. "Did you give him the package?"

Simmons stopped and dropped his head, "Oh Miss, I thought I lost it but Dave found it in the barn and gived it to Miss Veronica and since it had Mr. Darcy's name on it she sent it by post to Mr. Darcy."

"So he did get it?"

"Yes, Miss."

"Did he say anything about it?"

"No, Miss. Just that he received it."

"Oh," she said quietly.

"Was it important, Miss?"

"No, no... nothing important, only one of my books."

The memory of his day at the museum that was Chawton Cottage and the books in the library flooded is mind and he had to stifle himself not to divulge the secret Mr. Darcy had entrusted to him. He took a deep, shuddering breath and added quietly, "Mr. Darcy holds your books in very high regard, Miss."

As they walked back across the grassy meadow the talk turned to modern technology. Simmons tried to explain about computers and television but had little understanding of them himself so was unable to make any sense of them for her. Jane told him that Darcy had mentioned television when he was here. Simmons apologized for not being able to explain it.

Trains, on the other hand, were much easier for him to tell her about. He'd seen one when he went to Alton with Dave and Mark. "We ate in a restaurant there, Miss." A train, he said, was a vehicle with metal wheels attached to metal rails. Mr. Darcy said that the rails run all over the country and he had seen the ones that ran right by Alton. It was one of the ways people and freight were moved around. "There were trains and cars—that's the common word for automobiles—and jets and shops, Miss, where you can buy anything. The future was an amazing place and I'm grateful for the experience, however short the time." As he finished telling all that he could remember, they had reached the Great House.

Jane started up the steps to the front door.

Simmons, of course, would stay outside. He stopped her. "Miss Jane?"

"Yes?"

He removed his hand from his pocket. "I thought you would want these back, Miss."

Jane took the proffered items: Mr. Darcy's calling card and the gold crown she'd given the young horseman before he left on his adventure. She looked at him, a question in her eyes.

"The money is yours and he meant for you to have the card."
He shrugged slightly.

Jane nodded and thanked him, then went into the house
and talked to her brother about Lord Moore-Jeffries' request to
have Simmons go to Rosemont Hall and take care of the racehorse. Edward had a vague recollection of his Lordship men-
tioning it. He gave his blessing and the use of his carriage, so
Jane and Simmons could make whatever arrangements needed
to be made.

Simmons was thrilled when Jane told him of her brother's
words and the two oddly connected friends left for Lord Moore-
Jeffries' estate.

Sitting atop the carriage with his valuable charge inside
Simmons was mindful of Mr. Darcy's concern should the carriage overturn and Miss Jane be injured or killed. He drove
very carefully, unwilling to be the cause of changing his friend's
destiny.

Chapter 40

Windsong Manor ~ Hampshire, England
Summer, Now

Walking slowly along the dirt road, Eliza's hand in his, Fitz asked, "What did you and Jane talk about?"

"What do you think we talked about?"

"Yeah, I was afraid of that."

"She only said good things."

"But you didn't?"

A small smile was her only response. "She did tell me that she doesn't love you and she was pretty sure you don't love her."

"What made her tell you that?"

"Like I said, we talked about you."

"She must have had a reason to be that specific. What had you said before that?"

"I didn't say anything." She chuckled, "Oh yeah, Simmons introduced me as your wife, a misconception I immediately corrected."

Fitz shook his head. There were any number of women who would have jumped at the chance to claim to be his spouse, but the only woman he actually had considered might become his wife had adamantly denied it. Fitz didn't say it but he wondered or maybe hoped that Jane felt Eliza had protested too strongly.

"She said you probably appreciated that she took care of you and was nice to you."

Under his breath he said, "Sometimes."

Eliza chuckled. "That's what she said too. *At times* she was pleasant."

Quietly they continued their slow walk, each deep in their own thoughts. Eliza broke the silence. "I've been trying to figure out why I got so upset about you calling me Jane. I mean, rationally it's not that big a deal... or shouldn't be. But when you told me about the possible paradox of the business card, I realized why your slip of the tongue, if that's what it was, hurt so much."

She hesitated and he used the break to ask, "Why?"

"Because I've fallen in love with you."

"I thought you didn't believe in love."

"Yeah, well I don't believe in the fairytale kind. My mother tells me I'm too analytical; maybe I am, but being logical and rational has always worked for me."

"Sure it did, it kept you from getting emotionally involved with anyone."

"Yes, and that was fine with me. Anyway, mom and dad knew they were soul mates because after their first date they felt like they'd known each other all of their lives. Remembering that made me realize that love isn't the silly schoolgirl, head-over-heels feeling. The real thing isn't accompanied by hearts and flowers. Truth is that logic tells me love is what I've been feeling all along, relaxed and content."

He grinned. "Logic, huh?"

"Yes. When we're together I feel so comfortable; it's like, like—"

"Like you're home?"

"Yes!" She stopped walking, and he stopped as well. She looked up at him. "That's exactly it. I hadn't thought of it that way, but you're right. I feel like I'm home when I'm with you. Like it's where I belong."

A small smile brightened his eyes and curved his mouth slightly. "Me, too."

She dropped her gaze. "Doesn't this scare you?"

"Oh, I don't scare that easily."

"Yeah? Well it scares the hell out of me."

"Why? What are you afraid of?"

"You, the relationship, the possibility that—" She stopped.

When she didn't continue, he asked, "The possibility that what?"

"That you actually do love Jane, that you'll turn out to be someone other than who I think you are, that it won't last, that you'll leave, that something will happen to you. Take your pick."

Fitz stepped in front of her taking hold of her hands. "Lizzy, I wish you'd believe that I don't want to live in the past. I want to live now and build a future with you. Except for being responsible for bringing us together in the first place, Jane Austen has no part in it. As for not being who you think I am, I'm afraid you've already seen pretty much the worst of me. My egotism, my selfishness, my moodiness. You've experienced my temper and my suspicious nature, which tends to make me jump to conclusions. I just hope that you see what good there is, too and allow it to override all of that."

"Jane says your nature is changeable."

"See? Even she knows who I am."

"She says you have a tender heart."

He shrugged off the compliment. "A heart that belongs to you, if you'll have it." He paused. "I can't offer any guarantees—we both know there aren't any—but I can tell you that I don't intend on going anywhere."

"The road to hell is paved with good intentions. No matter what—"

He interrupted her with a kiss; accepting it with uncompromising pleasure Eliza kissed him back. He really could get what he wanted without saying anything. The conversation had ended and she didn't want to talk about it anymore either.

Resuming their walk, he admitted, "You know I considered asking Simmons to give the card back to Jane and tell her to hide it again. But I don't even understand the whole paradox thing, so how could I expect him to understand it or to explain it to her?"

"It's probably better that you didn't. I think we just need to move past what might happen and deal with what does happen."

Fitz said, "I'm afraid that what's going to happen is that I'm going to wake up one morning and not know you."

She shrugged. "We can't control what Jane and Simmons do." She paused. "All I know for sure is that I want to be with you, whether it's for years, days or just a few hours."

"Me, too."

They started walking again, "You know, Thelma said something that might be the answer."

"Do I really want to hear what Thelma had to say?"

She squeezed his hand. "Maybe just this once. During the authentication process they discovered that Jane's letter had been sealed twice. There were two separate wax stains and the chemical composition of the two different wax pieces they found matched each other. The conclusion was that Jane had sealed it, opened it and resealed it. Maybe she put the card back."

"I guess we'll never really know." Just outside the kitchen door, he said, "I'm hungry. Linda and Roger gave the staff the evening off since they weren't going to be here and I didn't want them to reverse it just because we are. So we can go out or I can make a couple of sandwiches."

"Sandwiches sound good."

The room was flooded with light as he flipped the switch by the kitchen door. Fitz went about fixing two sandwiches, and then added some dill pickles and potato crisps he found in the pantry. He finished preparing the meal by pouring a glass of wine for each of them.

They sat at the island, leisurely enjoying their light meal. Eliza showed him the sketches she'd done on her walk and said that she was looking forward to adding the paintings to her on-line gallery.

As he poured the last of the wine he suggested they take it into the drawing room where they would be more comfortable. They switched off the light and left the kitchen.

As they made their way along the hall to the drawing room, Eliza said, "Why do you smell like lavender?"

Fitz stopped near the foot of the stairs, reached into his pocket and extracted the small bunch of fragrant herb. "I picked them for you when Simmons and I went to Chawton Cottage today. It's from the plant near the kitchen door; I thought you might get a kick out of it."

She took the flowers and inhaled their essence "I love lavender. Thank you." She stood on tip toe and kissed him. "Hey, tomorrow let's go to Chawton and you can show me the Cottage and Great House."

Fitz looked down at her. "You know what? We've already spent too much thought and discussion on Jane Austen. I think we should save that for a future trip."

Eliza's lower lip protruded in a slight pout. "But I want to see where she lived and where you slept."

He took the wine glass from her hand and set both glasses on the table nearest them. He slipped his arms around her and kissed her.

His breath warm on her cheek, he said, "Well, I've decided we need to concentrate on us. And to that end—" In a swift, smooth motion he lifted her into his arms and started to walk up the stairs. She wrapped her arms around his neck.

In a New York tinged southern accent she intoned, "I feel like Scarlett O'Hara."

Exaggerating his already soft southern drawl, he said, "Well, Miss Scarlett, I guess that makes me Rhett Butler."

She whispered in his ear, "Does this mean we're going to do what they did?"

"Frankly my dear, it does, indeed."

A small whimper escaped her throat as she nestled her face into his neck.

Chapter 41

Chawton Cottage
Summer, Now

An early morning rain left the air fresh and clean and puffs of white clouds dotted the cerulean sky. Eliza and Fitz came around the corner hand in hand. Fitz stopped.

Eliza looked up at him. "What's wrong?"

"Now that you've badgered me into this, you aren't going to get all moody and pouty are you?"

"Badgered? You considered it badgering?"

His pseudo-glare gave way to a rakish smile. "Okay, now that you've *seduced* me into it." He looked at her with a raised eyebrow. "You aren't going to get all pouty are you?"

"Not unless you get all emotional and mushy."

"When have you ever seen me get mushy?"

"I've seen the tears in your eyes when you talk about her."

"Well, then maybe we shouldn't do this."

"Afraid you won't be able to control yourself?"

Fitz slipped his arms around her. Cupping her curvaceous backside in his hands, he drew her as close to him as he could. "I'm already having trouble controlling myself." He kissed her, as their lips parted he whispered, "We could just go back to the house."

Pulling away, she said, "Later," then turned and skipped across the street. She stopped on a patch of grass and stood looking up at the building she'd seen so many times in photographs. This was Chawton Cottage, Jane Austen's house.

Fitz caught up with her there. "Well, here we are."

"It must be weird for you."

"Nope."

"How is that possible?"

"Eliza, I've been here so many times I'll be surprised if the docents don't recognize me."

"I don't know how it's not weird for you. It's kind of weird for me and I only heard the story."

"I got past weird a long time ago. It's just a house."

"But it's *her* house."

"It *was* her house."

She took his hand and walked ahead. "So you can point out all the things that are different and tell me what they were like. Come on."

Grudgingly he followed her.

They were greeted by a sign perched on a weathered wooden stand, suspended in what appeared to be a wrought-iron frame announcing that they were at Jane Austen's House.

"That wasn't here," Fitz said with a sarcastic grin.

She gave him a dirty look. He looked down and told Eliza that the concrete walkway hadn't been there before. With every step he pointed out a multitude of minutiae that were either different or had not been there at all, which was much of it.

After about fifteen minutes of his constant observations, she finally said, "Okay, you win. Don't tell me what's different, just let me look." She waited a few minutes, then asked, "Can I ask about things?"

"Of course, I was perfectly willing to tell you what the differences were."

"I didn't mean I wanted a continuous diatribe."

He grinned. "Whatever you want, dearest."

She stuck her tongue out at him.

They continued their tour with only an occasional comment from him or a question from her. For Eliza this was where Jane Austen had walked, lived and written. For Fitz it was simply a memorial to her.

Inside the house Eliza wandered from room to room, Fitz following close behind. The costume room was upstairs next to the Admiral's room, where brother Frank had stayed. It held examples of the clothing Austen would have worn during her tenure in Chawton. Fitz had only glanced in the room once and found that all the dresses seemed to be reproductions. He hadn't recognized any of them, so he had simply ignored the space. So they were both surprised to find tucked in a far corner, *out of the light* the plaque said, a pink silk gown embroidered with rose buds. The sign said it was the only dress known to have belonged to the famed author. Mention of it being made and worn for Lord Moore-Jeffries Michaelmas Ball the autumn of 1813 had been found in letters to her sister and nieces. It bore a striking resemblance to the one Fitz' great-great plus grandmother had made for the first Rose Ball. The one Eliza wore to Fitz' modern day Rose Ball.

"Look at that."

"Yep."

"That's some coincidence."

"Yep."

"It's so weird."

"Yep."

"Bizarre almost."

"Yep."

"Is that all you're going to say? Yep?"

"Yep."

She wasn't going to get more out of him and in truth had no idea what she expected him to say about it. Following Fitz out of the room, she thought that she preferred to think of it as serendipitous rather than a simple coincidence.

Eliza stood at the window in Jane's bedroom and looked out onto the yard and bake house.

Fitz walked up behind her and put his arms around her, resting his chin on the top of her head. She leaned back against him. *Just like the morning she had appeared at Pemberley Farms, it felt natural, right. This is where she belongs, in my arms.*

His romantic thought was lost when she asked, "You don't feel strange being here in her bedroom?"

Stridently he insisted, "That wasn't her bed, that chair wasn't here, the painted screen is gone and you have her vanity. So this is just a room in the house as far as I'm concerned. It bears little resemblance to the room where I recovered from my injuries."

"And she took care of you."

He turned her around and looked deep into her eyes, "Are you trying to get me to say or do something to prove your theory that I'm in love with her?"

"No. I don't think so. It's just that it was only, what, ten days ago, that you were telling me all about it. You made it so vivid and you were so emotional that it's hard to believe none of this means anything to you."

Fitz switched places with her and sat on the deep window sill. "Like I said, it's just a *museum* now. It's the same location but it's not the same place. I'm not sure how to explain it beyond that."

Eliza suggested, "It's her house but not her home."

He brightened. "Yes! When Jane and Cassandra were here it was warm and appealing. Now it feels like what it is: a museum. In fact, it isn't quite as inviting as the library exhibit in New York."

Because he was sitting down they were at eye level. She looked directly into his sea-green eyes and whispered, "Is that how you feel about her, too?"

"What do you mean?"

She looked around and gestured slightly with her hands. "All of this—the pictures, the stories, the books—they're all *about* Jane Austen but it's not her; it's not the Jane you knew."

He had tried to put it into words many times, and now Eliza had said it exactly right; none of it was the Jane he knew and never would be. All he could say was, "Yes."

She took a step closer to him and put her hands on either side of his face and kissed him, "I love you, you know." He took her in his arms and there in Jane's bedroom kissed her. He smiled. He'd finally found a woman worth pleasing.

Eliza pulled away quickly at the sound of people in the room. Three teen-age girls were looking at them, smiling and giggling. Eliza blushed, but Fitz remained sitting on the window sill with his arms around her.

With his slow southern drawl and a sparkle in his eyes, he said, "Good morning, ladies. Enjoying the tour?"

One of them said, "We are now." They all giggled until one ducked into the closet next to the fireplace and the other two followed.

Eliza leaned over and gave him a quick kiss. "I guess maybe we should have gone back to the house."

"It's not too late."

"As long as we're here I might as well see the rest of the place."

Before either of them could say anything else the teenagers were back, looking at the bed and the interior of the wall where it was exposed to show the construction that was used in building the house. One of the girls kept turning her head and looking at Fitz. Finally she whispered something to the other girls. All three turned and looked at him.

Eliza whispered in his ear, "Why do they keep staring at you?"

"Maybe they've never seen an American before." He glanced over at them and they were still looking at him. "What is it, girls?"

One of them pointed to the closet. "There's a picture of you in there."

Fitz laughed. "I doubt that very much."

"Go look."

Eliza and Fitz looked at each other and went into the closet. On a small display table, exhibited under glass was an oriental box, a small bouquet of dried flowers and a poem. Those three pieces were separated from the other two items in the case by an extensive printed explanation.

This box from Frank, Jane's Admiral brother was found recently behind this slat in the closet when some restoration work was being done. Inside the box was a poem written in 1813 by Edward James Austen, son of Jane's eldest brother,

James. The poem is her nephew's acknowledgement after find-ing out that his Aunt Jane was the authoress of Sense and Sensibility and Pride and Prejudice.

The box and the poem have been authenticated, and the flowers have been dated to about the same period. As for the other two pieces, the gold chain is of high quality but is not in the fashion of the Regency era. The portrait is a watercolour done on hand-made paper of all natural fiber, painted with organic pigments mixed with water and gum arabic which, although relatively common in the early nineteenth century, shows none of the style or design of the period.

We have no idea who the subject of the portrait was or who the artist was but it is evident to us that it and the chain had very special meaning to Jane. Although we cannot authenticate the two items, because they were found in the box with other verifiable pieces and were apparently hidden by Jane Austen sometime between 1813 and 1817, the year of her death, we have chosen to include them here.

After they both finished reading Eliza spoke first. "I assume the chain is the one you gave her?"

He nodded. "Yes."

"I gave her the picture yesterday."

"How? Why?"

"I dropped my portfolio, and it fell out. It's the one I told you about, that I did the day we met at the library. She liked it so much I said she could keep it. It never occurred to me that it would be here."

"Why didn't you tell me about it?" His voice held a tinge of anger and suspicion.

"We were kind of busy last night and to be perfectly honest Jane Austen was not foremost in my thoughts." She paused a fraction of a moment. "Was she in yours?"

He smiled, the bit of anger gone. "Absolutely not!"

She smiled at him. "Good answer."

Eliza looked again at the printed card inside the case and before they left the small enclosure, she said, "She died in eighteen seventeen. Simmons said you told him he could come back then. Because once she's gone her legacy is secure?"

"Yes."

"I didn't understand the significance of the date. It's sad. She was so young."

"Yes, but her death is also part of her legacy."

As they came out of the closet holding hands, they glanced back at the memorabilia and realized they were both inexplicably and permanently linked to Jane Austen. They went downstairs, not bothering with the rest of the house.

As they stepped into the street Eliza started to laugh.

"What's so funny?"

"I still think it's weird that you'd rather be with me than with her."

"Well, get used to it lady, because I do." Slipping his arm around her waist, Fitz asked, "So what would you like to do with the rest of the day?"

Eliza smiled mischievously. "Need you ask, Mr. Darcy?"

"To the Manor it is."

Chapter 42

Eliza and Fitz ran up the steps of the Cliftons' manor house, having every intention of going directly to the bedroom, but that plan came to an abrupt halt when they were waylaid in the entry by Bobby.

"This package came while you were out and the messenger said it was important."

Eliza noticed, as the Cliftons' houseboy handed it to Fitz, that it was from the British Library. "Must be the book."

"Probably." He started to set it down on the table at the foot of the stairs.

Surprised, she asked, "Aren't you going to open it?"

"We already know what it is."

"But they said it was important so maybe there's something else in it."

He grinned at her as he picked up the package again. "Well, if you'd rather I did this instead of—"

"I want you to do both."

Quickly Fitz tore open the flap of the envelope; the three small volumes with Jane's lovely embroidery were bundled with bubble wrap along with the brown-paper wrapper. Fitz handed them to Eliza, who removed the bubble wrap as he unfolded and read the single sheet of paper that was with them.

"Well?" Eliza asked impatiently.

He laughed. "Your friend Thelma—"

"She's hardly a friend."

"Whatever. She's going to be greatly disappointed by the Library's conclusion."

"Why?"

A strange look crossed his face. "Because the British Library, in its wisdom, has determined that this book is a superb reproduction of the first edition of Jane Austen's *Pride and Prejudice*."

Eliza giggled. "How did they reach that conclusion?"

"It doesn't say. She writes that I can call if I have any questions."

"That's it?"

"Basically."

"It certainly doesn't explain why they said it was important."

"It doesn't explain anything."

Eliza opened the first book and read the inscription aloud. *"My dear Mr. Darcy,"* She stopped for a moment. "Jane said that you're *my* Mr. Darcy."

He raised an eyebrow. "Am I?"

"Time will tell," she said with a sweet smile. She continued reading the inscription.

My dear Mr. Darcy,

*If any one faculty of our nature may be called more won-
derful than the rest, I do think it is memory. You have given
me cherished memories to last a lifetime and for that I thank
you with all my heart.*

Yours affectionately,
Jane Austen

"It certainly sounds like she could have written it," Eliza
concluded.

"Because, as we already know, she did write it."

"I don't understand... why are they saying it's a reproduction?"

"Well, I suppose I could call and ask. Of course, that would
mean a delay of our planned activity."

"Are you so mercurial that you'll lose interest in that activity because of a slight delay?"

"Mercurial?"

She smiled. "Aren't you even a little curious as to why they
think it isn't real? I mean, it's weird."

"You're weird." Fitz leaned down and kissed her nose. "For
you, my lovely, I will investigate." He paused. "I'm only doing
this to please you, because frankly, I don't care." He dug the cell
phone out of his pocket.

"You're using a cell phone?"

"Thought I might try joining the twenty-first century."

"How's it working for you so far?"

"Jury's still out." He dialed the number on the British
Library letterhead. "Ms. Hart? This is Fitzwilliam Darcy. I got
the book and wanted to thank you for getting it back so quickly."

Eliza watched as he listened to something the woman was
saying. "Ask why they think it's phony." He gently laid his
finger on her mouth for quiet.

"Thank you, Ms. Hart. It is a beautiful piece, but I'm curious as to how you arrived at the conclusion that it's a reproduction." He listened. It seemed to Eliza to be taking forever; after all, how many reasons could there be for assuming a rare first edition was a reproduction? Fitz asked one more question, listened intently, then thanked her again and disconnected the call, slipping the phone back into his pocket.

"So why did they decide it was a reproduction?"

"It's new."

"What?"

"It's too new. In fact the reason we got it back so soon was they didn't bother to do any testing on it. The fabric of the cover and the silk embroidery thread are not faded or frayed. The paper of the pages isn't worn or yellowed and the ink hasn't oxidized. Most particularly telling, she said, is that the spine is intact which, to them, meant the book had never been read. Since books in those days were very expensive they tended to get passed around to family and friends, but this one is untouched. So the resulting conclusion was that it is a reproduction because it's brand new.

She did say that it was such a good reproduction that even the font looked exactly the same and typographical errors made in the original were included in this. But as splendid as the book is, she said, it is most definitely a reproduction."

Eliza looked at the books in her hand, knowing full well that they were a first edition of *Pride and Prejudice*, covered and embroidered by the author herself. She looked inside at the inscription: *Yours affectionately, Jane Austen.*

She looked up at him. "Did she say anything about what's written inside?"

"Again she said it was a superb recreation of Austen's handwriting. She stopped just short of calling it a forgery. However, since the ink had obviously been used within the last few days, Jane couldn't have done it. As for the words themselves, they are, in fact, Jane's. It's a quote from *Mansfield Park*, which she finished in the summer of 1813."

Eliza chuckled. "Even with the evidence staring them in the face they couldn't see it."

"They're scientists so only see things as they actually are, not how they might be. To them the book couldn't possibly travel through time and just appear here, so there was only one *logical and rational* explanation." He grinned.

Acknowledging his jab with a sarcastic smile she asked, "So what was so important?"

"Because of the circumstances surrounding their acquisition of it, they wanted to get it back to me as soon as possible." He paused. "She did admit that if she hadn't talked with me before she started the investigation, she would have been completely baffled. That Klein woman told them that it had been in my family for generations, but when she asked me about it, I told her the truth, that I'd received it as a gift a few days ago."

"You're right about Thelma. With all the experts from the British Library telling her it's not real, she'll have to believe it but she's going to be really disappointed. She was so sure. I almost feel sorry for her, especially since she was right about all of it. Kind of anyway. All she ever really wanted to prove was that Jane Austen's Mr. Darcy was based on an American." She curtsied, "And you are an American, Mr. Darcy."

With a twinkle in his eye, Fitz teasingly asked, "Yes, but who's Mr. Darcy am I? Yours or Jane's?"

She turned serious. "I've actually thought about that, and I think you're both hers and mine."

He didn't know what to say in response so said nothing.

Still holding the small hand-covered volume, Eliza ran her hand over the raised letters spelling out his initials and looked up at him. "I guess this means it's all over."

Taking the book from her and setting it on the table, he brought her hand to his lips and kissed it. "Except for us. We're just beginning."

Epilogue

Chawton, England
Summer, 1813

Standing barefoot at her bedroom window, her nightgown falling gracefully from her narrow shoulders, Jane absently braided her knee-length hair. The moon was but a sliver in the night sky, and the stars were so bright it looked as though the sun was shining through holes in black velvet. Draping the braid over her right shoulder, she went to her dressing table.

She removed Fitzwilliam Darcy's calling card from the top drawer of the vanity and slipped it into the letter she had written him before he left Chawton Great House in the spring of 1810. Frank's decision to go after the American had made it impossible for him to receive the letter, so here it was, forever in her possession, never to be seen by him. The red wax dripped onto the paper, melted from the flame of the single candle illuminating the room. Black soot swirled around the A as she pressed her seal into the molten wax. Tying the green ribbon around it and his note to her, Jane slipped them behind the mirror. She supposed she could have added them to the box with her other mementoes and she probably would eventually, but for now she liked having them close. She did enjoy looking at them from time to time, particularly the one written in his own words by his own hand. These small tokens of remembrance were all she had of him, all there would ever be.

She moved back to the window and looked into the infinity of the night sky. Her throat tightened and a tear fell on her cheek. Her heart raced. The image of him at the wall when she saw him through the tear in the fabric of time just before the brilliant light flared and closed the portal brought tears she could not stop. He was gone with his true love and she would never see him again.

As a shooting star streaked the nighttime sky she made a wish for their every happiness.

Books by
Sally Smith O'Rourke

The Man Who Loved Jane Austen

The Maidenstone Lighthouse

Christmas at Sea Pines Cottage